Praise for *Big Woods*

"*Big Woods* is brilliant! Cobb has crafted a haunting thriller that dives deep into grief, family connections, and the dreadful power of fear. The novel succeeds as a rich exploration of emotion and a not-so-distant time while also shining as a riveting page-turner."

—Owen Egerton, author of *Hollow* and
writer/director of horror-comedy *Bloodfest*

"Stephen King's *Stand by Me* collides with Gillian Flynn's *Sharp Objects* in this exceptional thriller. Gutsy, gripping—and pitch-perfect in its resurrection of an era long gone."

—A. J. Finn, #1 New York Times bestselling
author of *The Woman in the Window*

"*Big Woods* is a nuanced family story and also a heart-stopping thriller with surprising twists. Cobb taps into the fabulous '80s sensibility of *Stranger Things* and also into our deepest fears about safety, evil, trust, and the power of faith in what we don't understand. I couldn't put it down."

—Amanda Eyre Ward, author of *The Nearness of You* and *The Same Sky*

"Compulsively readable."

—Rosamund Lupton, *New York Times* bestselling author of *Sister*

BIG
WOODS

MAY COBB

*don't ever
go in*

BIG
WOODS

MIDNIGHT INK
WOODBURY, MINNESOTA

FIRST EDITION
First Printing, 2018

Book format by Bob Gaul
Cover design by Shira Atakpu
Editing by Nicole Nugent

Midnight Ink, an imprint of Llewellyn Worldwide Ltd.

Library of Congress Cataloging-in-Publication Data
Names: Cobb, May K., author.
Title: Big woods : a novel / by May K. Cobb.
Description: First edition. | Woodbury, Minnesota : Midnight Ink, 2018.
Identifiers: LCCN 2017061594 (print) | LCCN 2017056590 (ebook) | ISBN
    9780738759234 (ebook) | ISBN 9780738757810 (alk. paper)
Subjects: LCSH: Missing children—Investigation—Fiction. | Sisters—Fiction.
    | Widows—Fiction. | Texas—Fiction. | GSAFD: Mystery fiction.
Classification: LCC PS3603.O225554 (print) | LCC PS3603.O225554 B35 2018
    (ebook) | DDC 813/.6--dc23
LC record available at https://lccn.loc.gov/2017061594

Midnight Ink
Llewellyn Worldwide Ltd.
2143 Wooddale Drive
Woodbury, MN 55125-2989
www.midnightinkbooks.com

Printed in the United States of America

To my parents, Liz and Charles, for everything.
To my sisters and best friends, Beth, Susie, and Amy.
And to my husband, Chuck, maker of shooting stars.

1

Sylvia

October 1989

Who will save the children? That's the question I wake up with this morning, the thought that comes barging in without invitation and stays parked there, like the neighbor's fat cat I can't seem to shoo away from my garden. I'll be seventy-five this month, old enough to leave so many thoughts behind, but this one curls its way around the edges of my mind like the ribbons of cream in my afternoon cup of Earl Grey. I rise and do what I have done every day since living alone. I part the yellow ruffled curtains that rim my second-story picture window. I look out the window and beg the sunlight to give me strength enough to start one more day. The sight of the rose bush helps, as does the view of the crumbling red brick wall. Both have always made me feel like I live somewhere enchanted, somewhere far away and storybook, like France, perhaps, or maybe Ireland. Anywhere but here, this greasy-spoon town.

I complete my morning ritual by kneeling next to my bedside table, lighting an amber-scented candle, and saying a simple prayer, the prayer of St. Francis, which I've said every morning for as long as I can remember. "Lord, make me an instrument of your peace. Where there is hatred, let me sow love. Where there is injury, pardon." And so forth. I'm a believer, but I don't believe in everything that everybody else in this town seems to. Things aren't so black and white, so fixed, so certain.

I do believe in the message of hope, though, so each morning I pray, rounding out my morning ritual as if by completing these modest tasks my day will hold some shape. A useless hope, as it never does, the day giving way and deflating to the endless quiet of widowhood. I kneel and complete this simple prayer, but this morning, I add another, more urgent one to it: Who will save the children?

————————

It was the latest poster that got to me. There hadn't been a new one up in a few years and I had hoped that it was finally over. But last Saturday, as I did my usual grocery shopping in the next town over—for the freshest tomatoes and peas—I couldn't help but see it. Amidst the wall of frayed missing children's posters, still white but beginning to yellow, their shining, helpless faces calling out to me—a blizzard of despair—there it was. A new one. Bone-white, crisp, and tacked up next to all the others.

Lucy Spencer. Blond Hair. Age 10. Missing since September 29th, 1989.

It was then I knew there was no turning back. I had to find a way to tell someone who would listen. The children wouldn't be safe until they stopped them. Until they stopped *him*.

Lucy

Friday, September 29th, 1989

One red sock, one orange sock. One red sock, one orange sock. One red sock, one orange sock. This is how she kept time that day walking the short distance to the bus stop. Lucy always had a song or a jingle in her head. It was her dad's day to dress her, to make sure she ate her breakfast, to make sure she caught the bus, and that's how she ended up wearing mismatched socks. Her mom would die, but Lucy liked it. It made her feel like Punky Brewster, which made her feel older than she actually was. One red sock, one orange sock. There were just a few more blocks to go, but there was a car driving up real slow behind her and she felt scared, so she put on her Walkman headphones and pushed play. The song was "We Built This City," and she loved it. Loved the idea of a city built on rock and roll. She'd recorded it from MTV onto her cassette deck, and as she stepped over the cracks in the sidewalk, she wondered if she would ever get to see a city. Dallas maybe, which wasn't all that far away. Her older sister, Leah, had been there once, with her best friend, Nicolette. They had gone to the Galleria Mall, and she told Lucy how awesome it was and brought her back a pair of fluorescent orange sweatpants. Leah had a lime green pair, and they sometimes wore them to match. Leah Lucy, Lucy Leah.

Lucy kept walking, then started walking faster, and the car zoomed past her—a tiny dark green convertible. She was almost running, not paying attention to the cracks anymore. The bus stop was just around the corner, but the car had turned around and was inching up beside her. One red sock, one orange sock. She now started saying *"Christmas, Easter, Happy Times,"* the chant Leah had taught her to say over and over again when she would wake up with a nightmare, or was afraid of the dark. *"Christmas, Easter, Happy Times, Christmas, Easter, Happy Times—"* But he was getting out of the car, the man with the moustache. He was getting out and coming closer and she couldn't round the corner in time. She couldn't find her voice to scream and it suddenly felt like she was trying to run through Jell-O.

3

Leah

MY SISTER LUCY WENT missing when I was fourteen years old. She was ten. Lucinda Rose Spencer. To us, Lucy. Or Lucy Belle, or sometimes, just Lu. The morning she vanished could've been considered an ordinary one; that's what I told the police later that day as I sat between my parents on our orange nubby sofa, my eyes trained downwards to a strip of sunlight that slashed through our wooden floor. I watched the shadow of leaves tickle the polished hickory boards as I answered their questions.

It was an early fall morning, but the summer was still hanging on, having baked the sidewalks kiln-like, so that even the mornings were stifling, not crisp and cool just yet. When Dad woke me up, my room already felt stuffy. It was a Friday, and I woke up thinking about the weekend, about seeing Scott, my new boyfriend, about what I should wear to school that day.

The day was ordinary, but I remember this: the smell of Aquanet burning on my curling iron. Me, spending too much time in the bathroom—the peach-tiled one I shared with Lucy—fussing over my bangs, trying to get them just right, a restless primping. If I hadn't stayed in there so long. If I hadn't pulled and tugged on my shirt so much—my favorite one, a yellow button-down Guess shirt that I knew Scott liked. If I hadn't been so vain...

If, if, if.

I remember grabbing my books and the lanyard, chewed up by Lucy, that held my keys, and walking through our breakfast room just off the kitchen, and seeing Lucy's half-eaten blueberry Pop-Tart (which I considered grabbing but didn't, having just brushed my teeth) and Dad's toast—too much of it still there, his tan coffee mug still full and steaming. They must have left in a hurry, I remember thinking, and if they had told me goodbye, I just hadn't heard it.

I stepped outside and waited on the curb for my carpool ride, fiddling with the worn corners of my paper sack book cover. The last ordinary morning of my life.

When a month would pass and there would be no news of Lucy, I'd watch from my upstairs window as the sheriff coasted up our steep driveway in his big tan Impala (his off-duty car; it was after church on a Sunday). He'd step inside our foyer with his hat in his hand and talk to my mom—my dad was already gone by then. He'd tell her to start preparing for the worst: none of the other children who'd been taken had been found alive.

Later that evening, my mom would click the door shut to Lucy's room, as if closing off the possibility of Lucy's return.

And I might've started to believe she was gone from us forever, too, if it hadn't been for the dreams.

———————

The first time Lucy broke through—which is how I had begun to think of it—it wasn't even nighttime. It was in the middle of a hot, lazy afternoon nap. I'd fallen asleep on the couch in the upstairs playroom—a huge room lined with windows—when I had the first dream. In the dream, Lucy was just outside in our treehouse calling for me to join her. "Lee-yaah!!! Come down! I'm making mud bombs!" I watched Lucy from the second-story window as she hurled little clumps of red clay down at imaginary enemies, her hair wild and curly with sweat and her heart-shaped mouth coated in a string of slobber as she mouthed the sounds of bombs exploding. I raced down the stairs and out into the courtyard, but by the time I reached the edge of the lawn, the sky had suddenly turned a dark violet. I strained to see Lucy, but the lights from the house didn't reach that far and I was too scared to go any farther. Sweat stung my armpits and I willed myself to inch closer, but by now it was completely dark and no matter how many times I cried out for Lucy, nothing but the sounds of crickets chirping answered me back.

When I woke up, the sun was setting and I had that empty feeling that I always had after a nap—that I'd slept the day away and missed out on something huge. Since Lucy had gone missing, waking up was one more thing I now dreaded. Especially in the morning. Coming out of sleep was like reliving the moment I first heard about Lucy all over again. I'd sink back into the covers and slip into a black despair as the layers of reality settled in around me that my sister had vanished.

It had been over three weeks, and there was still no trace of Lucy.

But then the dream came rushing back, and with it, a warm feeling spread over me and a certainty I couldn't shake: *Lucy is still with us, Lucy is alive.*

4

Sylvia

I LIKED IT HERE. At first. We moved from Des Moines, Iowa, in the spring of '42. We arrived in the evening on the heels of a rain shower, and what I remember most about our first night in East Texas was the air: how stepping out of the car was like stepping into a warm bath. I inhaled the sugary-sweet air. It was intoxicating. The moon was bright and it made the magnolia blossoms that lined our driveway glow like lanterns, welcoming us. Or so I thought.

I was twenty-eight; John was thirty. We had just gotten married that February, on Valentine's Day, in a small white chapel with a bright green lawn. John and I were ancient to still be unmarried by our parents' standards, but it was only because we had met later in life than most couples.

We were both in college. John was finishing up his electrical engineering degree, and I was working part-time as a clerk in the library, my hand growing used to the pleasant, dull rhythm of stamping books for checkout. I took a handful of classes in my spare time, with the idea that I might become a school teacher one day. World history, English literature, and biology were my favorites. But when John graduated and landed the job at the steel plant in Texas, it made sense for me to move on from college.

I had always pictured, or hoped, that we would move to someplace even larger than Des Moines. To California or, closer to home, Chicago. Not to a town of fifty thousand. But it was the best offer John had received and after he visited there by train once, he came home to our tiny walk-up apartment, clasped my face in his broad hands that always smelled sweetly of pipe tobacco, and promised me I would love it there.

Our plan was to start a small family, and my early years in Longview were dreamy. When John was at work, I busied myself with gardening. Small rows of tulips in the side yard, at first, and then roses in every shade I could find. I imagined myself being the sort of woman who would have a cutting garden, who would always have fresh flowers on the table, and for a while, I was that sort of woman.

Our house was the very best part of the move, a caramel-colored stucco, three-storied home with a Spanish-tile roof—the kind of roof that never needs mending. It was in the oldest neighborhood in town, and the streets were as wide as rivers and lined with sheltering oaks. The third story was reached by climbing a long, creaking staircase and the whole floor was a large, light-filled room with dormer windows. It became my sewing room. I spent my mornings in the garden, and when the sun turned into a torch, I would go upstairs and knit baby blankets and booties, and cut out pink hearts from old quilting material of my grandmother's, which I planned to use as a nursery decoration.

Sometimes during John's lunch breaks I would drive over to the steel plant and we would have a picnic lunch on their campus, which had a sprawling park, and stroll alongside the pond beneath giant pines, holding hands. I would bring us toasted ham-and-cheese sandwiches and a pint jar of lemonade to share.

I made friends with some of the other wives whose husbands worked at the steel plant, and they showed me how to play the domino game Forty-Two, and how to fry a chicken and make sun-brewed iced tea.

On weekends John and I would set off in the car on long, meandering drives over the blacktop roads. The trees—elm, oak, and pine—were so ancient that they were stooped over, their tops weaving together like clasped hands, forming a tunnel over the country lanes. We used to marvel at the majesty of it, imagining that we might be led to some magical place if we drove through the green corridor.

————

Those same trees feel claustrophobic to me now. Suffocating. And when I think of all they've seen and all they've witnessed, they seem downright menacing.

5

Leah

Halloween
Tuesday, October 23rd, 1989
Lucy missing 1 month, 2 days

Mom turned the porch lights off early tonight. The police have urged everyone to stay in for Halloween, but she was worried there might be some brave trick-or-treaters, so after dinner, she snapped the shutters closed, killed the lights in the entryway, kissed me on the forehead, and went upstairs to watch TV.

I'm in Dad's study—a small nook just off the den.

He hasn't slept at home in over a week. He can't bear to be in the house anymore, to look at the walls that are filled with pictures of Lucy, or to eat in the breakfast room—the last place he saw her. Mom doesn't know this, but while she was fixing dinner, I snuck upstairs to call him at his office where he's been sleeping.

"Hey baby," he answered, his voice slurry with alcohol.

"Dad," I said, cradling the phone to my ear, "can you come home, just for tonight? Please? It's Halloween. For me?"

He promised he would, so I'm up waiting for him, sitting on his brown leather loveseat, sawing my way through a bag of creamy candy corn that Grandad brought by earlier today.

Dad's an architect, and his study is a light-filled room with high, rectangular windows running the length of the walls. Through the windows you see a sea of green trees. It's a calming room. And modern compared to the rest of our old rambling, two-story Colonial.

Lucy and I used to love playing in here. We'd sit at the slate-green drafting table, shoulder to shoulder, and doodle, using Dad's silver compass to make big, perfect circles. We loved all of his tools and instruments, especially the giant pink eraser, the way it became red-hot as we ran it across the paper and shed its crumbly shavings, which Lucy used to scatter over sheets of construction paper coated with glue.

Just next to the drafting table, perched on top of an ornate, black lacquer desk, is Dad's computer, a Commodore 64. He's always been fascinated with electronics, so we were one of the first families in town to own one. Lucy and I really didn't know how to use it—and we weren't supposed to mess with it—but we'd pretend we did and would spend Sunday afternoons playing secretary.

Light is streaming through the windows, and though it's cool outside, the room is warm and toasty as the sun sets, making me feel drowsy. I stare out the window and a breeze combs through our maple tree, shaking the leaves. On the windowsill there is a gold heart-framed picture of me and Lucy taken on our first camping trip at a nearby lake. In the picture, I'm carrying a four-year-old Lucy on my shoulders. She has pulled her grin wide with her index fingers, making a clownish face. We are underneath a feathery pine tree, next to our bright orange tent, and we're wearing matching tube socks, to ward off chiggers. Our faces are hot-pink from the sun. One of a hundred weekends we spent like this together.

I stare at the photo, and reach out to touch Lucy's face. "I won't give up," I say out loud. The room grows stuffy and orange with the setting sun, so I stretch out on the loveseat and drift off to sleep.

––––––––––

The house is dark. The only light in the study comes from the Commodore, the blinking orange cursor. The cursor starts to move; my name is being spelled out:

L E A H.

I grab the keyboard and start typing: *Lucy! Is that you?*
My heart thrums in my chest. The cursor blinks.

Y E S.

I can tell that it's Lucy, that she's typing with just her pointer finger, the only way she knows how. And the caps lock must be pressed down.

I MISS U. I MISS MOM AND DAD.

I quickly type: *We miss you so much! We love you! Where are you?*
I have so much to say but I'm afraid to type any more in case she's trying to write me back. But the cursor just keeps blinking, blinking at me, a teasing, winking eye.

My breath is thin and my hands hover over the keys, but then the cursor starts moving again:

UNDERGROUND.
BY THE WOODS.

My fingers grow cold over the keyboard. I'm just about to ask more but the screen goes blank and the computer zaps off. I try to power it back up, but it won't come on.

When I wake up, the study is dark with just a slice of moonlight turning the walls silver. My heartbeat is ragged and is pounding in my temples. The computer is on. I try to remember (but can't) if it had been on before I fell asleep. I walk over to it and try to type to Lucy, but she doesn't answer back.

6

Sylvia

Sunday, October 15th, 1989

Today after lunch, I clear the table and shake the breadcrumbs from the tablecloth. I wash the dishes by hand, the warm, lapping water putting me in a daze. I do some more tidying up and work a crossword puzzle, but then I set it aside and do what I've been putting off doing since I saw Lucy's poster.

I walk across the room to John's old roll-top desk and fish out the key from the back of a drawer. I climb the narrow stairs leading to the third-story sewing room. I don't come up here very much anymore, unless I need to do some mending.

I reach the top of the landing and open the door. The room smells closed-up and musty, so I throw open the windows and let the room suck in the cool autumn air.

In the corner, behind bolts of dusty fabric, I find the rusty metal file box—the box I promised myself I'd never reopen—and with the key clasped in my hand, I turn the lock. My fingers brush against the file I know to be Delia's—I can feel the weathered, hand-made map to the cemetery she drew for me late one night—but I don't let myself look at her file just yet.

I put on my glasses and search for the file marked "CHILDREN" and pull it out, fanning the contents across my work table: newspaper clippings, photographs, and, of course, my own handwritten notes. I begin to read and allow myself to remember.

———

The first child to go missing was Eleanor Jackson, age six. Blond hair, blue eyes. From the small community of Starrville, like all the other children who disappeared would be. Until Lucy. In the picture that the family selected for the poster—the same one that would be flashed on the nightly news and in the newspaper—Eleanor's eyes were almost gray, the blue was so deep, and her lopsided grin revealed a recently lost tooth.

She was taken right from her own backyard one summer afternoon, August 7th, 1980, while her father was away at work. Her mother, Helen, had just stepped inside to make Eleanor a peanut butter and jelly sandwich. She was watching Eleanor run through the sprinklers from the kitchen window. She turned to open the fridge and grabbed the jar of Welch's grape jam. She slid the knife through the jam and spread it across the bread, and when she turned back, Eleanor was gone.

That winter, in Big Woods, when the leaves from all the trees had thinned, the police would find what was left of her: a row of teeth and a tiny gold cross, a gift from her grandma.

The following summer, three more children went missing. Their remains would all be discovered, too, in Big Woods, in a small clearing, all next to the same markings spray-painted in white: the inverted pentagram, an upside-down cross, the numbers 666, and some other wretched symbols I would learn about; we all would.

———————

My breath catches; I have to stop reading. I close the file and put it away. I don't know if I can go on with this. The room is too cold now—I don't know how long I've been up here, the leaves are starting to turn gold from the sinking sun—and I sit there holding myself, rocking back and forth, working my own gold cross necklace between my fingers as if it's a talisman, as if it can ward off the evil that's sure to come.

7

Leah

Friday, September 29th, 1989
Lucy missing 3 hours

When I first heard about Lucy, when my parents suddenly appeared together just outside my third period classroom door and led me out into the hallway to tell me, I didn't believe that something horrible had happened to my sister. The possibility crossed my mind for a second, but I shoved it away, wanting to believe another version. Wanting to pick another reality, like Lucy was always doing when she read her Choose Your Own Adventure books. If the story ended too quickly, Lucy would cheat and flick ahead to see the correct route to take to reach the end. That's what I was doing in my mind as my parents were telling me, and my mind fixed on what I believed could be the better version.

"Lucy ran away from home," I said.

"Why on earth would she do that, honey?" my mom asked, her eyes suddenly filling with hope.

"Maybe she's just trying to get attention," I said. But as soon as the words left my mouth I could hear how lame they sounded. Attention was all we Spencer girls ever got. We were the complete and total center of our parents' lives. I decided not to confess that Lucy and I had planned to run away one day this past summer. It was only out of boredom that we did it, and we were back home within the hour, scorched from the August sun and quenching our thirst with icy popsicles while watching *The Price Is Right*.

I kept this tidbit to myself, but I did tell them about our secret hideout, and soon I was leading my parents and the police to the empty lot a dozen houses up the street from ours. It was two lots, really, perched atop of one of the highest hills in town.

Lucy and I used to pedal our ten-speeds up the hill and collapse in the field. There is a cluster of overgrown honeysuckle vines in a far corner, and we'd huddle underneath the twisted branches and pretend it was a cottage for the muses from our favorite movie, *Xanadu*. Sometimes, we'd leave tiny bits of candy bar or half-finished bottles of Orange Crush to try and summon the muses home.

When we arrived at the spot, there was no sign of Lucy. I showed them the tangled dome of honeysuckle—our own private Narnia— and remembered the first time I taught Lucy how to drink the honeysuckle's nectar. I had plucked a creamy-white blossom off the vine, showing her how to tug gently at the green tip, pulling the stem slowly through the flower until it came through the bottom and yielded a drop of sugary nectar. Our fingers were threaded together and I remember the look on Lucy's little cherub face that day—one of trust and rapt amazement at my trick. I'd felt all-powerful that afternoon as the guide and protector of my sister's tiny universe.

The memory of it and the thought that I may never see Lucy again sent me into convulsions, and I wailed and cried a cry that sounded animal-like, a howl that surely couldn't have been my own.

8

Sylvia

AFTER MY THIRD MISCARRIAGE, we stopped trying. Something in me had shifted. I could no longer deal with the heartbreak or the lost look in John's eyes, which was as much a look of utter sadness for us both as it was a look of failure over how he could comfort his new, broken wife.

We lost the first baby just after I had tested positive at the doctor's office; we didn't even have time to pick out a name. I was pregnant just three months later, though. Getting pregnant wasn't a problem for me, but staying pregnant was. I bought a yellow baby quilt the color of lemon chiffon and embroidered it with the initials "JP" in a pastel green near the top, next to a baby elephant. Josephine if she was a girl, or Joseph for a boy.

I carried the baby nineteen weeks. We had just started to tell our friends and family when, one morning while doing the dishes, I felt a twinge in my stomach and then a warmth spread between my legs. John was at work. I drove myself to the doctor's and he performed a

D&C. I was shaking afterwards, and the nurse called John to come and pick me up.

"We'll just keep trying, Sylvie," John said on the way home, his voice steady and sure. The doctor suggested we wait a little longer before trying again, and we did.

By summer, I was pregnant again. It was a boy, I just knew it, and we named him Peter. We would call him Pete for short, and, as if we were both trying to will him into existence, we began readying the house for his arrival. I began monogramming everything I could find—pillowcases, sheets, baby towels—and John went to the hardware store for sky blue paint and painted his nursery. I wanted to decorate it in blue and white, to match the gingham wicker rocker that had been my grandmother's.

I was nearly five months along when we lost Peter. One night a pain shot through my back like a drill and I couldn't walk. John and I rode in the ambulance to the hospital, a fervent prayer hissed through my clenched teeth: *Please let him live.*

I had a rapid-spreading kidney infection, and by morning, Peter was gone. A boy, just like I had thought.

I cannot describe that day. The way the medication held me hostage between sleeping and waking—a drug-induced purgatory. A chaplain stopped by, but it was of little comfort; people came from our church, but John turned them away at the door. After a few days I was released and we went home. John closed the door to the nursery, packed up all of Peter's little things, and dropped them off at our church for donation.

———

For a long time, I couldn't eat or sleep. Grief riddled my body and if John hadn't forced me to take small sips of chicken soup, I probably wouldn't have survived. It was December, and winter was already unnecessarily harsh, making it easy for us to both shut in and turn away from the world. We didn't put up the tree that season, and I was grateful for a friend who brought us plates of Christmas dinner leftovers, the only way we marked the holiday that year.

Then spring came, and I began to garden again with a gusto that surprised me. I drove to all the surrounding towns and visited their nurseries, looking for inspiration. I planted a stand of pink crepe myrtles along the back fence and filled in a bare patch with as many gardenias as would fit. I rimmed our towering oak with layering rings of hostas and orange cannas. I planted a rainbow of lantana in front of our stone fence, preferring perennials to annuals—things that will return, as opposed to the things that leave us forever.

I enjoyed picking out the plants, having small exchanges with the nursery owners, learning tips about the native species and such, but in the process of driving to and fro I also discovered my newest love: transplanting. I would spy an old, creaking homestead from the road, park the station wagon in the shade, and carry my trowel and sack through the field. I never failed to find a long-abandoned patch of bulbs—tulips, irises, or daylilies—and would gently dig them from the earth, nestling them safely in my brown paper sack. I didn't think of it as stealing at all; to me, it was rescuing.

The rhythm of planting, of turning the warm soil over in my hands soothed me. Dare I say it healed me, even. And on one day in mid-April, the 11th—what would've been Peter's due date—I found myself driving on a back country road to clear my mind when I came across a dilapidated rust-colored barn. The remnants of a farmhouse stood nearby—just a brick chimney and an old washtub remained—but right out front where a walkway used to be I was greeted by the most glorious plot of paper whites, their tops so bright they looked like a cluster of stars.

When I returned home, I dug a special row and planted them in Peter's memory, tamping down the soil, saying a special prayer for him and saying goodbye to the life we would never have.

9

Leah

Friday, September 29th, 1989
Lucy missing 4 hours

We walked down the hill toward home. My face was hot with tears and I clutched my stomach. Dad wrapped his arm around my back; Mom walked up ahead with the officers, the heels of her tan work pumps striking frantic notes along the pavement.

Neighbors were beginning to stream out of their homes to join the search party. We passed by the Holts' house—an elderly couple— and they were standing in their yard being interviewed by the police. Mrs. Holt used to babysit us and she craned her neck around to look at me, but I avoided her gaze and looked straight ahead instead, trying to hold onto the image in my mind of Lucy standing in our driveway waiting for us, safe.

When we reached our driveway there was no Lucy, just more police.

We all sat in the living room—my parents and me on our sofa, directly across from the two lead officers on the case, Sheriff Greene and Officer Watts.

Sheriff Tommy Greene had gone to high school with Mom and Dad. He had been a football star and was a friendly acquaintance, somebody my parents would wave to in the grocery store.

"Leah," he said, his voice calm and steady, "can you tell us what you remember about this morning? About Lucy? Was there anything unusual that you can think of?"

He had kind eyes and hair the color of pennies, and there was something about him that I trusted. I bit my lip and looked down. When I spoke, my voice came out reedy and thin, but I told him every detail that I could remember about the morning, which wasn't much. He gave me a conciliatory smile and nod. Officer Watts just stared at me openly, with something like disapproval on his face, his mouth curled in a snarl. He was fat and balding and seemed like a jerk. He kept his radio up so we heard every beep and blip—it was jarring—and at one point he got up and stood by the front door as if we were just wasting his time.

———————

Earlier that morning on the drive home from school in our cramped navy blue Honda Accord, my parents told me what had happened as I picked at the peeling window tint.

Dad had showered while Lucy and I were both still asleep. Mom was just leaving for work when he stepped out of the shower; they kissed goodbye. Dad woke us up and while I was getting ready in the bathroom, Dad and Lucy sat around our scarred wooden table, eating breakfast together. Halfway through breakfast, Dad grabbed the newspaper and went upstairs to use the restroom. By the time he came back down, Lucy was gone. He raced outside calling out to her, then started running to the bus stop. By the time he got there, he saw the back of the bus pulling away and figured she was on it safely, on her way to school.

"We thought she might've fallen asleep on the bus again," Mom said. Dad was being quiet. I thought I could hear him crying.

It had happened before. One day last spring, Lucy's school had phoned Mom to let her know that Lucy had been late to school that morning because she had fallen asleep on the bus. The bus driver had noticed her in the mirror once he was several blocks away from the school. She was curled up on one of the back seats, sucking her thumb with her headphones on, her Walkman playing softly. The driver patted her gently with his large hands, careful not to frighten her.

When Dad called Mom at work this morning to let her know, they agreed to first meet at the bus barn. I could imagine Mom gearing up for a fight with the bus driver. As the principal of All Saints', a private all-girls' high school, she was used to issuing harsh words when need be. But when they got there, there was no sign of Lucy.

They went straight to the police station and then immediately to get me.

Anger flashed through me. I was mad at Dad for not catching up to her, mad at Lucy for always darting off, mad at myself for staying in that damn bathroom.

"So you didn't actually see her get on the bus?" I asked, my voice shrill. As soon as the words came out I wished I could've snatched them back.

"No, honey," he said. He was sobbing. I saw his hand fly up, motioning for Mom to pull over. She did and he climbed out of the car and down on all fours and vomited into a strip of bleached grass.

"You know how she was always begging us to let her make the walk alone, Leah, insisting that she was old enough," Mom said, her voice pinched with alarm.

————————

Now Dad was up from the couch, pacing the living room and pulling at his thick, black, wavy hair.

"As I explained to your parents earlier, these first twenty-four hours are the most important," Sheriff Greene said while jotting down notes in his notepad.

"Well then DO something, Goddammit!" my dad said, his voice cracking with pain. He pounded his fist on the coffee table, making the ashtray jump and scatter ash over the glass top.

"Carl," my mom said, a warning.

Sheriff Greene didn't flinch, he just nodded. "Believe me, Carl, we're doing everything we can to bring Lucy home. There's still the possibility that there's been no foul play. That she just went exploring and will be back. From what you all have told me, Lucy is adventurous. But we're treating this very seriously."

Sheriff Greene stood up to leave. "If you think of anything, Leah, give me a call." He handed me his card and when his hand brushed mine, it was calloused and warm.

10

Sylvia

WHEN THE GARDEN WAS filled, it was time to move on to something else. The constant activity had lifted me up. I could greet John after work, with dinner in the pan, and look forward to hearing about his day.

We slowly began to enjoy our life together again as a couple without children. We flew to Ft. Lauderdale once, when John had time off, to visit my sister, Evelyn. John treated the three of us to meals of grilled seafood at a different restaurant each night, and we spent lazy afternoons at the beach, letting the sun broil our skin while sipping on fruity cocktails.

Once we returned home, John painted the nursery in a creamy white and lined the walls with shelves made of chestnut to hold my growing collection of books. When he went off to work for the day, I would spend hours reading. I gravitated toward thick Victorian novels, books of poetry, and even some potboilers. But I found that if I had too much time on my hands, I could swiftly slip back into the quicksand of sadness. I needed some other way to fill my time.

————

I have always loved children—that's why I had originally wanted to be a teacher—but the thought of summers off scared me a little now. All that time alone. So when I saw a bulletin up at the library, *Become a Registered Nurse!* I knew it was something I wanted to try. I was still young, just in my mid-thirties, and the thought of going back to school excited me. I figured I could specialize in pediatrics and work with babies or children. Be useful somehow.

John kept saying that we didn't need the money, but he also knew that I needed to stay busy, so he agreed it would be best for me to enroll. And thank God for that. I would've never been able to stretch John's pension this long.

And, I would've never met Delia.

11

Leah

Friday, September 29th, 1989
Lucy missing 12 hours

We stayed up all night that first night. Sheriff Greene kept the search party going but urged us to stick close to home in case Lucy showed up or the phone rang. Dad prowled the front entryway like a panther, as if there was going to be a knock at the door at any second.

His nervous energy set Mom on edge, so she sat in the back den smoking Virginia Slims as I nuzzled into her on the sofa. She draped a homemade afghan over us, and we stared out the huge bank of windows, catching the occasional flashlight from the search party bounce through the woods behind our home.

Dad couldn't stand it inside any longer so he cranked up his vintage yellow pickup and circled the neighborhood, hollering out Lucy's name as if looking for a stray animal.

Mom went to the kitchen and pulled a bottle of sherry off the shelf and brought me a can of Coke and a package of Fritos. "You really need to eat something," she said, pushing the bag of Fritos toward me. I just shook my head; my stomach was in knots. But my mouth was dry, so I pulled back the tab on the Coke and took a swig.

I kept winding the afghan around in my hands, hooking my fingers through the holes. I couldn't stop fidgeting. Though no one had mentioned it—at least not in front of me—I couldn't help but think about Big Woods and the devil worshippers. The adults tried to keep us kids sheltered from the grim details, but everybody in town knew the stories. A few years ago in Starrville, a tiny town next to ours, a bunch of kids had gone missing. Nobody ever found out who kidnapped them, but their bodies were all later found in Big Woods. People believed it was the work of a satanic cult.

Growing up, I'd always heard stories about Big Woods. At slumber parties kids would tell ghost stories about it, and even before the kidnappings there had always been spooky tales about cults and devil worshipping out there.

There's an old village out there called Shiloh, with a decrepit schoolhouse that everyone says is haunted. It blew up at the turn of the century, but some of the red brick walls are still standing. High school students used to party out there after football games, and they'd say that there's still textbooks scattered all over the floor from the day of the explosion. But now, nobody goes out there anymore.

I've driven past Big Woods a few times with Mom and Dad; it's on the way to Grandpa's deer lease. There's no sign announcing it, but you know once you're out there: the trees are thick and tall and next to the old schoolhouse, there's a cemetery with black gates that are always chained up.

A kid in my school, Nathan Blackhill, lives on a farm that touches Big Woods and he's always telling these wild stories about it. He says that during a full moon, he can hear screams all the way from his house. He's explored it on foot during the day and he swears that he's found old shacks that have been spray painted with devil worshipper symbols and upside-down crosses. He says he always finds piles of new clothes and cans of fresh Coke, as if somebody's just stepped out. Nathan has lots of pimples and his face is always blushing (and he's never had a girlfriend) but when he starts telling these stories, everyone gathers around. I've always thought he did it for the attention, but now I'm not so sure.

I turned to Mom and asked her if she thinks Lucy was taken by devil worshippers. Her eyes were red-rimmed and bloodshot, making them bluer than they normally were, almost supernaturally blue. "Oh, honey. The sheriff hasn't said anything like that. You know that nothing like that's happened here in Longview." She was working her cigarette between her fingers and wouldn't meet my eyes.

"I'm not thinking that, and neither should you." She took a long drag off her cigarette and pulled me into her.

12

Sylvia

AFTER THE FIRST CHILDREN went missing, we started hearing about the devil worshippers, and everyone in town became really afraid. My neighbor started to bring his cat inside during the week of Halloween, and people stopped letting their children out to trick-or-treat.

My tiny Episcopalian church, St. Paul's, wasn't as fervent as some of the other churches in town, but my minister did hold a call to prayer one Wednesday evening to offer folks some solace. The bigger churches in town banded together with the smaller, rural churches, including the Starrville Church of Christ, and held weekly prayer vigils for the missing, and later, for the dead.

I passed a vigil on my way home from the store one Friday evening. I had started to push myself, to work up the courage to go out again at night. It was being held at East Texas Methodist. Children and adults were clutched tightly together in a prayer circle, swaying side to side on the slender sidewalk between the church and the highway.

Some were waving signs that read HONK FOR JESUS! and GOD=HEAVEN, SATAN=HELL, YOU CHOOSE! My windows were rolled up, but I could hear them chanting back and forth as the youth minister stood in their midst shouting into a bullhorn, riling up the crowd. A young boy was sitting on the curb, setting a Ouija board on fire.

Sticks of candlelight cast an eerie glow across their faces, so that all I could see were bare teeth and flickering eyes. Something about this sight made me shiver as I drove past and my heart didn't stop racing until I was back at home safely with my garage door shut.

13

Leah

Saturday, September 30th, 1989
Lucy missing 1 day

I wake to the sound of dishes clattering in the kitchen. My face is damp with drool and Mom has slipped off my Keds and tucked a pillow beneath my head. I'm downstairs, on the couch. I must have just dozed off, because Mom and I had watched the sun come up together.

There's a knock at the door. It's someone from a church group; they've stopped by to bring us a box of donuts. Mom slides a powdered sugar one onto a plate and pushes it toward me.

I'm starving and I devour it so quickly it makes me cough. Dad brings me a glass of chocolate milk and we all sit around the breakfast table as the morning sun—orange as a peach—bleeds honey-colored light through the windows.

The doorbell rings. Dad hops up; it's Sheriff Greene. He steps into the breakfast room. I'm steeling myself for bad news.

"We may have something," he says, looking at each of us. His hair is still wet and he smells like aftershave and fresh soap. "A neighbor lady, Katie Whitaker, down the street, says she saw a strange car circling the block yesterday morning. She didn't get home until late last night, so we are only just now hearing about this."

My heart begins to flutter. Mrs. Whitaker is a retired accountant who lives six houses down in a small house with yellow shutters. Just around the corner from the bus stop.

"Said she was in her breakfast room watching for the mailman when she noticed an olive green car driving past, slowly. Possibly a Karmann Ghia. Wasn't sure." His eyes are tired. He's been up all night, too.

"She only noticed it because it's such an unusual-looking car, but also because it circled the block a few times. She didn't get a license plate, though, so it could be tough to find a match. This could mean nothing, of course, but we're going to follow up on it."

My hands grow sweaty, I feel like I'm going to be sick. Mom takes a drag off her cigarette and Dad stares out the window, doe-eyed. The sheriff pauses in place for a moment before nodding at us and turning to leave.

The milk curdles in my stomach. I don't know what to think, but I can't stop seeing Lucy in my mind, being driven off in that car.

14

Sylvia

Sunday, October 1st, 1989

Today is my birthday. Seventy-five: a milestone. Since John died, I haven't seen much point in celebrating birthdays. After he passed, I would get invitations to lunch or to tea. And at first, they were genuine, but then they began to feel stiff, obligatory, and after I was shunned, the invitations thinned out and then stopped altogether.

I now mark it the same way every year: I pad to the mailbox in my house slippers—there will be a card from Evelyn and another one from the March of Dimes. I might have something sweet to eat, if I have the energy to make it.

Today I pull an apple pie from the oven. I found a bushel of pink ladies from a nearby farm stand this weekend, and so this morning I sliced them up into thin discs and tossed them in my cream-colored mixing bowl with cinnamon, lemon, and a little brown sugar—I like mine tart, the way they make them in the north, not so sugary—and filled them into a store-made pie crust, no longer having the pep to make my own.

Today I do this because it is a milestone, but also, I do it for Delia. We have the same birthday week. Hers will be October 8th. Exactly one week apart.

Delia. That's not even her real name—I never knew it, that's just the name I gave her—but I was able to draw out some facts, like her birthday, for instance, and when I told her late one night at the hospital that we shared this week, she smiled.

The warm yeasty smell fills the kitchen. I take the pie from the oven and let it rest on top of a hand towel, and decide to brew a pot of fresh coffee, which I only drink on special occasions. I shake the bitter grounds into the filter and then sit at the table and watch as red hummingbirds light on my feeder. The kitchen window is open and a quick rush of wind sweeps through, giving me a chill and making the pile of dried curled leaves clatter along my sidewalk.

The summer Delia vanished she was nineteen, going on twenty. I bought her a card that year when I hoped she might still be alive. But it's here, in this house somewhere, never sent. This year she would've been thirty. She might've been a wife, perhaps, or even a mother by now.

When the coffee is done, I pour myself a cup, top it with cream, and set out a plate for the pie. I also set one out for Delia, and say the words aloud to her that I've been saying every year since she vanished: "I'm sorry I couldn't save you."

15

Leah

Friday, October 6th, 1989
Lucy missing 1 week

Lucy has been missing for a week. Other than the car—which we've heard nothing else about—there haven't been any new leads. Mom and Dad and I have stayed at home, huddled inside our quiet house, waiting for the phone to ring, waiting for something to break the silence. I've started to hate the mustard yellow wall phone itself, the phone I stare at, willing it to ring, willing for Lucy to be on the other end, but it just hangs there. My parents won't let me take calls, and no one is allowed to make calls unless it's to the police, for fear that we might miss something.

Dad's big blue eyes leak with tears all the time, and every morning around the time that Lucy went missing, he marches back and forth to the bus stop, as if trying to retrace what happened. Mom and I watch him from the kitchen window. One morning Mom ran out after him in her rust-colored robe and caught his arm. I cracked open the window to listen.

"This isn't your fault, Carl. None of this is anybody's fault." But Dad tore away from her and kept walking. She's been in that robe every day, only changing once into normal clothes when she had to take more photos of Lucy to the police station.

They stay up most of the night talking in angry tones, and Dad has started drinking again, something he swore off years ago. Once, when Lucy and I were little, we went to a backyard barbecue with Dad while Mom was away on business. He drank too many margaritas and passed out in a hammock while he was supposed to be watching us. Lucy and I made our own way home that night, with Dad staggering in hours later. This had terrified him, so he quit completely after that. Yesterday morning, though, I could smell the sharp fumes of gin in his orange juice at breakfast and he goes through the days glass-eyed in front of the television, or shut off alone in his study, compulsively sketching pictures of Lucy that he hopes will bring her home.

Mom's co-workers have been bringing by gooey casseroles and leaving them on the porch with notes pinned to the top, but this morning she insisted on making a proper breakfast, so she pulled out her cast iron skillet and fried a neat row of bacon and a batch of fried eggs. We sat around the breakfast table and ate in silence.

————

Mom and Dad have drifted back upstairs to take a nap, but I'm wired, I can't sleep. I climb the stairs and for the first time since last Friday, I allow myself to go into Lucy's room.

I pause at the door before walking in. I stick a bare foot onto the carpet and run my toes along the seafoam green shag as if testing the temperature of pool water. I suck in a deep breath and step into the room.

It's raining out, and big drops of rain thud against the tall, thick windows, making the room feel like it's rocking, like how you feel inside a car as it's being pulled through a car wash.

I cross the room and throw myself on the bed and snuggle underneath Lucy's Strawberry Shortcake comforter. I breathe in and I can still smell her—that little Lucy smell that is perfectly her own—a mix of Juicy Fruit gum and baby shampoo, which Lucy swore made her hair softer. My Lucy Belle. I can't stop crying but I don't want Mom and Dad to hear me so I sob into Lucy's pink chenille pillow and find myself talking out loud to her. "Where are you, Lucy? What happened to you?"

Lucy and I like to joke that we are twins; we have the same birthday, December 8th. We were born four years apart, so we're not really twins of course, but Lucy and I believe we can read each other's minds and we're closer than any other sisters I know.

It might be hard to believe that we are born on the same day, but Mom planned it that way. She had me by C-section and though Lucy wasn't due until Christmas Eve, the doctor gave her the choice of when to schedule Lucy's birth and she thought it would be neat if we shared the same birthday. And it is neat. We get to have a joint party every year with our friends—usually at the roller rink if it's chilly out, or if it's nice we have a party at our house. Mom bakes us each our own birthday cake: a yellow butter cake with chocolate frosting for me and a vanilla cake with pink frosting for Lucy. We each get a small pile of presents—usually new clothes—but we also always get our favorite gift: a matching brand-new Swatch watch.

I notice I'm twisting my own Swatch around on my wrist (a simple one with a teal-colored band and a Pepto-Bismol pink face) and a panic shoots through me when I realize I don't even know if Lucy is wearing hers. I jump out of bed and go over to her creamy white vanity to look for it.

It's gone, and for some reason this makes me feel relieved. It makes me feel connected to her somehow. I run my finger along the stack of other Swatch bands. Some are spiky, from when she was little and had to punch holes in them to make them fit.

We are both tomboys and it shows in the things we have in our rooms. Lucy is forever making stuff with her hands, and her vanity bursts with her creations: friendship bracelets—both the kind made from colorful thread and also the kind with safety pins and little glass beads—and leather wallets and belts. A tangle of her leather-making tools are scattered over the surface—little mallets and letter stamps and strips of leather that she dyes in deep tans in Mom's art shed.

Above her vanity is a poster of Ralph Macchio. I reach up and touch a torn corner. She had it pinned up, I knew, both because she thought he was cute, but also because she wanted to be him. There's a brick wall in the backyard and we used to balance on it, facing each other with one leg raised, trying to pull off moves from *The Karate Kid*. Just beyond the wall is our tetherball court. In the summer we'd spend hours out there trying to one up each other, but I can't think about that now, the fact that I might never get to let Lucy win another game.

I flop back onto her bed and scan the room as if searching for clues. My eyes rest on a stack of letters on Lucy's bedside table.

I rearrange the pillows behind my back and unfold the letters like an accordion over the bedspread. The edges of the envelopes are rubbed soft; I can tell that Lucy has read them over and over. I open a few and read them, but then toss them aside. Reading them makes me shudder as I remember our last fight, which hadn't been as much of a fight as it had been me just being flat-out mean to Lucy.

Last summer, when we returned home from camp, Lucy got a string of letters from pen pals. All boys. Though we're both tomboy-ish, Lucy's always been more girlie than me, especially this past year—I've held onto my gawkiness longer than most. She's just plain cuter, with her golden curls and almond-shaped caramel eyes, and she's always got a flock of boys around her, even in grade school.

She was lying on her stomach in bed, her legs kicking lazily behind her, chewing bubblegum and reading the letters when I walked in. I was suddenly filled with jealousy and became irrationally mad at her. The only letters I ever got were from my bunkmate, Margaret, a nerdy girl who wears Coke bottle glasses and who is always citing scripture. I couldn't stand it—this attention that Lucy always got from boys—so I started stomping around the room.

"What's up your butt?" Lucy asked, an eyebrow raised.

"Nothing! But do you always have to smack your gum like that?"

"Sorry—"

"You're SO gross, Lucy. Everyone is sick of you." I started kicking at Lucy's dirty clothes pile. "Just look how messy your room is. Mom's gonna have a cow when she gets home."

Lucy looked confused and hurt, like I'd just slapped her. "Le—"

"What?" I snapped. "I don't even wanna BE here when she gets back."

I pedaled off on my ten-speed, the warm air sucking at my damp shirt, and kept riding until I reached the nearest vacant lot. I threw my bike down and fell to the ground sobbing, hating myself for being so senselessly mean to Lucy.

I didn't apologize to her or ever tell her why I was really upset; I was too ashamed. But as I'm lying here now in her bed, I start bargaining furiously with the universe: *If you will let her come home, I will never be mean to her again.*

————

When I finally did get my first boyfriend, Scott, just this past summer, I couldn't understand what all the fuss was about. Hanging out with a boy was like hanging out with a girl, but you're just more aware of what your hair looks like, what your clothes look like—you wouldn't wear your headgear in front of a boy—you see everything through their eyes.

Scott's a soccer player, a year ahead of me, handsome in a traditional way with wavy blond hair and hazel eyes. At first, I couldn't believe he asked me to be his girlfriend. My new friend, Ali Sherman, is girlfriends with Scott's best friend, Brett, so I figured it was just out of convenience that he had asked me, but honestly, I didn't care. I was just happy to finally have a boyfriend, someone's name I could scribble on my book covers.

Scott's dad is an orthodontist and his mom is one of those perky moms always trotting out cookies or brownies and smiling constantly. She still cuts the corners off of Scott's toast and embarrasses him by calling him Scottie.

Scottie. I can still hear his name in Lucy's giddy voice. She liked him, and used to run around the house teasing me, saying with a mouthful of giggles, "Leeeuh's gonna marry Scot-teee!"

————

The rain has let up. I get out of bed and walk to the window and look out over the backyard. The sky is a gray cloak pushing down, but just above the clearing in the woods where Lucy and I play, the sun has started to crack through. The ground there is a carpet of red leaves, matted down by the rain, but the sun is now trickling down a halo of yellow light. My eyes fixate on this spot, and something about it sends a shiver up my spine.

16

Sylvia

THERE ARE NO STRAIGHT roads through Big Woods. It's hard to tell where you are and where you've been once you start driving into it. The roads are narrow and twisty, the sunlight snuffed out by the trees. Some of the street signs have been knocked clean off; others dangle from their metal rusty poles like loose teeth, so it can feel disorienting, like you're driving through a maze.

After the children's bodies were found, I drove out there; I had to see it for myself. I had never been out there, never had a reason to go out there, and didn't know all that much about it.

As best I could tell, half of it is in one county and half of it is in another. Oil and gas leases make up most of the area, but there is also private land with long driveways that wind through thick brambles. Some have mailboxes and others just have threatening signs tacked onto trees that say things like NO TRESPASSING: WE DON'T DIAL 911.

And who knows who actually owns what piece of land. It's just a tangled net of forest that stretches between Starrville and Longview, pulling the two towns together.

There was that single article in the paper—Is Big Woods a Haven for Devil Worshippers?—but other than that, the police didn't release much information about where the bodies were found.

The day I went out there was in summer. I parked next to a gas well and started walking through a scorched field. Locusts scattered in the fried grass; their buzzing gave me chills. I tried to imagine where the bodies could've been found, but it's twenty thousand acres deep and when I heard the low rumble of a truck pass by not once, but twice, I ran as fast as I could back to my station wagon. My heart was hammering as I fumbled with the keys, but I managed to get inside and slam down the beige lock.

17

Leah

Saturday, October 14th, 1989
Lucy missing 2 weeks, 1 day

A cold front blew in today, tossing up the unraked leaves in our yard. The sun is setting and Dad's built us a fire—the first one of the season. We're in the back den, huddled around the television, watching re-runs of *Dallas*.

I can't keep warm (our big old house is drafty) so I've pulled a blanket around my shoulders, and Mom has brought me some hot chocolate. I cup it in my cold hands and stare into the mug and watch as the top layer of mini-marshmallows bob and dissolve into the choc-olate. Mom and Dad are sipping brandy and for a moment, I forget. For a moment, things almost seem normal. But then there's a loud knock at the door.

We all jump up and rush to the front of the house. It's the sheriff. My stomach does flips. Dad shows him into the front parlor and then motions for me to go elsewhere so they can talk.

"It's okay," Sheriff Greene says. His voice is thick. He looks at each of us and clears his throat. "Leah needs to hear this, too." He looks up at my parents. "We may have a lead."

A knife twists in my gut.

"I know this might sound crazy, but a psychic lady is claiming that she knows where Lucy is. She says that she keeps having visions of a little blond girl next to a creek."

Mom's eyes go wide and Dad starts quickly nodding as if he wants the sheriff to hurry up and spit out the rest.

"She's been talking to us for the past three days and we think we've finally narrowed down the location. She's helped us in the past," he says, turning up his palms and shrugging.

"Is she alive?" I ask, my voice a screech, the words spilling out before I even realize it. Mom and Dad both look at me and then look back to the sheriff.

"Well, sometimes she can tell and sometimes she can't. And, unfortunately, this is one of the times that she can't," he says, folding his arms across his chest and tucking his hands into his armpits. "She says she sees her sleeping, but that's it, that's all she can see."

"Where ... " my father stammers. "Where does she think our Lucy is?"

"Well, we can't say for certain, this isn't an exact science, mind you, but the location she's describing sounds like it's at Caney Creek, near Kilgore. Near a little white church in the woods. So we'll look there first."

The sheriff starts shifting his weight from one leg to the other. "We are going out there in the morning, first light. And this psychic,

51

she thinks it would be helpful if y'all would come along, too." He looks up at us sheepishly.

"Yes, of course, Tommy," Mom says, pulling her robe tighter around herself.

"Good. Meet me at the station at seven, and y'all can ride in the cruiser with me."

Blood is roaring in my ears and I can't make out the rest of what is being said. The sheriff leaves and I follow Mom and Dad back to the den, trailing behind them with my head spinning.

Dad flips off the television and we sit in the dark. The fire is starting to go out. It's trying to cough and spit its way back to life, but Dad lets it smolder and die down. My hot chocolate goes cold. I can't finish it. I leave Mom and Dad and go upstairs. I climb in bed and even though it's nowhere near bedtime, I want to sleep. I want to wake up and have it be morning and for us to go and find Lucy.

18

Sylvia

I REMEMBER MY FIRST day at the hospital. I parked in the employee parking lot and walked up to the peach brick building. I was issued a crisp white time card and was excited to punch it for the first time. I was promptly introduced to Dr. Sloane, the OB/GYN who I would work under for years. He was a kindly man. They wouldn't all be.

We were in the Labor and Delivery ward. I was not a delivery nurse; I was in charge of helping the mothers just after labor, when they were settled into their rooms with their tiny, screaming newborns. I would wash their faces, help them to the restroom, and bring them their meds.

I took to it right away—it was like a second skin, like I knew exactly what to do. And after attending to the new mothers for even just a few nights, they began to feel like daughters to me. Some were in their glory, others were startled and frightened, and if it worried me, I would jot down my home number for them. Most of the fathers were perplexed, but I would say to each of the women, loud enough for the men to hear (whether it was the case or not), "You know exactly what you're doing. You're a natural."

Sometimes, if I could tell the families didn't have much, I would slip them extra samples of formula or give them a small care package of things I had assembled at home from odds and ends: blankets, pacifiers, and diapers. I would try to do extra little things, like bring in baked goods, or in the summer, fresh fruit. You weren't supposed to, but I did it anyway and I hope it brought them some comfort.

And of course, when I could tell that the new mothers needed rest, I would lift their baby from them and take them to the nursery, whispering blessings over them as I carried them down the hall.

When the mothers would have cesarean births, they would stay with me even longer, and this was the case with Roz Spencer. I only worked the delivery ward on weekends by then, but I could tell right away that she was the type who was used to doing everything, and even after the C-section, she still had a flurry of commanding energy about her, a strong, capable presence. I met her husband, too, a darkly handsome man who I could tell had a good heart. They mostly kept to themselves but during the night while he was sleeping and she was in the throes of pain from trying to nurse, she'd have me keep a cool washcloth over her forehead and she'd ask me to tell her stories about my childhood, about my time on the farm in Iowa.

When it was time for Roz to be released, I was sad to see them go, but I knew that the little girl was going home to a blessed life.

I wasn't working by the time Lucy was born, but I saw her birth announcement in the paper; this was back when folks still did that sort of thing.

Years later I saw the three of them together at the supermarket. The older one, Leah, was pushing Lucy in the stroller while Roz was picking out tomatoes. I'm not sure if Roz recognized me, but she smiled when she saw me and gave me a little nod.

I don't think she'd recognize me now, now that I've let myself go, and I've always hoped and prayed that she didn't recognize me in that TV clip. My hair was white by then—frazzled and stringy and whipped by up the wind—and I looked like a disheveled mad woman standing there in front of the police station. There was a cascade of people swarming around me shouting in the background, and the reporter got knocked over so that the footage of me looks even more chaotic.

They didn't name me by name, thank goodness, but the local news station played that clip of me over and over again for what felt like weeks. I'd wince every time it flashed on the screen, and would want to plug my ears so I wouldn't have to hear my own voice, high and shrill, making the bold statement that would have me shunned.

19

Leah

Sunday, October 15th, 1989
Lucy missing 2 weeks, 2 days

The creek is swift today from all the rain. I've crossed over it before and it's usually clear and calm, but today it's boiling, a tan and foaming mudslide. The banks are high and tree roots jut out of the rust-colored clay, threading over the creek and catching debris.

My Keds are grass-stained and soaked through. I'm shaking, it's so cold; I should've worn my boots and a heavier coat. Sticker burrs grab at my ankles but I've given up on bending down and plucking them off.

We got to the station early this morning, at six thirty, but everyone was already there waiting for us on the steps outside. When I got out of the car, I could feel a charge in the air, a buzz running through the group, all nervous energy and excitement.

The psychic was standing on the bottom step. She introduced herself as Carla Ray. She looked to be in her late forties with lanky brown hair that dropped to her waist. When she stuck out her arm to shake hands with my parents, her tiny wrist reminded me of a stick doll's. She was wearing smoke-tinted glasses and a long necklace with a chunky rock. I held out my hand to greet her, but to my surprise she grabbed me into a tight hug. She smelled like talcum powder and rose perfume, and she hugged me hard, as if she were trying to take something from me.

The sheriff came over and cleared his throat, breaking up the embrace and announcing it was time to head out. Dad rode up front with Sheriff Greene and Mom and I climbed in the back. His cruiser was a warm oven. The seats were old, cracking leather that smelled stale, but it was neat and tidy and I noticed an air freshener pinned to our back vent that pushed out an aroma like Big Red gum.

The ride out to the creek was so smooth, it felt like we were almost gliding. We pulled into a muddy field and when I stepped out of the car, it didn't feel real to me. It felt like I was watching us all on television.

A heavy-set officer in a tan uniform hurried across the field to us. He had thinning red hair and was breathing hard by the time he reached us, his glasses fogged over from the effort.

"Pleasure to meet y'all," he said, grinning at us expectantly. "I'm Sheriff Randy Meeks. My fellows and I thought we'd come out here to help." He nodded to each of us, and when Dad offered to shake his hand, Sheriff Meeks took it and clapped Dad on the back as if they were getting ready to watch a football game together.

"Sheriff Meeks is with the Starrville Police Department," Sheriff Greene explained. "Some men from the Kilgore force are out here as well."

———

We've been here for half an hour. We're walking side by side with Sheriff Greene. Just up ahead a cluster of officers and volunteers are fanning out in different directions with packs of search dogs. Carla Ray is up front, leading the way, making hand gestures and sometimes pausing to look up at the milky-white sky. We walk along the creek and my eyes stay focused there, watching it gurgle and spit up trash and faded beer cans.

We reach the small church and Carla has us all circle it a few times. She's standing on the north side, looking up at a stained glass window when a dog starts panting, then barking, then the rest of the dogs chime in with angry barks before bursting off toward the woods. The sheriff holds us back and lets Carla lead the officers into the woods first, her ropy brown hair swinging behind her like a pendulum. My heart is punching against my chest, a staccato, and I feel dizzy as we wait.

A few moments later an officer comes out of the woods holding up a blue converse sneaker, but it's too big to be Lucy's. It's a boy's shoe, a teenager's. They bag it up anyway and we continue milling around until I see Carla Ray shaking her head while she's talking to an officer. The sheriff breaks away from us to go and talk to her.

After a moment we all walk back to the cruiser. Dad opens the door for me and shuts it and walks to the front but Mom calls for him, motioning for him to come over to where she and Sheriff Greene are talking.

I see Mom light a cigarette and I see her arms flail up and down in exasperation. I can't hear them over the engine, but I hear the words *fucking* and *quack* shoot out of Mom's mouth. She can be astoundingly direct sometimes, and I see Sheriff Greene slump down in reaction to her words and stare hard at the ground, frowning and quickly nodding. Dad looks crestfallen.

They walk back to the car and Mom slides next to me in the backseat. Her mouth is a tight line and she squeezes my hand as she explains,

"The psychic lady is saying that she is certain this is where she claims she saw Lucy, but now she's saying that Lucy's not here anymore."

I lean into Mom and rest my head on her amber fur coat and let the tears spill down my cheeks as we drive back to the station.

20

Sylvia

I GOT THE CALL about John at nine a.m. on a Monday morning. Poof. He was gone. No warning. I had just finished working the night shift and had stepped inside the house to fix myself a ham sandwich. I was just about to take the first bite when the phone rang.

It was Jeanie, his secretary. I couldn't make out most of the words from the roaring in my ears, just these: *heart attack, paramedics did everything they could, he didn't suffer.* My head was a blur. I ended the call and sat there with the phone cradled in my hands for the longest time before heading back up to the hospital where they were taking his body.

The cardiologist, a tall man with thinning hair, met me in the waiting room and explained that, in his opinion, even without an autopsy (which I declined, I knew it wouldn't change a thing), John had suffered an inevitable, massive heart attack—something I later learned they called the "widow maker."

A widow at thirty-seven. I was too young to just stop living but too old to start over. I didn't know what to do with myself. I took a leave of absence until further notice. Dr. Sloane was very understanding and told me to take as much time off as I needed.

———————

I thought about what to do next. I considered retiring early—I could've, there was a small insurance policy as well as John's pension—but I was worried it wouldn't carry me through. And I considered moving to Florida to live with Evelyn (she had offered). But the idea of living in Florida was much better than the reality of living in Florida: I kept picturing sunny days at the beach, but Evelyn's place was a hard twelve-block walk from the shore and she spent most of her days inside her coral-painted condo watching game shows and fussing over her five cats. I knew we'd make each other crazy.

Two weeks after John died I drove out to the plant to clear out his desk. They had left everything untouched, which was a sensitive gesture but made it all the more gut-wrenching.

I went while everyone else was out to lunch and filled three cardboard boxes with his things: our wedding picture, his grandfather's pocket watch, the last ledger he had written in. I drove home and started in on his things downstairs: his jacket, his billfold (still in a plastic bag from the hospital), and his shoes—immediate stuff that I couldn't bear to look at anymore, things that made me still believe I'd hear him pulling in the driveway. I sealed them up and set the boxes out in the garage.

21

Leah

Thursday, October 19th, 1989
Lucy missing 2 weeks, 6 days

After that morning with Carla Ray, Dad became more unhinged. He began drinking openly at breakfast, cracking open bottles of Pearl Light and barely picking at his food. He believed Carla Ray, I could tell, and this morning while Mom was outside sweeping brittle leaves off the front porch, Dad stepped into his office and called the sheriff to see if she had anymore updates. But we would never hear about Carla Ray again.

This afternoon while I was laying on the couch reading, Mom announced that she and Dad would be returning to work in the morning. I thought it was too soon, but I knew she was trying to shake Dad out of it. She explained that she was just going in for a half-day to clear off her desk to get ready for the following week. Mom didn't press me into going back to school just yet, but she insisted I go to the Fall Harvest Dance with Scott tomorrow night. I wasn't ready to face all of my classmates, but I was itching to escape the house and the sticky, heavy air that had grown between Mom and Dad, so I agreed.

———————

Now it's Friday, midmorning. Grandpa's here with me while Mom and Dad are at work. He is a grouchy widower and smells like Folger's instant coffee and Skoal, but he always lets me do whatever I want, so I like it when he babysits. I just finished a whole box of Fruit-Rollups and an entire sleeve of Pringles and now we're watching television together. Grandpa has turned it to *M.A.S.H.*, which I secretly hate, but I play along anyway, not wanting to hurt his feelings.

I feel sorry for him, even though he's grumpy. He has been stopping by every day since Lucy vanished, and he now has a far-off look in his eyes and seems even more bewildered than usual, so I feel even sorrier for him. I lean into him and let his rough hands tousle my hair.

When Mom gets home a few hours later, Grandpa snaps out of a nap and smooths out the wrinkles in his button-down shirt before kissing me goodbye and leaving. Mom juggles in some grocery bags and starts dinner. I watch as she shakes three pork chops in a large paper sack filled with flour, salt, and pepper. She then drops red potatoes into a pot of boiling water and begins chopping vegetables for a salad.

Once the potatoes are finished, I pitch in and begin mashing them, mixing in cheddar cheese and butter and spooning them into a serving bowl. As Mom begins frying the pork chops, I set the table. This is the first family dinner we've prepared since Lucy's been gone, and my hands tremble as I set out three plates instead of the usual four, but I fight back the tears and try to slip into a routine of quietly working next to Mom.

Dinner is starting to cool, so we begin without Dad. I look out of the corner of my eye and study Mom's profile. In the late-day light she looks older. Her eyes are swollen and puffy as if she's been crying all day, something I hadn't noticed until now. Mom catches me staring at her and puts down her fork. She draws in a deep breath but then tears fill her eyes. It's one of the few times Mom has let me see her cry.

"Oh, honey." She takes my hand. "What are we gonna do without our Lucy?"

I'm about to answer but the moment passes as soon as it had arrived. Mom jumps up and clears the table and says with a forced cheerfulness. "Now, I bet you need to start getting ready for that dance tonight."

I go upstairs and get dressed. I choose a simple black shirt. The only festive clothing I can muster enough energy to put on is a pair of acid-washed jeans. I pull my hair up in a banana clip and run a light layer of mascara over my lashes. I wait upstairs, staring out the window, watching for Scott's headlights to appear.

22

Sylvia

AFTER BEING OFF FOR a month, I went back to work, and it was the only thing that kept me going.

That first year was the hardest. Weekends were especially tough, so I made sure I went to church each Sunday. At first, I hated the pitying stares and I didn't find comfort in other people the way that some folks might, but I kept it up anyway, just to keep me out of the empty house.

On a bright January morning, almost a year to the day that John passed, Dr. Sloane pulled me aside and asked if I would mind filling in for the hospital's psychiatric unit. They were in need, he explained, and were having a hard time finding a replacement. I would need to commit for at least a week and it would be all night shifts. At first, I thought it would be grueling, but I actually found it to be a relief: no more lonely nights at home.

———

The psych unit was located in the basement of the hospital. You had to punch in a security code to enter, and a set of double glass doors whooshed open, slapping sheets of hot, antiseptic air in your face.

It was much like nursing on any other floor—you made your rounds and took care of your patients—except it was a locked unit so security guards had to wheel in the food carts and sometimes you had to watch your back. I got jumped once by a wiry man who was coming off of heroin, but the orderlies happened to be right there and restrained the guy right away.

When the patients first came to us they had usually been off their meds and acting out in public, so they were brought in to get leveled out again. Some were homeless, some may have been living in shelters, and others might have been at home, just disregarding the doctor's orders so that when their bodies got free of the meds they were out of control.

When they first arrived, we were ordered to sedate them pretty heavily, so they were docile, for the most part. It could be demanding at times, but the challenge of the work helped lift me out of my grief. Also, the pay was nearly double because the work was so dangerous, and if I worked holidays (which I usually did), I got paid even more. It was a cash cow, but that's not the reason I stayed on that week and then on permanently for twenty-seven more years.

I stayed on for the camaraderie.

The floor was supervised by the chief nurse, Hattie Banks, a formidable woman with a head of tight black curls that were just beginning to turn silver. She smelled like fresh-pressed laundry and the lilac lotion she was always working into her hands. Hattie had run the unit for nearly twenty years and was its first black female supervisor. She and her team were efficient. They were experienced psychiatric nurses and knew what to watch for—the side effects of the medicine, the swift changes in patients' behavior—and to me, they were role models and sources of assurance. I knew they had my back and I'd never worked with nurses with that level of expertise.

The unit was overseen by a short, cranky, red-faced man named Dr. Marshall who was disliked by most. But he did his rounds in the morning and we rarely had to see him on the night shift.

And everyone knew it was Hat's floor. She was tough on the outside, and at first, I didn't think she liked me all that much. But late one night we got to talking and figured out that we had a lot in common. Reading, for one.

The night shift could be strangely serene, so you could bring in busy work. Most of the patients were knocked out and sleeping. It was lights out at ten thirty. Some of the patients were allowed to go to the rec room to watch TV or play games, but most were not able to because of the heavy medication, so a hush would fall over the floor.

Hattie would do needlepoint and I would crochet, or write letters to Evelyn. Most of the other nurses would huddle around the coffee-pot and gossip, but Hat and I would sit in a quiet corner and swap magazines—I'd bring in *National Geographic* for her and she'd bring in *Reader's Digest* for me—and we'd tell each other about our lives.

She was my one true friend after John died, and in many ways, Hattie saved my life.

23

Leah

Friday, October 20th, 1989
Lucy missing 3 weeks

I'm back home early from the dance; my heart is still racing.

———

Scott picked me up earlier in his black Nissan truck. It's small but souped up with big tires and a loud stereo system that makes the dashboard glimmer like a Christmas tree. Scott just got his license, and he's proud of the thumping bass and likes to crank it up so that other cars notice. I could hear his stereo from down the street but thankfully he turned it down before pulling into our driveway.

"Please be safe," Mom called out to me as I was walking toward his truck.

When I got in, Scott didn't ask me a bunch of awkward questions, he just sweetly squeezed my hand and set it on his knee, holding it there until we got to the church where the dance was being held.

We pulled up to the white-rock building—the dance was in the basement—and Scott turned to me, saying, "Look, we don't even have to go in if you don't want to."

I considered leaving, but I also didn't feel like driving around for hours alone with Scott. "No, I can do it. Let's go."

It was still stifling outside, but when Scott led me through the thick wooden door to the basement, it was freezing cold and dark. Strobe lights beamed off the walls pulsing to the music, and the odor of the smoke machine made me feel dizzy. He took my hand and led me around the room. All eyes were trained on me. I was mostly met with sad, pitiful smiles and half waves until Ali burst in front of us with a pushy, over-exaggerated hug.

"How *are* you? I am *so* sorry, sweetie." Ali was a cheerleader and was always making big displays of emotion, trying to grab the spotlight. In that instance, I cringed; I couldn't remember why we were friends, or what I even liked about her. I started to answer Ali but she was already chatting up Scott, thanking him for bringing me to the dance.

The next song that came on was the Cutting Crew's "I Just Died in Your Arms Tonight," and I was relieved when Scott pulled me away from Ali and onto the dance floor. I clasped my hands around his neck, still sweaty from the night heat. We tried to settle into a groove, but the song really was too fast, making it awkward to keep time to. Scott kept stepping on my toes with his Cole Haans and we both became flustered, so we followed the other fumbling couples off the dance floor.

I looked around the room and saw my old best friend, Nicolette, in the corner with her boyfriend, Damien. She was looking up at him and twirling her hands through his hair as he held her close, his arms roped around her back. I left Scott by the drink stand and went over to her.

We'd been best friends since third grade. We had the same homeroom class that year and were seated next to each other according to the roll call: Nicolette Rossi and Leah Spencer. I liked how different Nicolette was from the other girls—she was easily the prettiest girl in the class with raven hair and a Liz Taylor smile, but also, there was something wise about her and she possessed a mischievousness that I envied. On the playground during recess one day, she turned to me and asked if I would be her best friend. "Forever and ever, promise?" Nicolette had said, flashing her wide grin. Lucy was my best friend but Nicolette was irresistible so I said, "Yes, forever and ever."

We became inseparable. We went to slumber parties and birthday parties and were friends with other girls in our class, but we kept a moat around our perfect friendship, not letting anyone else get too close to us.

Mom and Dad adored Nicolette, and her parents, Nick and Florence, would clasp my cheeks in their hands and call me Little Bella every time I saw them. They were originally from Italy. Mr. Rossi was a well-respected heart surgeon and when he came to Dallas once for a conference, he fell in love with Texas, with the wide-open skies and barbecue and decided to bring his new bride to America. Soon, they had Nick, and then Nicolette, their offspring just as dazzling as they were.

I loved going to their house. It was always warm and open with company drifting in and out—their windows and doors were always open, too—and the air was thick and dreamy with towering houseplants and sliced fruit resting in glass bowls, the sounds of classical piano always tinkling in the background from the stereo. Just outside their back door, there was a crushed granite path that led to a huge, jungly garden and a glittering pool.

When we hit middle school, Nicolette blossomed overnight, becoming bustier and more like a teenager while I was stuck with my flat brown hair and training bra and braces. Nothing bad had happened between us—we didn't have a fight or anything—but during the summer before eighth grade, we started drifting apart. Instead of spending endless hours with Nicolette by her pool reading *Seventeen* magazine, I watched her being swarmed by eighth-grade boys and even some high school boys. She always tried to include me, but I felt left out and awkward watching her make out with a handsome boy while I sat parked in my swimsuit in a lawn chair, dazed by the sun, sipping on a Sprite.

When we got to high school, we slowly went our separate ways. Now she spent all her time with Damien, a hazel-eyed junior with curly blond hair. Damien was edgy and good-looking and drove a black convertible Mustang.

And I joined the yearbook staff and fell into the group of giggly girls I had always tried so hard to avoid.

———

As I got closer to Nicolette and Damien, I saw him point in my direction and whisper something in her ear. Nicolette broke away from him and looped her arm through mine, guiding me toward the bathroom so we could talk. It was as if no time had passed between us.

"Have you guys heard anything at all?" she asked.

"No. Nothing," I said, my throat tightening into a lump.

"I'm so sorry, Leah. Lu is like a sister to me, too. I really don't know what to say."

She pulled me into her and we both started sobbing. She took my face in her hands and wiped away my tears while smoothing out my bangs. "My parents really want you to come to the house. Mom wants to cook for you. Whenever you're ready, okay?"

We walked back inside the dance. Scott was talking to Damien. They were discussing Lucy, I could tell, because as soon as we walked up they both fell silent.

The DJ then put on "With or Without You" by U2. I looked at Nicolette and saw a look of concern flash across her face. U2 is Lucy's favorite band. As the opening notes of the song filtered through the room—the haunting sound of the keyboard like a call from the sea—I felt my stomach coil into a knot and thought I might be sick. I raced for the door, across the dance floor, and tried to push my way through the couples that had already started to lock together and sway. The lyrics rang in my ears as I scanned the room for the exit, and all I could think was this: Lucy might never get to go to a high school dance.

Scott was right behind me and pushed down on the metal bar that clanked open the heavy door that led outside. We stepped into the parking lot. He wrapped his arms around me tightly, letting me cry. After a moment, I looked up at him. He leaned in to kiss me, but I just shook my head.

"Can we just go?" I asked.

————

Scott is driving toward my house, and I thought he was taking me home, but now he's turned down a cul-de-sac a few blocks up. It's a quiet and dark circle, with only one house set far off the road. He puts the truck in park in front of an empty lot and kills the engine but leaves the stereo playing. He fumbles through his cassettes until he finds one and jams it into the tape deck. He lowers the windows. The air has cooled but the night is still a hot, panting thing.

He pulls me into him and we start kissing. John Wait's "Missing You" is playing softly, and for a moment I let myself go, for a moment I enjoy being wrapped up in Scott's arms. He feels solid, secure. He reaches for my hand and places it on his thigh, then takes his own hand and slips it up the back of my shirt. His fingers feel like warm velvet; my heart is a jagged drum. But when he starts fumbling with my bra clasp, I jerk away.

"It's been a while," he purrs, and starts tracing his fingers back up my spine. Suddenly, I can't breathe. Suddenly, his truck seems too tiny and I feel overpowered by his cologne—Benetton—he always wears too much, and I find myself annoyed with him, irked by the cheesy song he chose, the very normal, predictable song he always plays when he wants to make out. All at once I feel repelled by Scott, by what his life is—normal—and what mine will never be again. There is a gap between us now that I can't name, and I can't wait to get out of his truck.

"I'm sorry, I just can't."

"But you don't have to be home for another hour at least. I miss you, I—"

"What's your problem, Scott? Just take me home," I snap, sounding more annoyed than I intended.

He just sits there with one arm dangling off the wheel, his face in a pout, sulking, so I open the door and get out, slamming it shut behind me. I decide to walk home. Scott idles for a few angry moments before peeling off. It's dark out, the streetlights casting puddles of light on the road, but when I get to the darkest spots I pump my legs as fast as they can go. I'm still just a few blocks from home and mad at myself for not letting him drive me. The hairs stand up on the back of my neck as I race home. Between pools of streetlight, I race in the dark, running faster.

Is this what you felt, Lucy?

I hear a car door shut. I whip my head around, but I can't make out anything. My calves are on fire, but I run as quickly as I can down my street and up my long driveway. Mom has left the porch light on, thank God, and I race toward it and fumble with the key in my pocket. My hands are shaking but I jam the key in the lock and open the door. Safely inside, I lock the door behind me and collapse in the entryway.

24

Sylvia

HATTIE LIVED IN THE small farming community of Easton, ten miles south of town. On Saturdays, she'd invite me out there and the drive was luscious—the pine trees thinned and the flat highway started to undulate over vivid green hills that rolled out like an emerald quilt. I would crank the windows down and breathe in the tangy air of the thick vegetation. Wild bushes, their tendrils waving in the wind, stood next to native fruit trees and vines. Orange persimmons, fat as baseballs, would roll into the road.

Hat's place was neat and tidy—a small, cream-colored wooden house with red shutters. A spray of metal butterflies hung by her front door and her house was set on twenty acres, far off the highway on a blacktop road that curled around like a half smile.

Her husband, Teddy, was gone most weekends long-haul truck driving, so it was usually just us and her granddaughter, Cynthia, who she kept on Saturdays. Hattie needed the company, too.

We would mostly talk about her gardens. Like me, she had a flower garden, but also, in the back of the property, she had a massive vegetable garden and we'd walk the rows and fill baskets full of turnip greens that she'd fix for our lunch.

We'd sit on the back porch while the greens soaked in her white enamel sink and drink iced tea and pass the time, watching Cynthia spin cartwheels in the backyard, the red and white beads at the end of her neat braids click-clacking together as she spun. Honeysuckle vines, thick as ropes, strangled the chain link that fenced in the yard.

Easton was an all-black community and her great-grandfather's church—which he built as a newly freed slave—sat in the middle of town. It had been burned to the ground twice by the KKK. She told me about the prayer circles, how the congregation would ring around the burned church and pray, pitching in double their tithes and some their entire paychecks to rebuild. She talked about how the insurance company would cover the cost of reconstruction, but how that check always fell short and how they would have to raise additional funds to rebuild the children's center, to order new hymnals, etc. And she told me how the police offered little solace from the terror that struck their hearts. But, she said, with a smile spreading across her face, "The Lord always rebuilds, every time, our house of worship and our spirits."

Farther afield, an ancient pecan orchard stood and when it was in season and the pecans dropped to the ground, we'd spend the day gathering them up in woven baskets and later cracking them on the porch so Hattie could make us her aunt's recipe for pecan tassies—little discs of the most buttery, delicious dessert that ever passed my lips.

At the very back of the property, as the hill dipped down, there was a large stocked catfish pond. Sometimes we'd walk down there with Cynthia and watch as she'd scatter feed over the water and squeal with delight when the fish would light the surface. Teddy loved to fish and one Sunday while he was home, he caught a bathtub's worth and invited me out for a fish fry. They became like family to me during those first few years.

I loved the thick warmth of springtime on her back porch and I was never ready to leave, but as the sun would begin to set, turning the sky into orange sherbet, I'd give little Cynthia a kiss goodbye and climb into the station wagon and head for home, a sinking feeling spreading over me as I drove back to my cold, lonely house.

25

Leah

Wednesday, October 25th, 1989
Lucy missing 3 weeks, 5 days

The first person to get a black rose in their locker was Brandi Miles. It happened on my first day back to school, the Wednesday before Halloween. Ali told me in the girl's bathroom just after fourth period, her eyes darting around underneath the sickly fluorescent light.

"They say she screamed when she saw it! Can you imagine?" Ali was talking fast and chomping ferociously on her gum. "Everyone is saying it's from devil worshippers! I'm SO scared, Leah! I mean, what if it happens to me? I've got blond hair and blue eyes, too!" she said, flipping her hand through her sheets of golden hair.

We had all heard the rumors that if a girl finds a black rose in her locker, then she will soon disappear. This had never happened to anyone we actually knew, of course, but the rumors still persisted. The cloying smell of Lysol mixed with hairspray was making me feel claustrophobic and I wanted to get out of there.

"She brought it straight to Principal Davis, of course," she continued. Ali would've kept talking but the school bell buzzed, cutting through her monologue. "Oh! Gotta run to English!" She turned in the mirror and primped her hair, smiling at her reflection before sprinting off.

Brandi was a senior and captain of the drill team. She had thick, bleached-blond hair that she teased up into a mountain every morning before school. Her eyes were pale-blue and she was tall and thin and would glide down the halls with model-perfect posture.

Because she found the black rose so close to Halloween, everybody thought it was just a Halloween prank, but one week later, at night, when Brandi came out of drill team practice, she went to her teal-colored Suzuki Samurai and all of the tires were slashed. Someone had picked the passenger's side lock and there was a note on the seat, scribbled in red marker that read:

> *Heat and power*
> *This dead flower*
> *By this curse,*
> *I make it worse*

The police came to the parking lot to dust the car for fingerprints and take photos, and after that night, her parents escorted her to and from practice.

26

Sylvia

THEY SAY THAT GOD is most present where he is most needed, so I guess that's why there are so many churches in this town. I thought it was strange at first: all the churches crammed into such a small place. They are seemingly on every corner, sprouting from the earth—both monolithic churches with chalk-white steeples that shoot to the sky and also the smaller, homier churches.

But it's not these churches that bother me, it's the splinter groups around here—what I call the basement churches, some of them formed in secret—that bother me the most. I'm leery of anyone who feels the need to shut off from society and make up their own rules.

27

Leah

Friday, October 27th, 1989
Lucy missing 4 weeks

Dad hasn't slept at home all week. Mom made some lame excuse about him working late for a deadline, but I know he's just passed out drunk on his couch at work. He comes home in the mornings to shower—all rumpled hair and bleary-eyed—and gives me long, tight hugs that leave me feeling both anxious and drained.

Mom has become closed in on herself, dragging paperwork home from school and sitting at the dinner table hidden behind mountains of manila folders, a pen jammed behind one ear, deep in thought. I can tell she's half waiting to hear if Dad's truck will pull up in the driveway, and half just trying to distract herself.

It's Friday night tonight and Ali invited me to the football game earlier today at school. I said no, I didn't want to go; I didn't want to leave Mom all by herself.

"Scott really wants you to be there," she said, her jaw squared, clutching a pile of books to her chest.

"Well, then why doesn't he ask me himself? He's barely looked at me all week," I said, my voice coming out whinier than I meant it to.

"Oh, Leah, you know how guys are. Just come, it'll—"

But I cut her off by fake-coughing into my arm and squinting my eyes up at her. "I'm really just not feeling all that well, okay?" I said. Ali is a sucker when someone is in need.

"Oh! I'm sorry!" Her eyes spread wide with concern. "Well, you just take care of yourself, sweetie. I'll call you tomorrow to check on you," she said, blowing me a kiss before turning to leave.

The sun set hours ago, outside it's so dark, the night sky is a purple bruise. My stomach grumbles and I'm just beginning to wonder about dinner when Mom comes downstairs.

"I'm ordering us a pizza. Sound good?"

"Definitely!" I stand on my tiptoes and kiss her china doll cheek.

While we wait for the pizza to be delivered, I go into the kitchen and pull out some Tupperware. I grab a box of lime Jell-O from the pantry (Mom's favorite) and tear open the bag and shake the emerald crystals into the bowl before mixing it up with water and putting it in the fridge to set. Mom steps into the kitchen and smiles when she sees the ripped-open Jell-O box. She pours herself a short glass of sherry and studies me for a second, her eyes smiling.

We nearly eat the whole pizza. Afterwards, she stays seated at the table and begins sifting through more paperwork. I don't want to move an inch so I keep picking at the pizza, lifting up brick-red discs of pepperoni and pouring the grease out and eating more. I've guzzled nearly half the two-liter bottle of Coke that came with the pizza when Mom starts rubbing her temples and says she's going upstairs to bed.

I clear the table, dump everything into the trash, and sweep the powdery crumbs off the table with my hands. When I'm sure she's upstairs with the TV on, I step into the kitchen and call Dad at the office. He doesn't answer. I hope for just a moment that this means he's on his way home, but after a while, when I don't hear his truck rumble into the driveway, I go upstairs. I pause at Mom's door. She's fallen asleep with the TV on, the remote still clutched in her hand. Her bedside lamp is on and the ashtray is in the middle of the bed, pinning down the *TV Guide*. I go over to her, click off the lamp, shut off the TV, and move the ashtray before climbing into bed and snuggling into her warmth.

28

Leah

Sunday, October 29th, 1989
Lucy missing 1 month

Dad hasn't come home all weekend. Mom and I don't discuss this, but we both stay coiled, waiting for the back door to open, waiting for him to come strolling in. We sit at the breakfast table and I crunch through a bowl of sugary cornflakes while Mom opens the Sunday paper.

She flips through the sections briskly, barely skimming the stories, but then pauses on something, furrowing her brow. She refolds the newspaper, pushes back from the table, and pitches it in the trash before I have a chance to read the comics. I trail behind her and am about to fish it out of the trash but it's landed on a layer of wet coffee grounds, so I leave it.

"I'm going to take a bath," Mom says, clearing the table and taking my cereal bowl to the sink.

I cross the room and twist the knob on the dining room television set. I'm trying to find something interesting to watch, but it's just live broadcasts from local churches. Religious stuff has always made me squirm. Grandma and Grandpa used to take me to church with them sometimes, but Mom and Dad aren't very religious. We're members of the Episcopal Church because Mom is principal of the school, but we only go for the holidays.

Once when I was eight, I asked Mom if she believed in God. We were out for a walk, it was a fall afternoon and we were strolling down a wide street. I remember the way the sunlight played tricks on the leaves shimmering in the trees—it felt like we were walking through a bowl of Fruity Pebbles—and I looked up at Mom and asked her if she believed in God. She went quiet for a moment and wouldn't meet my eyes. She was still staring off when she answered me.

"I believe we evolved from soup of the earth." And the way she said it, I knew it was the end of the conversation. The thing about Mom that I and all the other kids at her school respect is this: she doesn't bullshit you. I'm not sure what I believe yet, but I do believe in a higher power, a force of good.

I turn the TV off and climb the stairs. I can hear Mom's voice, so I step into her room. She's in the bathroom with the door closed; it smells like she's smoked a hundred cigarettes. The olive green phone cord is pinched in the door, pulled tautly like it's about to snap.

"No, YOU listen to ME," she says, her voice sputtering in anger. She must be talking to Dad. "I don't give a rat's ass what you—" The floor creaks underneath my feet; she can hear me so she shifts away from the door so I can't listen to their conversation. I can imagine her in there with the receiver cupped to her mouth, the open window rustling the pages of the neat pile of magazines, and smoke streaming from her nostrils.

I go to my room to lie down. A while later, I hear a car in the drive so I jump up and run to the window, thinking it's Dad. It's the sheriff. My stomach churns. I see the front door swing wide open. Mom is already downstairs, and I hear her ushering him inside.

I creep downstairs sock-footed and eavesdrop on the other side of the thin door.

"How've you been holding up, Roz?" the sheriff asks.

"Same," Mom says, her voice blank.

"Carl still gone?"

"Yep, 'fraid so."

"Listen, I'm sorry you had to read about it in the paper this morning before I got to you—I don't know who spoke to the press. I came here straight after church so we could talk about it," Sheriff Greene says.

"Just tell me everything, Tommy, shoot it to me straight."

"Look. Lucy has been missing for over a month. I didn't think her case was connected to the others, but now …" He's stumbling around for the words. "Now I do. There has been suspicious activity in the area recently, more signs of Satanism and such, and—" He starts stammering again.

"Jesus, Tommy, just spit it out! What kinds of signs?" Mom says, exasperated.

He blows out a heavy breath. "We have been taking reports of dismembered pets, cats bagged up and nailed to trees. And it's not just in Big Woods this time; it's been happening here in Longview, too. There's been other signs as well. We've seen more spray-painted markings around town, upside-down crosses and pentagrams. Just like before."

"So what does any of this have to do with Lucy?"

"Forensics indicated that all of the other children whose bodies we found had been murdered within a month of their disappearance. So if it's the same people or same cult we're dealing with who took Lucy, I'm afraid, Roz, that it's time to start preparing for the worst."

I hear the sound of my Mom's back slide down the wall. I hear her stifle a sob that comes out anyway, as an ugly snort. I stifle my own cry—a white-hot piercing pain that tears the back of my throat—so I won't be heard. And finally, I hear the strike of a match as Sheriff Greene lights Mom's Virginia Slim.

They are quiet for a few moments before Tommy says goodbye and opens the front door.

I run around to the bottom of the stairs and sit there. Mom walks over to me.

"What did Sheriff Greene want?" I ask.

She studies me for a second before answering, and swallows hard. "Honey, the sheriff thinks it's time we start saying goodbye."

My eyes burn with tears. She doesn't tell me about the devil worshipers, or go into details, and I don't have the strength to press her. I sit there limp, the breath sucked out of me. Mom slumps down next to me on the stairs and hugs my shoulder hard. The sun has splashed warm light across the stairway and we sit there in its warm glow.

29

Sylvia

Sunday, October 29th, 1989

The local newspaper hits my front door this morning with a thud, jostling me out of sleep. No matter how many times I've called the paper to complain, the paper boy still sails it up toward the front door, rattling it with a whack, never failing to pry me from my dreams. I stopped taking the daily paper years ago—it's useless—but I do read the circulars in Sunday's paper, and the local food writer who has a Sunday column is actually decent.

It's been raining all night, so by the time I climb downstairs to get the paper, it's swollen, thick with rain, the sleeve half on. I bring it inside to the kitchen table and set it on the tablecloth to let it dry. I walk over to the stove, turn on the teakettle, and drop a slice of bread in the toaster. As I'm waiting for my toast to be ready and the water to boil, I sit down to read the paper.

I unroll it and my stomach churns: her face is bloated with the rain water so that her features are blurry, but the image is not so smeared that I don't recognize her immediately. Lucy. Her picture is underneath the headline that screams out at me: MISSING GIRL'S CASE MAY BE LINKED TO AREA'S PREVIOUSLY UNSOLVED MURDERS.

Of course it's connected, I think to myself, I already know that, but I read through the rest of the article.

It talks about recent activity in and around Big Woods, signs of "definite cult activity, possibly Satanic rituals," but doesn't go into much detail other than that. Sheriff Greene has declined to comment, but an unnamed source from the police department says, "Activity has ramped up in the Big Woods area, just like before. We have evidence of ritualistic-type ceremonies being held out there, it appears to be the working of a cult—same signs and symbols as before. They will strike again—it's what we're most worried about."

Details from Lucy's life are offered up: she comes from a caring family, her parents aren't under suspicion, and she was last seen on Friday, September 29th, the morning she walked to the bus stop and never made it.

There are comparisons between Lucy's case and the cold cases, and even a quote from one of the murdered kid's parents: "Please, for the love of God, find these monsters."

The same unnamed source comments on Lucy's case, "At this point, we're following all leads, but we're worried about this suspicious activity, and we've increased patrolling in Big Woods. If anyone out there has any information, please call us."

I look down again at Lucy's face, one of her eyes engorged from the wet paper, and I know what I have to do.

30

Leah

Halloween
Tuesday, October 31st, 1989
Lucy missing 1 month, 2 days

UNDERGROUND.

BY THE WOODS.

Even though the screen is blank, the orange letters flash like neon through my mind. I want to scream, to shout up to Mom's room but my mouth is dry, like it's filled with sand, so I follow the trail of moonlight to the bottom of the stairs and let the rail guide me up toward my parents' bedroom.

Their room is dark so I click on the bedside lamp, waking Mom up. She rolls over and looks up at me, concerned.

"What is it, sweetie?" she says, her blond hair frizzy with sleep.

"Mom, Lucy is trying to talk to me. I had a dream—I—"

But Mom cuts me off. "Oh honey, come climb in here with me."

I stand there, not moving. "No, Mom, I'm serious. I just had a dream about Lucy, it's my second one, actually, and she told me where she is. She was typing to me through the computer. She said she misses us. She's underground somewhere, by Big Woods."

Mom sits up in bed in her faded baseball t-shirt. Her eyes are searching mine, but then she just looks down at her hands. "Leah," she says, "I am so sorry, sweetheart. I know this is hard for you, it's just ... terrible ... but ... "

Anger rises in the back of my throat. "The dreams are REAL, Mom! Get up! Let's go find Dad and go out there!"

She shrinks into herself and tears form in the corner of her eyes, but she shakes her head and wipes them away. "Come here, sit down," she says, scooting over and patting the wrinkled spot next to her. "We can talk about this more in the morning."

I look at her with a steady gaze, but then turn to leave. My eyes burn with tears and I go to my room, slamming the door behind me.

31

Leah

Wednesday, November 1st, 1989
Lucy missing 1 month, 3 days

I wake up in a ball, still dressed in my clothes from the night before, on top of my unmade bed. My pillow is soggy with sweat. I'm jerked out of sleep by the sound of Mom clanging dishes around downstairs. I rub my cheek; there's a deep groove in it from my watch. I stayed up late last night compulsively checking it, hoping that Dad might come home.

When I wake my first thought is of Lucy, of how to get to Lucy. Last night I considered grabbing Mom's keys and trying to drive the Honda myself, but I was too afraid to go out into the night alone, and the Accord is a stick shift; I haven't quite mastered that yet. I'm just one month away from getting my hardship license. In Texas, you can apply for your hardship license when you're fifteen and both parents work. This was our plan so I could drive us to school. We had already picked out the car over the summer, a Ford Tempo, and Lucy chose the color—sky blue—and had a plastic tray of cassettes she couldn't wait to play on our drives: The Thompson Twins, OMD, and Michael Jackson.

"We can take turns who gets to play DJ," Lucy had said, but she knew she'd be the one picking the songs.

I get dressed for school and go downstairs.

"Pop-Tart's in the toaster. I'm going to shower," Mom says, emptying the remains of the coffeepot into her metal-green thermos, curls of steam rising from it like smoke signals. Her mood is chilly.

"Okay."

"And honey, please don't mention any of that stuff from last night to your father. It'll just make things so much worse," she says without meeting my eyes.

I'm running late, so I snatch my Pop-Tart out of the toaster and fold it into a paper towel and walk outside to wait for the Weavers, my carpool ride.

I've been carpooling with the Weavers since middle school. Their youngest daughter, Becky, and I have known each other since kindergarten. We aren't all that close but she lives nearby, so they've always given me a ride.

They pull to the curb and I climb into their burgundy Lincoln Town Car. The upholstery is pulling away from the roof and sags, looking like hundreds of deflating maroon balloons. Mrs. Weaver is always smoking and when I climb in and sit on the spongy back seat, ashes float up and pepper my jeans. Mrs. Weaver has five kids and always seems spacey and distracted, her frosty, white-blueish hair always whipped up in frantic waves on top of her head, so that's probably why I blurt out the request before I've even fully thought it through.

"Mrs. Weaver?" I say, leaning into the front seat.

She fiddles with the radio dial, turning down the sports station she keeps cranked up. "Yes, hon?"

"Can you drop me off at my Dad's office after school today?"

"Sure, no problem," she says, "Just remind me at pick up."

———————

My morning classes drag by. I sit in second period History tracing ink-filled initials on the side of my desk and absentmindedly picking at a wad of dried gum stuck next to it. When I bump into Scott in the hallway just after class, I think about asking him to drive me to Big Woods, but he is still sulking and this makes me not want to share anything with him. And I can't wait to tell Dad. I know he'll believe me, and I spend the rest of the day picturing the two of us bumping along Seven Pines Road in his truck, the road that leads to Big Woods.

———————

Mrs. Weaver parks in front of Dad's office and leaves the car running. I grab my backpack and hop out.

"Want me to wait for you, in case he's not here?" Mrs. Weaver asks through a cracked window.

I hadn't considered this a possibility. "Okay," I squeak back.

The office is dark, the front blinds are pulled shut. I use the key on my lanyard to unlock the front door. I step in and the smell of stale beer and Corn Nuts hits me in the face. My face flushes with frustration. The receptionist desk is empty—Dad hasn't used a secretary in years, he prefers to do his own books, take his own calls, work in solitude. I gulp and walk down the narrow hall, following the river of industrial pea-green carpet that leads to his office.

His back is to me and his feet are propped up on the desk. Willie Nelson's "Stardust" (Dad's favorite) is playing on the 8-track.

"Dad." My voice is strained. He doesn't answer. I keep talking to the back of his head, hoping to get through. Empty amber beer bottles teeter out of the top of a brown plastic trash can and an open bottle of Jack Daniels sits open on his desk, most of it drained.

"Dad, I know where Lucy is. I've been having these dreams about her, and in the last one she told me she was in Big Woods." He doesn't move. I walk over to him and shake his shoulder. His boots slide off the drafting table and he slowly spins around in his buttery tan leather chair to face me. His eyes look like they've been stung by chlorine and when he sees me, his mouth forms a sloppy, lopsided grin. "Ahhhh, Looo-see," he says and shuts his eyes.

I realize how lost he is. I can't reach him, so I kneel down and tug his boots off and pull on his arm until he is alert enough to let me guide him over to the couch. I cover him with a blanket and walk down the hall, biting down hard on my bottom lip so Becky Weaver and her mom won't see me cry.

32

Leah

Thursday, November 2nd, 1989
Lucy missing 1 month, 4 days

The next day after school when the Weavers drop me off at home, I'm walking up the driveway, wading through a pile of crispy, ruby leaves when I spot Dad's lemon yellow truck. A warm feeling spreads across my chest.

I walk along the side of the house and pause at the dining room window. I can see Mom and Dad in the kitchen, standing shoulder to shoulder over the sink; I see Mom give him a playful bump with her hip and I hear laughter. I open the side door, dropping my backpack with a thud to announce my presence. Dad rounds the corner and drapes a damp kitchen towel over his shoulder and walks to me with his lanky arms open.

"Hey, sugar," he says and kisses the top of my head. Then he lifts me up and twirls me around like he used to when I was little. "I'm home, and I'm staying home," his voice buzzes in my ear. He sets me down and looks at me level with his crystal blue eyes. A smile spreads across my face and I burrow my head into his arms.

Mom is humming a happy tune in the kitchen, and when Dad steps out to take the trash, I go to her with my palms up and shrug. "Well?"

"I don't know, he just showed up at school today with a bouquet of flowers, and took me to lunch and apologized," Mom says, her cheeks flushing pink. "Says he hasn't known how to deal with any of this. I didn't go back to work; we came home together to talk," she says, glancing out the window, making sure he's still outside.

While Mom slides a roast out of the oven, Dad and I set the table. His olive-toned skin is gleaming, he's freshly showered, and he's whistling as he neatly folds the napkins and presses the silverware on top. I keep checking his eyes—looking for a sign that he remembers me stopping by his office last night, that he remembers what I told him about Lucy, and I almost whisper to him to ask, but I swallow it back down. I don't want to spoil his happiness and I don't want him to leave us again.

Also, a murky, gloomy feeling has begun to tug at me: I'm beginning to wonder if my dreams about Lucy are just my imagination.

———

Last night, when I got home from Dad's office, I waited until Mom went upstairs and then I snuck into Dad's study and tried to write to Lucy again on the computer. I sat down and typed on the chocolate brown keys: *Lucy. Lucy, if you're out there, I need to know. I need to know if this is real.*

I trained my eyes on the blank space beneath my words, willing Lucy to write me back until my vision went fuzzy. I sat back in the chair and pulled my knees into my chest, rocking back and forth, waiting. But nothing. No answer. The pain of it made me want to smash the keyboard and kick the monitor, but instead I went over and threw myself down on the loveseat. I formed myself into a tight ball and a heavy sadness poured over me as thick as mud, pinning me in place for hours.

33

Sylvia

A LOT OF OUR patients were escorted in by the police—if they had been picked up in public, for instance—and this was how we got Delia.

It was a Friday night, just before midnight. February 23rd, 1979. The police had picked her up on the side of Highway 80, and two sheriff's deputies were holding her by the elbows as they brought her in. She was shaking, dirty, and disheveled. It looked like she had been dragged across the ground. Bruises covered her arms like tattoos and her eyes kept darting back and forth. She kept looking over her shoulder when there was no need: we were in a locked unit.

She was talking really rapidly as if she was in a manic phase, saying over and over, "You have to hide me! They are going to kill me, you have to hide me, they are after me. They know everywhere to look."

Even in the state she was in, I could see that she was beautiful. She had long, raven hair and perfect teeth. Her eyes were black discs, like obsidian, smoky and deep. She was stunning, and I would have the strange thought later: I can see why they took her.

Hattie was in charge of the intakes and in Delia's chart, under possible diagnosis, she scrawled down *paranoid schizophrenic, possible drug abuse*. Before they left, the police told us that a trucker had picked her up ten miles out of town and had given her his trench coat, but that she had gotten scared and jumped out of his truck a few miles away from the hospital. Under the dirty coat, she only had on a torn slip. She had no personal effects, no ID, and when Hattie asked for her name, she looked back at the police and just shook her head, so Hattie marked down *Jane Doe*.

"Alright, we'll take it from here, thank you," Hattie said, dismissing the officers. She put me in charge of Delia, and together we escorted her down the dimly lit hall to a room, the other nurses casting glances at her.

Once we were in the room, Hattie gave her a thin gown and asked her to change behind the flimsy cotton curtain. While she dressed, Hattie got the shot ready—a high dose of Valium—but when we tried to give it to her, she folded her arms across her chest and shook her head. "No, no, no!" she shrieked at us. "I'm not crazy. But you have to hide me." Her teeth were chattering and she kept talking fast and wouldn't calm down, so Hattie nodded her head at me and I held her arms down as Hattie slid the needle in her vein.

Almost instantly, this calmed her down, and I stayed with her until she drifted off into a fitful sleep.

34

Leah

Friday, November 3rd, 1989
Lucy missing 5 weeks

Mom has been frying chicken since she got home from work, dropping flour-coated pieces into the cast-iron skillet that glistens and pops with grease.

Dad tosses a salad of crunchy shards of iceberg lettuce with carrots sliced so razor-thin they are almost translucent. He coats it in a creamy layer of ranch dressing, and sets it in the fridge to chill.

My stomach groans with hunger and by the time we finally sit down to dinner, I'm so ravenous that Mom passes me a steady stream of chicken legs. My teeth tear into the crunchy skin and I let the grease dribble down my lips.

Mom reaches over and grabs Dad's hand. "Honey, your father and I thought it might be nice if we went to the park tomorrow for a picnic," she says, both of them beaming at me.

Saturdays at the park used to be our family ritual, especially in the fall. Mom would spread out a checkered blanket and we'd picnic next to the pond under swaying cypress trees. We'd always bring a sleeve of stale bread to feed the ducks, and we'd spend the afternoon playing tag football until Lucy and I called time, our lungs burning and our cheeks ruddy with wind. We'd wander off, leaving Mom and Dad sprawled and lazy on the blanket while we built fortresses out of the orange pine needles that blanketed the ground.

"Sure, sounds good," I say, nodding and reaching for more chicken.

"Great! We can take the leftover wings and I'll make potato salad and pie!" Mom says, cheerily. Dad adds something about making a thermos of hot chocolate, but I've tuned them out. Their voices now sound distant and the edges of the room go soft as a plan to get to Big Woods hatches in my brain.

35

Sylvia

THE NEXT NIGHT WHEN I came on, I went straight to Delia's room to check on her. I pulled her chart and saw that she had been given Valium all day. There was an order to give her another high dose, but I didn't rush that. Something about what she said last night had stuck with me. Her fear had seemed real, and I wanted to see if she would talk to me.

I rapped lightly on the open door and said, "Hello, dear. How was your day? Did you get enough to eat at supper?" She had been staring blankly at the mute television, but she turned her head and her eyes found mine. They were still dilated from the meds, but she was becoming more alert, her body ready for the next dose.

In her chart, there were instructions to bathe her, but the daytime nurse had marked down *Patient refused*. Her hair was still a rat's nest and I couldn't imagine a girl that pretty feeling good like that, so I gently asked her if she'd like a bath. She nodded yes. While I was filling the basin with tepid water, she peeled the covers back and sat on the edge of the bed like a toddler. I walked over to her with a towel and when I looked down, I could see through the open gown that there were black marks—bruises like a crow bar on the inside of her thighs. I went to shut the door to the room, and turning back to her, I asked, "Who did these things to you?"

You think abusive husband or boyfriend, but when I asked her that, she just slowly shook her head.

She pulled her knees into her chest and began rocking back and forth, biting her lower lip. "There's no safe place, everywhere I go they find me." She was crying now, her voice turning shrill. "They are powerful and they are the law, they will get away with this. They will kill me and get away with it." She kept saying this over and over and muttering other things under her breath, and moaning, and was becoming agitated again like she was going to hyperventilate.

"Who? Who are you talking about?" I asked. But she wouldn't answer, she just kept rocking back and forth.

I shut the water off and drained the tub. I brought her a warm washcloth instead and helped her sponge off, then gave her a clean, fresh gown. I filled the syringe and she held her arm out for me. Once she was calm, I took a brush and gently teased out the knots and tangles in her hair and tucked an extra blanket around her.

36

Leah

Saturday, November 4th, 1989
Lucy missing 5 weeks, 1 day

I open my eyes and it's early. I can tell by the light; my cherrywood floor mirror hasn't yet grabbed the sun and sent it splashing across my room. I check my watch: 7:25 a.m.

Soon I hear the muffled sounds of Mom and Dad coming out of sleep. Last night I waited until Mom and Dad had turned in before I crept back downstairs and filled my backpack with supplies: two packages of Fritos, a can of Coke, a pair of gloves, and Dad's Swiss Army knife. When I got back to my room, I shoved my backpack underneath my bed and laid out my clothes for the next day.

We are supposed to leave at ten. I stay frozen in place, staring at the wall until Dad pokes his head in, all perky, and says, "Shake a leg, buttercup! Breakfast is on the table!"

105

I roll over and clutch my stomach. "Dad, I'm sick. I threw up all night." And then for safe measure, I add, "And I've had diarrhea all morning."

He winces and calls downstairs for Mom, who rushes up and looks both concerned and crestfallen. "Oh, Leah, I'm so sorry," she says, leaning over me and placing the back of her hand to my forehead. "You do feel a little warm, so you must have a stomach bug."

"Sorry, Mom, y'all just go without me."

"No way, sweetie," she says, "It wouldn't be the same. I'll start unpacking the car."

"Mom! I'll be fine. You won't be gone that long."

"Well, let me see if I can get your grandfather on the phone."

"Mom, seriously, I'm fine. I'm almost fifteen. Plus, I don't want to give this to Grandad. I'll stay in bed and you can set the burglar alarm before you leave. I promise I'll be fine, I just want to sleep."

Mom looks at Dad and he shrugs, saying, "Might as well take advantage of such a gorgeous day. I'll bring you some Gatorade from the store, Lee."

Mom leaves and returns with a glass of water and a sleeve of Saltines. She drapes a damp washcloth across my forehead and squeezes my hand goodbye and says, "We won't stay that long, we'll be back by noon."

———

I check the time: 9:45. I walk over to the window and watch Mom pack the trunk with the wicker basket and thermos. I hear Dad punch in the alarm code and shut the door and watch as he shuffles to the car with his sunglasses on and the picnic blanket shoved under his armpit.

I glance at my watch. It's 9:48. I spring from bed. I have just over two hours. I get dressed, pull my hair into a ponytail, and put on a baseball cap. I sling my backpack over my shoulder and race downstairs, grabbing Dad's keys off the hook as I go.

It's sunny out and a warm wind blasts the back of my neck as I climb in the truck. I twist the keys in the ignition and the truck springs to life, the cushioned seat humming underneath me. I put it in reverse and ease down the drive.

When I get to the first stop sign, though, the truck grumbles and stalls. I jam it into park and then crank it back up again. It starts right away, but this spooks me and for a second I think about turning back, but I press on.

I stick to the back roads, not wanting anyone in town to recognize me. I creep up to an intersection and hit a red light. There's a car next to me, and I feel their eyes on me, but I force myself not to look over, my heart drilling in my chest. I pull the baseball cap down farther and sit straight up, trying to look older.

My mouth is watering—I haven't eaten a thing this morning—and when I pull through the intersection and pass by the Dairy Queen I'm tempted to get a cheeseburger, but I check my watch again: it's 10:00, I don't have time.

As I leave Longview behind, the road slims down to two lanes and I feel a small relief knowing that no one can pull up next to me anymore. I reach in my backpack and find a sack of Fritos and I eat them all, licking my fingers.

I'm almost to Big Woods when I realize that I don't have much of a plan of what to do once I'm out there. Big Woods is enormous, but I'm just trusting that Lucy will guide me once I'm there.

The trees are starting to thicken. I check the time: 10:13. I spot the turn-off on Seven Pines Road and carefully throw on the turn signal before making a right. The sun is bright and the sky is open with no clouds, but once I turn down Seven Pines, the road becomes even narrower and the tall trees cast shadows over the road so that it suddenly seems like dusk in the middle of the day. I have to blink a few times to clear my eyes of the sun spots.

I ease off the gas and crank down the window so I can listen. A dog is barking in the distance, but I don't hear much else. The smell of burning leaves fills the truck and I drive past an old man in coveralls tending a fire in a rusted barrel. He looks up at me and I wave, but he just stares back at me with hard eyes and turns away.

I keep driving down the tar-topped road. It dips down even farther. The surface is pock-marked with craters and entire chunks of road are missing so that I have to swerve to miss the holes. I squeeze the steering wheel even tighter for balance. So far, all I see are tiny roads leading to oil and gas wells. I start to see a few mailboxes, but the driveways are so long and winding I can't see any homes.

The trees are really thick now, their shaggy trunks coated in ivy, and the sun cuts through the pines in thin, jagged lines, making me feel even more disoriented.

I look at my watch: 10:24. I have just over an hour left. "Guide me, Lucy. Give me some sign," I say under my breath. I come upon a road that veers off to the left and decide to swing down it. It's just a dirt road and even more narrow than the last one. Tree branches scrape the truck and I feel like I'm being squeezed. My breath is shallow and quick and I realize there's no way to turn around if I need to.

I'm inching along the road when I spy a makeshift greenhouse to my right. It sits about a hundred feet away from a dirty trailer that faces the road. Next to the trailer is a pyramid of empty, crushed beer cans.

The greenhouse looks unusual—it's not like any kind I've ever seen before. We have one in our own backyard—an old glass one that Mom has turned into her art studio. But this greenhouse looks like a miniature A-frame house, like the bottom half of it is sunk into the earth. It has a little wooden door on the front that is closed, and like the trailer, it's covered in dark green mold.

I'm underground. By the woods.

I pull the truck over and kill the engine. I look all around but don't see anyone, so I open the truck and climb out and as I do the door creaks loudly. I can hear a cry from inside the trailer. I press the door shut as softly as I can and circle behind the truck toward the greenhouse. I walk past the mailbox and make a mental note of the name, *Haines*, scrawled in black paint on the side. I creep toward the greenhouse, but the leaves under my feet crack like a pop gun.

I get down on my stomach, so I won't be seen, and pull myself by my elbows to the little door. I reach up and grab the wooden handle, and as my palm catches a splinter, I hear the trailer door snap open behind me.

I scramble to my feet. A man steps out onto the rotted front porch. He looks to be in his early thirties. He's got thick black hair that's swept to one side like pudding and when he opens his mouth to speak, his parted lips reveal a ragged row of gold front teeth.

"You lost or somethin' darlin'?" He isn't wearing a shirt and he's got on a pair of dirty jeans with the top button undone and the belt splayed out to one side.

I swallow hard and just stare back. I can feel his eyes all over me and I'm suddenly aware of how my sweater has crept up around my waist, exposing my belly. I pull it down, not answering him.

From inside the trailer, I hear a baby crying and on top of that cry, a little boy shouting. I can hear the sounds of other children crying too, building up to a pitch until I see a silhouette pass in front of a window, followed by a series of slapping sounds and muffled cries.

I crane my neck to try and see around the man and into the trailer, but he shifts and slaps the door shut behind him, stepping toward me.

My mouth tastes like pennies and I stay rooted in the same spot. I can't help it, but I turn and look back at the greenhouse.

"Lookin' for somethin'?" He's getting closer. He keeps walking until he's right up on me. He reeks of beer and cheap cologne; his breath is stale and hot on my face. I can't decide if I should risk turning my back on him and running for the truck so I just stare blankly at the ground.

"You're awful pretty to be out here all alone, doncha think?" he says with a crooked smile. My stomach turns sour and I'm about to respond when I hear another cry from the trailer, a little girl's cry. I can't place it for sure as Lucy's but I can't swear it off either.

"Is your wife at home? I'd like to speak to her," I manage to ask, the words coming out soft and small. I want to lunge for the trailer, and as if he can sense this, his face darkens and he reaches up and places a strong hand on my shoulder.

"Wife's not feelin' so well. I'm gonna kindly ask you to leave," he says, turning me around toward the truck and giving me a firm shove. I walk as fast as I can without looking back. When I reach the truck, I turn around and he's standing right behind me.

"You best be findin' your way outta here," he says, his mouth a sneer.

I climb into the truck, my hands are shaking, I close the door. My window is still down and the man leans in and shakes his hands beside his face, saying, "Or the devil worshippers will get ya!" He steps back, clutching his dirty belly and howls with laughter.

I roll up the window and put the truck in reverse, backing out slowly the whole way until I reach Seven Pines Road. As I'm slipping the gear shift down into drive, a mud-covered black truck with its headlights on approaches me. It slows down as it passes by and almost comes to a stop. I try to look through the windows but I can't—they're too heavily tinted—and then the truck speeds off.

My hands are still trembling when I check my watch: 11:35. Just enough time to beat Mom and Dad home. But when I pull up to the main road, I find myself turning left instead of right, toward the police station and Sheriff Greene, the only adult who I think will listen.

I ease out onto the country highway and roll down my window and release a deep sigh. Warm air hits my sweat-soaked neck and I'm peeling off my damp baseball cap when I hear a loud rumble behind me.

I look in the mirror; it's the same black truck. I'm pretty sure I'm being followed.

37

Sylvia

THE OTHER NURSES, I could tell, didn't believe Delia. They were rough and coarse with her; they thought she was a floozy and a looney. Not that she told them much, but everyone on the floor had heard her that first night she came in. And then folks whisper. But I believed her, and Hattie did, too. And because we showed her a kindness, she trusted us. Especially me.

At night, when she was certain that the others were sleeping, I would step into her room and we would talk; Hat would cover all of my other rounds. Delia would speak in a whispered voice while fingers of moonlight poked through the chunky slats of the venetian blinds.

Once she had drifted off into medicated sleep, I would find a quiet corner in the lounge and write down everything she had told me.

It was on the third night, when I delayed giving her the meds even longer—hoping for a longer window of clarity—that she began to tell me her story.

They raped her, they tortured her, they beat her. They took what little shot she had at a life and snuffed it out, these men. When she first told me about them that night, I doubted it because it was so unbelievable, but only for a minute: sometimes you just know when you're hearing the truth. And off her meds, she was as clear as a bell.

I started out gently, by asking her questions about herself.

She was nineteen. She had been working as a dancer at a night-club—a strip club—and had graduated from high school the spring before. She had been a good student, she was smart, but her family was quite poor and she hadn't come from a good home. Her mom had run off when Delia was still little and her father was a mean, bit-ter drunk who despised all women, even his own daughter.

The strip club was set back off the highway in a low-roofed, black-bricked building. Delia started stripping there the summer after high school. She wanted to save enough money to move to Dallas. She had dreams of becoming a model and going to college. On her first few nights, she was shy about taking off her clothes, but she soon learned if she had just the right amount of beer before she went onstage, she could look out and the men's faces would blur together into a comic nothing.

At first, she thought the men were just really good tippers, so she'd give them her special dance and treat them extra nice, but one night after the club closed, when she was walking across the gravel parking lot to get into her car, the man she knew as Sheriff Meeks ap-proached her. She assumed he was going to ask her for a special favor—something she would never do and something her boss for-bid—but when she opened her mouth and said in her friendly, open way, "Hey, Sheriff," he began reading her her rights and arrested her.

In the car, on the way to the police station, she kept asking him why she was being arrested. All he would say, in a nasty voice, was, "You know why."

He was fat with thinning red hair, his face pocked with dark brown freckles. She was crying hysterically by the time they got to booking, her vision a blur of hot tears. Did someone plant drugs on her? One of the other girls? Out of jealousy? Even then, she knew she hadn't done anything wrong and figured she would come out all right.

When the sheriff ushered her into the police station, there was another deputy there, as if he had been waiting for her. They took her fingerprints and mug shot and when she asked again why she was being arrested, the sheriff said, "You've violated state and county law. At the strip club, it is illegal to show your private parts." So they booked her on trumped-up charges about her being too risqué (which she hadn't been).

That first night in jail, when she begged for water, they gave her some in a dirty glass, spiked with drugs. And from then on, until she escaped, they kept her drugged up and locked away.

They only kept her sober on Fridays, just before their Friday night rituals.

————

Sometimes when we were talking, Delia would retreat from me, too exhausted to go on. Other times, the horror of what she was remembering would send her into an agitated state and I would give her her meds and leave her be for the night.

Certain details were fuzzy, just out of her mind's reach, and she would knit her brow and just shake her head. But she was clear about the men involved: Sheriff Randall Meeks and his deputy, an oil man (his first name was Charlie, she recognized his voice from the strip club), and a preacher (she didn't know his name and never saw his face; they all wore hoods while they raped her).

38

Leah

Saturday, November 4th, 1989
Lucy missing 5 weeks, 1 day

The black truck is still behind me. I hit the gas and try to speed away but the truck speeds up, too, and as it's approaching, I try and make out the license plate number. But just as it's coming into focus, the truck swerves and makes a U-turn, heading back for Big Woods.

My heart is thundering in my chest as I pull into the police station. I park as far away from the entrance as possible. As I'm walking to the front door, I pass by a huge magnolia tree, the shade of which has killed the grass beneath it. Curled up at the base is a tanned, homeless man smoking a cigarette, his head propped up by an Army green duffel bag. I guess it's my nerves but for some reason I find myself saying, "Hello!" in a chipper voice and waving at him enthusiastically. He rolls up on one elbow and gives me the peace sign.

I climb the concrete steps and walk inside. My pulse quickens as I approach the front desk, and when I ask to see the sheriff, my voice sounds mousy and small, like someone else's. The clerk nods and disappears down the hall. I sit down in the corner on a fake leather bench. The cushions have split open and I pick at the cottony-white fibers until Sheriff Greene comes out.

"Leah," he says, his voice warm and deep. "Want to chat in my office?" He tilts his head in the direction of his office and I follow him down the wood-paneled hall.

His office smells like furniture polish and is neat and tidy. On the wall, I study a row of pictures—one of him in his high school football uniform and one from a family cruise in which he is hugging his tanned, blond wife and two sons. A turquoise globe sits on a corner of his desk next to a crystal paperweight that catches the light from the overhead fluorescents.

The sheriff looks concerned but before he even asks why I'm there I find myself telling him everything—about Big Woods, about the black truck, about Mr. Haines, and about the dreams. He takes notes the whole time I'm talking and when I mention the dreams, he doesn't break my gaze or look at me like I'm crazy, he just nods his head as if in understanding.

"This Mr. Haines," he asks. "Did you by chance get the spelling of his name?"

I smile and write it out for him. "Good, that's great," he says. "I'll check it out and if this man is connected at all to Lucy's disappearance, I *will* find out." He leans back in his chair and folds his hands behind his head. "I've got another question for you, Leah."

"Sure, of course," I say, sitting straighter.

"How did you get out to Big Woods and to the station all by yourself?" My cheeks burn and I dip my head down before stammering,

"Umm, well I do have my learner's permit and my parents—" My throat sticks on the word *parents* and I look at my watch: 12:05.

"Want me to call them for you?" he offers.

"That'd be great," I say, sheepishly.

"Tell you what, your house isn't all that far from here. I trust you can make it home by yourself?" he asks, a trace of a smile warming his face.

I nod yes and stand to leave. Sheriff Greene picks up his phone and cups it in his hand and says, "Drive straight there and I'll call them and fill them in. And try and smooth things out for you," he says, adding, "And Leah, please promise me you'll never go out to Big Woods alone again." His eyes are searching mine for some kind of compliance, so I nod my head in agreement before heading down the hall.

————————

When I pull in the drive, Mom and Dad are both waiting for me out on the lawn. Mom's arms are crossed tight across her chest, her face is creased with worry, and as I step out of the truck they both stride over to me and fold me into their arms.

They lead me inside. "You must be starving, sweetie," Mom says and busies her panicky hands by warming up butter in a skillet to make my favorite lunch, grilled cheese. Dad leans back against the counter, his pale blue eyes searching mine. My stomach grumbles at the smell of the sizzling butter. I keep expecting them both to explode on me, but they tiptoe around me, treating me not like I ran away, but as if I still have a stomach bug. I'm grateful for whatever the sheriff told them.

I scarf down my grilled cheese and move to the living room. Mom hovers in the doorway, biting her nails. I can tell she has something to say but doesn't want to say it in front of Dad, so she makes an excuse about folding the laundry and leaves the room. Dad's got a football game on and I stretch out on the couch next to him and put my cold feet on his warm lap. When I'm sure Mom's out of earshot, I ask, "Dad, you believe me, don't you? About the dreams?" His eyes are far off, staring somewhere between the Texas Longhorns football game and the fireplace.

"I don't know what I believe anymore, baby," he says, his voice soft and distant, the sturdy knot he'd tied himself back into already beginning to unravel after my stunt this morning.

I roll over on my side and curl up and drift to off to sleep.

———

I wake to the sound of my parents chopping vegetables. It must be near sunset, because the room is a dark cave with just thin slits of sunlight creeping through the shutters. Mom and Dad are talking in hushed tones and the radio is on, tuned to a classical station.

I step into the dining room and the table is set for dinner so I sink down in my chair. Mom and Dad carry in platters of food and just after we start to eat, Mom clears her throat and sets down her fork and says, "Now that you've had some rest, we'd just like to say that we're not mad at you, Leah. Your father and I are just thankful"—her eyes fill with tears—"that you're here, back home, safe, with us." She looks at Dad expectantly, but he just nods quickly and chokes back his own tears.

After supper Mom brings out dessert, the apple pie left over from the picnic, and is just beginning to serve it when the phone rings. Dad wipes the corner of his mouth with a napkin and leaps for the phone.

"Spencer residence," he says, breathless. "Yes, yes, she is ... hang on." He's standing between the kitchen and the dining room where the wall phone hangs. Mom jumps up and pushes away from the table, but Dad shakes his head. "It's actually for Leah. It's the sheriff."

I take the phone from Dad and step into the kitchen, cradling the phone to my ear.

"Listen, Leah, I'm sorry but I drove out to Mr. Haines's property this afternoon myself and he checks out. The children you heard were his foster children, and I'm absolutely certain he in no way had anything to do with Lucy's disappearance."

"But what about the greenhouse?" I ask, stepping farther into the kitchen until the cord strangles the wall. "Did you investigate that?"

He sighs. "I'm sorry to tell you this, but there was nothing there. I had a look around inside and it's just an old greenhouse. They don't even use it anymore. And there's no trap door, it's just a big mound of sod with weeds growing over it—the land hasn't been recently disturbed."

I slump into the wall, still holding the phone.

"I'm sorry, kiddo, I wish I had more good news," he says. "Would you mind putting your mom on the line for me?"

"Sure," I say, my bottom lip quivering. "And thanks for checking it out anyways."

I walk out of the kitchen and pass the phone to Mom, who's already standing. She takes it and steps into the kitchen, gently pushing the door shut behind her. I can hear soft murmurs, and I can picture Mom twisting the phone cord around her finger like she does when she's having a serious conversation.

————

Later that evening as I'm about to drop into sleep, Mom comes in my room and sits next to me in bed. She's wearing a lavender cotton nightgown and smells like pink Dove soap. She smooths down my bangs and strokes my hair for a while before saying, in a low voice, "I can't believe you went out there all by yourself!" She shakes her head as much as a reproach as wonderment.

"But that's not what I want to talk to you about. Your father and I both know that you've been through enough already," she says, still stroking my hair. "The sheriff, umm … Tommy, well, he suggested," she says, fumbling around for words. "He thinks that maybe you should go and talk to a counselor. About the dreams, about Lucy, just about everything you've been through. Your father and I agree with him. We think it might help, Leah. Just think about it, okay?"

I roll over, turning away from her. I'm silently counting the yellow wildflowers on my wallpaper, fighting back tears. I'm stung that the sheriff doesn't believe me, that Mom and Dad don't believe me.

Mom starts to rub my back, and at first, I want to twist away from her, to punish her, but I don't have the energy. I stare at the wallpaper feeling foolish and betrayed. She rubs in small, soothing circles. My eyelids grow heavy and I fall into a numb sleep.

39

Sylvia

ACCORDING TO DELIA, THESE men were all part of a secret society—a sex ring, presumably run by the sheriff—and every Friday night they would meet out at a cemetery where they would conduct dark rituals and force women into performing sex acts with them.

On the first night she was raped, the sheriff and his deputy led Delia out of her cell and out the back door of the police station. At first she thought she was going be released, but then they dragged her by the handcuffs to a black Chevy Blazer, threw her in the back, and shackled her legs.

They drove out of town and turned down a long blacktopped road, then down a red-dirt lane. Her hip bumped against the metal truck bed as they hit craters in the road.

They yanked her out of the car and dragged her toward the cemetery. There was a fire pit with a huge bonfire raging and a great big circle of stones around the fire. There were other women there, all strapped to the stones, naked and terrified. The preacher seemed to be the master of the ceremonies, and when they tied Delia to a stone and unshackled her legs, he started to say strange, mysterious words over the fire, words she didn't understand.

That first night, she struggled to break loose. She fought them and kicked at them when they removed the shackles and tore off her clothes. She screamed until they stuffed a filthy rag in her mouth, but after that first night she learned to stop fighting—they would be finished with her quicker that way and there'd be less punishment—so she learned to let her body go slack and let them have their way with her, their stale, putrid breath fuming in her face.

They treated the women like animals, she told me. While they were tied to the stones, the men would force themselves into the women's mouths, and then rape them and do other horrid, vile things that she couldn't even tell me about. I could tell she was ashamed, but I tried not to make her feel any shame—I wouldn't shudder in front of her or blink. Instead, I'd say, "Go on, dear."

She told me about the rituals, about something called a blood ritual that the preacher would perform. One Friday, under a full moon, she saw him slit the throat of a white bunny and wipe the blood over the throat of one of the women. The next Friday, the woman had disappeared. Delia felt like they had murdered her during a sacrifice, and that they would all eventually be murdered.

Delia thought she was next; that's why she was so desperate to escape.

No one came looking for these girls. They were the forgotten, the "trash" in their small Christian town.

"I'm safe here, right?" she would ask me every night, heartbreakingly so, like a child, jittery and manic. Her thin body rocking back and forth in bed, her bony knees pulled tightly into her chest. It broke my heart to have to keep telling her over and over, "Yes, you're safe here. You're safe."

40

Leah

Sunday, November 5th, 1989
Lucy missing 5 weeks, 2 days

I wake to warm fingers brushing across my face. It's Lucy; she's giggling and trying to wake me up. Her breath smells like hot cinnamon; she's just brushed her teeth with her favorite toothpaste, Colgate Red. She tugs at my pjs and brings an index finger to her lips and says, "Shhhhh."

Other than that *shhhh*, we don't talk, or can't talk. She just keeps giggling. She's wearing her pink nightgown, the kind that collects static so that her hair stands up at wild angles, and every time I touch her, it shocks us. I can hear music playing in another room, and Lucy grabs me by the hand and pulls me out of bed.

My face is wet with tears. I'm just so happy to see her and we stumble into our yellow playroom. It's morning and the sun has filled the room with warm, silky light. The turntable is spinning and it's the soundtrack to *Xanadu*.

Lucy smiles when I realize it. It's our thing. We used to spend hours in our roller skates, skating up the drive to the side of our house, trying to gather speed so we could bust through the brick wall like they do in the movie, to get to the mystical place of Xanadu.

Olivia Newton John's voice purrs at me to take her hand, to believe we are magic.

Lucy dances around the room, smiling and giggling and then runs over to me and we start waltzing around the room.

The record keeps spinning, but Lucy breaks loose and runs out of the room. I go to follow her, but when I get to the landing, it's dark and there's no railing to the stairs. I stop because I could tumble down and when I wake up, I'm screaming her name.

41

Sylvia

THAT SATURDAY I DROVE out to Hattie's. It had snowed the night before; the ground was coated in a thick white layer as creamy and rich as vanilla frosting, so we spent all day huddled inside Hattie's kitchen, sitting around her enamel-topped table drinking coffee and trying to figure out what to do about Delia.

We knew we wouldn't have her forever. Our unit was a temporary one, a place to move on from.

"Let's wait and see about Dr. Marshall's diagnosis," Hattie said, clinking a tiny silver spoon against the inside of her coffee mug as she stirred in more cream. "He's going to evaluate her Monday morning."

We knew that based on his evaluation, Delia would be transferred soon, to the state hospital in Rusk or, if her case was less severe, she would be sent back to family, if they could find any, and seen on an outpatient basis.

We both fretted over either possibility. Nowhere seemed safe for Delia, unless she was with us. We talked about me taking her home and hiding her there; I was certainly willing to do it.

"Isn't it time we go to the police, tell them what we know?" I asked.

"Mmm…no, I don't think so, not yet." Hattie shook her head. "They'll just wanna know if she's crazy or not, so we have to wait for Dr. Marshall."

I knew she was right.

I didn't want to leave Hattie's, but outside the sky was turning a deep purple and snow flurries began skipping through the air, so I gathered my heavy winter coat and said goodbye.

———

That Monday I went into the hospital during the daytime, just before lunch, and requested a meeting with Dr. Marshall. He was in his office, hunched over paperwork, a pen jammed in his fat hand. He barely looked up when I walked in and motioned for me to take a seat.

"I want to talk to you about Delia," I said, my voice suddenly teetering.

"Yes, what about?" he said, the overhead fluorescents bouncing off his waxy, bald head.

I felt my throat harden—Delia had confided in me and Hattie, but I had to tell him what I knew. I didn't go into too much detail, but I told him that Delia believed her life to be in great peril, that she had managed to escape from a sex ring led by the Starrville sheriff.

He held my gaze for a moment, but then looked bored and continued filling out paperwork.

"The girl is not in her right mind," he said, licking the tip of his stubby index finger and flipping through paperwork. "I did a full evaluation this morning, and she's displaying all the symptoms of paranoid schizophre-nia—"

I opened my mouth to speak but he waved his hand, dismissing me.

"And I'm going to recommend that she be transferred to the state as soon as possible."

"But she's not crazy!" I said. My hands were shaking. "Her story is real, and it's our opinion—"

"*Our?*" Dr. Marshall asked with a nasty smirk on his face.

"Nurse Banks and I believe that she's a victim and yes, she may be suffering from post-traumatic stress disorder, but she's definitely in her right mind. We need to be going to the police, we need to keep her safe, we need—"

Dr. Marshall was up out of his chair, hands on the desk, lunging toward me. One thin strip of black, greasy hair ran over the crown of his head. "She's delusional!" he was practically shouting at me. "That's my diagnosis and it sticks! No more of this nonsense!" he said, waving me out of his office.

"But I'm willing to take her home! She can come and live with me," I said.

"Look, I don't know what is going on between you and this girl," he said, a distasteful look spreading across his face, "but you need to let this go."

———

That night and for the rest of the time Delia was with us, I stopped giving her the meds. It occurred to me later that of course Delia might've acted out more in front of Dr. Marshall, wanting him to believe she was truly insane so she could stay in hiding, but I wanted her to be as lucid as possible, to get as many facts for the police as I possibly could before she was transferred.

Her shots, though, were carefully measured out and recorded— controlled substances are monitored under a tight watch—but I would turn and empty the syringe into a wadded up towel on top of the laundry bin. One night, as I turned to do it, the door was still open and Laverne, another nurse, walked by and a look passed between us.

42

Leah

Friday, November 1oth, 1989
Lucy missing 6 weeks

Ever since the sheriff called, I've decided to start keeping a diary. I want to record everything that happens, especially my dreams, so I went to the top shelf of my closet and pulled out an old baby blue diary I haven't touched since fifth grade. It has a silver lock on it, and I wrote on the inside flap with magic markers, "NOBODY IS ALLOWED TO READ THIS. ESPECIALLY LUCY!" It had just three entries in it: what grades I had made that semester, what movie Lucy and I had just watched, and an entry about Jason Wesley, a boy I thought was cute.

I flipped to a fresh page and at the top I wrote: SUSPECTS. I wrote down the name Mr. Haines, even though the sheriff swears he's innocent.

On Tuesday, Ali came bounding up to me in the locker banks after fourth period. Her hair was pulled back tautly in a big red bow with frizzy rings forming around her face. She was wearing a multi-colored baggy sweater and she sashayed toward me and passed me a note. I read it during English:

Leah! Want to come over this Saturday night? I know things have been SO hard for you, but I would love it if you'd say yes. Brett and Scott are coming over to watch a movie. Well, Scott actually asked me to ask you to come, but I really want you to, too, and I really think you should! Mom says you can spend the night. Let me know!

I folded the note back up into its ruler-perfect shape and let out a sigh. I had no desire to go to Ali's, to get nauseous from eating too much popcorn and Cool Ranch Doritos and to spend the night trying to fend off Scott while Ali and Brett stayed lip locked underneath a blanket, but I found myself unfolding the note, and scrawling YES on the bottom.

I needed Scott to drive me to Big Woods.

That night I waited until Mom and Dad were asleep and I snuck into Dad's darkened study and turned on the computer. I looked over my shoulder to make sure I was alone before I started typing:

Lucy,

I know you're out there. I know the dream was real. I went out to Big Woods to find you, but I couldn't. But don't worry, I'm coming out there again Saturday night—I'm going to ask Scott to take me. If you can, tell me more, tell me where you are, anything.

I love you,
Leah

I left the message up all night so she could see it, but I made sure I erased it before Mom and Dad woke up the next morning.

———

On Friday night, the night before Ali's sleepover, I decided to sleep in Lucy's room. I walked over to her closet and turned on the light, like she used to at night, and pulled the door just so. Her room was starting to smell musty, so I turned the ceiling fan on low, even though it was cold outside. I climbed in her bed and turned toward the window. The moon was nearly full and so bright it glowed pink and had a halo around it. I stared and stared at the pink orb until I fell asleep.

———

I had a dream that night that Lucy and I were playing in the woods behind our house. It was chilly out, and Lucy was all bundled up, wearing her thick wool toboggan. She was tracing a circle in the dirt with a stick, but then tossed it aside and went into the house. A moment later she came back and held out her gloved hands and handed me a bracelet. It was her favorite: a silver cuff with a butterfly on it made out of turquoise. Mom and Dad brought it back from a vacation in Cancun as a souvenir. They'd given me a matching pair of silver turquoise earrings. The butterfly's wings are spiky, and Lucy and I used to pretend that it was her "weapon bracelet," like the one Wonder Woman wears.

"Here," she said, solemnly. She wouldn't meet my eyes. She looked forlorn and vacant.

"But it's your favorite."

"You'll need it," she said. And she was gone.

———

When I woke up, I rolled onto my side and stared at Lucy's night-stand. There, next to her little alarm clock, was the bracelet. A smile spread across my face as I slipped it on. I tried to remember if I had noticed it before I fell asleep but couldn't. But in that moment, I decided to believe that the bracelet had somehow come from Lucy, and this dream, more than any of the others, was the one I'd cling to the most; it was the one dream that nobody could take away from us.

I went to my room and started to pack for the sleepover—toothbrush, pjs, my retainer case. But I also grabbed my backpack and threw in a flashlight, a whistle, my compass from summer camp: things you would need if you were going to Big Woods at night.

43

Sylvia

ONE NIGHT WHILE I was sitting up late talking to Delia, a dark look crossed her face. She had started to look better, healthier. The color had returned to her skin, her cheeks were flushed pink from the shower and her hair was shiny and glossy with the drugstore shampoo I'd picked up for her. But when she started telling me about the children, all the color leached from her face and the bags under her eyes were so purple they looked like bruises.

She stared out the window as she spoke, gazing out over the dingy lights of town, a yellow neon sign from the corner liquor store and the flickering fluorescents of a nearby service station.

Sometime in the weeks before her escape, the men had started to bring children to their ceremonies. Young girls. Probably five and six years old. They forced the girls to watch, she said sadly, and she could still hear their constant, terrified crying, and the sick way the men would try and calm them down, and reassure them with cookies, candy, and soda.

She overheard the sheriff tell his deputy on the way out to the cemetery one night that he was done with these "sassy, older bitches," that they needed to start with younger girls, so they that they could groom them.

My stomach formed itself into a pit as she told me about the children, and a murderous rage I've never felt before or since shot through me. When she was done, I brought her a hot cup of chamomile tea, drizzled with honey, and I sat there and cried with her until she rolled over and slid into sleep.

44

Leah

Saturday, November 11th, 1989
Lucy missing 6 weeks, 1 day

The Shermans' house is a red-and-white brick mansion perched aggressively close to the street, pushily announcing its presence. No long, winding, suggestive driveway for them—just an immaculate, half-moon chunk of concrete that practically gleams in the sun and cuts through a yard so perfectly manicured that it almost looks plastic.

Mom dropped me off just as the afternoon sun was starting to drift behind the treetops, splintering light over the gray streets.

"I'll just get Ali's mom to bring me home tomorrow." I leaned over and kissed Mom on the cheek. "You know how she loves to make us pancakes for breakfast, so I'll have her drop me home after that."

Before I even shut the car door, Mrs. Sherman launched herself from the house in a lime-green pant suit and marched to us. Mom's eyes deadlocked straight ahead and she eased out of the drive, pretending not to notice Mrs. Sherman, who waved frantically after her.

She opened the door and guided me into their dramatic, polished foyer, placing a bony hand on my shoulder, her chunky gold ring digging painfully into the bone.

"Sweetie, how *are* you?" she asked in the same annoying tone Ali uses, as if there is something inherently wrong with me, like I'd been bit by a rabid dog or just had a lobotomy.

"I'm fine, Mrs. Sherman," I found myself saying, trying both to reassure her and to end the conversation.

"We've been praying for you, dear," she said and then shouted to the second floor, "ALI! Your guest is here! Get off the phone!" She turned back to me and smiled and motioned for me to have a seat in the living room.

Even though the Shermans' house is gigantic, it always feels strangely suffocating to me: wall-to-wall cream carpet blankets the whole house and there is all this wasted, unused space everywhere— soaring ceilings with weird ledges that serve no purpose other than to display dusty knick-knacks in front of tall windows that trap light, making their house feel perpetually hot. And the whole entire house smells chlorine-soaked, even though they cover their pool for the winter.

Ali leaned over the railing, the phone dangling from her hand and shouted, "Hey! Come on up!"

Mrs. Sherman shuffled out of the kitchen and foisted a tray of ham and cheese sandwiches on me. "Here, darling. Why don't you take those upstairs to Ali's room? I know you girls have a lot of catching up to do."

I nodded robotically and climbed the steps up to the second floor.

"Um, I'm so sure," Ali giggled into the phone. "Okay, gotta go now, Leah's here! But see you soon." Her face was flushed. "Sorry, that was Brett."

I handed her the tray of sandwiches and we plopped on her cushy bed and started attacking them. Her whole room was done up in Laura Ashley—her bedspread, curtains, and the wallpaper were all the same creamy-yellow tone with sprays of deep maroon flowers. Tacked up all over the walls were hand-made signs in bubble letters: Ali + Brett = forever! Ali LOVES Brett!

And then the cheerleading slogans: GO LOBOS! LONGVIEW LOBOS ARE THE BEST! Her green-and-white pompoms were tossed in a corner with a megaphone planted on top.

"So, there's something I've been meaning to tell you," Ali said, between mouthfuls of sandwich. "Scott's been talking to Kelly Hayes lately. I saw them in the locker bank together last week. He was whispering something in her ear and twirling her hair and she was like laughing hysterically!"

My face burned with anger.

"I know, ewwww, right?" Ali crinkled her nose up in disgust. "She's such a skank! I can't *believe* he's interested in someone on the whore core."

The whore core was the derogatory name given to our school's drill team. It was just understood that the rich, popular girls were cheerleaders or majorettes and everyone else was on the drill team.

I said nothing. I felt like I'd been kicked in the stomach, but I didn't want to show this weakness to Ali.

"So, I just thought you should know, Leah. And that's why I thought you should definitely be here tonight, to hold on to him. I mean, I'm sure you guys are totally fine but—"

Mrs. Sherman appeared in the door with two red plastic cups fizzing with Coke. "This is the last time I'll interrupt you girls tonight, I promise," she said, winking.

Ali rolled her eyes. "Anyway, there's something else we need to talk about, too," she said, chomping on ice. "The church wants to have a candlelight vigil for Lucy on Friday. And Pastor Mike wanted me to ask if you could be there to speak."

Just hearing Pastor Mike's name made bile rise to the back of my throat. He was the youth minister at East Texas Methodist, and the few times I'd been around him, he icked me out. Ali dragged me to a lock-in once—basically a co-ed sleepover at the church where nobody gets any sleep—and there was something too eager about Pastor Mike that gave me a hollow feeling inside. He's too chummy with the teenagers and tries overly hard to fit in and every time he shakes your hand he holds on to it too long, clasping his other, cologned hand on top and saying things like, "We'd love it if you'd join us on a Sunday, Leah."

"I don't know, Ali," I muttered.

"Well, I've been working on some t-shirt designs. Pastor Mike asked me to," she said, blushing and smiling. She pulled out her over-stuffed Bible and unzipped it, the gold cross on the zipper catching the sunlight, sending dizzying, gold glitters across the room. "And well, here they are," she said, thrusting it toward me. There were loose sheets of typing paper in there, assorted versions of the same messages like, FIND LUCY, BRING LUCY HOME, and LONGVIEW LOVES LUCY.

Before I could even respond Ali started up again. "And it's not just about Lucy, Leah," she said, twisting her James Avery charm bracelet around her wrist. "It's a whole movement of us standing up against the Satanists. We're brainstorming on some slogans for posters and I wanted to see what your vote would be: *Christian Youth against Satan*

Worshipers or just *Christian Youth against the Devil?*" She leapt off the bed and headed to her closet to pull out the posters. She was talking about the vigil as if it was another pep rally she was organizing—she had that same giddy, hungry look she gets when she's making posters at school: spread-eagle over the poster board, armed with a rainbow of tempura paint bottles.

My stomach lurched. I had to get out of there.

"I need to go to the bathroom," I stammered and headed down the hallway. I stepped inside the bathroom and shut the door. I collapsed on the fabric-covered toilet lid and rested my chin in my hands. I stared at Ali's sea of mint-green Clinique bottles strewn across the countertop. I had no desire to see Scott ever again and the whole talk of Lucy and the church was making me sick. I fake-flushed the toilet and fake-washed my hands and went back into the hallway. I picked up the wall phone and pretended to make a call.

When I got back to Ali's room, I clutched my stomach and said, "I'm not feeling so well. I called my Mom and she'll be here in a sec to pick me up, so I'm just going to wait outside for her."

Ali's mouth opened in an O-shape. "But what am I going to tell Scott?" she screeched at me.

I grabbed my overnight back and shrugged. "Goodbye, Ali."

———————

It was still light out, but the sun was beginning to slide behind the mansions in Ali's neighborhood so I walked as quickly as I could. And when I thought nobody was watching, I sprinted. Nicolette's house was eight long blocks away (she lived on the outer edge of the development), and I knew even if she wasn't home, her parents would be.

I made it to her block just as the street lights were starting to flicker on, my lungs on fire and my hair wet with sweat. I walked up the stone path leading to the front door and rang the bell.

Mrs. Rossi swung the door open wide and pulled me into her. "Oh, Bella," she gasped. Her breath was warm and tangy and her lips were stained with red wine. "We've been so worried about you," she said with her rich accent. "How is your fam-a-lee? How is your mother? Your father? Oh, I can't imagine what you've all been going through. Here, come, come," she said, taking my bag from me, pulling me into their brick-red living room. I could hear the sounds of a dinner party trickling from inside the dining room: silverware clinking, gusts of laughter, party music.

"Do you mind if I spend the night, Mrs. Rossi?"

"Of course not! You can stay all week if you like," she said, smiling. "Nicolette is getting ready upstairs. Damien will be here shortly. Go on up!"

I climbed the polished wooden staircase and went to Nicolette's room. She had her back turned to the door and was hunched over her vanity, applying makeup. A clove cigarette smoldered in the ashtray. The Rossis don't care if Nicolette or Nick smoke, and they share wine at dinner with them.

"Hi," I said.

She spun around, crossed the room, and grabbed me. "I'm so happy you're here," she said, her eyes searching mine. "Any news?"

Tears sprang to my eyes. I just shook my head. I wanted to tell her all of it—about the dreams, about the sheriff and my parents, about Ali—but I knew Damien would be showing up soon, ringing the doorbell, so I decided to wait until later.

"Your mom said I could spend the night. Do you mind?"

"Don't be silly! Of course not! Damien's taking me to Monaco's tonight. Wanna go?"

Monaco's Uptown is the only underage club in town. I've never been there. Neither has Nicolette, or any other freshman that I know of.

Before I could even answer, Nicolette said, "Here, let me give you a make-over."

She pulled back my hair with a headband and tilted her head before deciding where to begin. She shook a bottle of orange base and coated a makeup sponge with a few drops of it and rubbed it deftly across my skin. I looked around her room while she worked. When we were kids, she used to have Holly Hobby wallpaper up, but now it was a modern-looking white pattern with geometric shapes in primary colors. Her walls were covered in music posters, mostly of the band The Cure. She had a map of the world up, with thumbtacks marking the places her family has traveled. Nicolette never seemed to study but she was in all honors classes and was fluent in four languages and could graduate early if she wanted to.

She took a sip of something out of a coffee mug and passed it to me. It smelled sharp, and I looked at her with my eyebrows raised.

"It's just a little peppermint schnapps," she said, pushing it back to me. "Don't be such a pussy, Leah" she said, smiling, an old joke between us.

I took a small sip, the alcohol burning my tongue as it went down, and I made a spattering sound.

"Here, look down," she commanded and ran black liquid eyeliner across my eyelids. It felt thick and cold. She dusted my face with powder and rubbed pink blush into my cheeks.

She finished with some dark red lipstick and then slid a pair of black-laced gloves over my hands—like the ones Madonna wears—before she finished getting herself dressed. My face felt tight with the base on, like it was wrapped with cling wrap, like my skin couldn't breathe, but when I looked in the mirror I looked sixteen. I looked brave. I looked like I could be mean, even.

We heard Damien's Mustang roar in the driveway and I followed Nicolette, bounding down the stairs.

"Ciao Mama!" she called out and ran out the front door without waiting for a reply.

———————

Monaco's is downtown in an old loft. A man with spiky hair sat on a barstool outside and asked for our IDs (you have to be thirteen). Loud music rattled the giant windows. We went in and my breath stopped short for a second. It was wild. Throngs of older teens danced to a song I'd never heard, light pulsed off the walls, and there was a DJ in a cage. The walls were painted black with Day-Glo spots on them and everybody in there was smoking.

I found a wall in the back and stood there with my back pressed up against it, trying to look casual and cool. The DJ put on "Pour Some Sugar on Me" and couples dirty-danced and made out; it made me blush and I fidgeted with Lucy's bracelet. The place reeked of stale cigarettes and fresh smoke, the grime of teenage sweat mixed with perfume.

Damien pulled Nicolette into a corner on the dance floor. I felt self-conscious watching them. My eyes scanned the room and I saw Nicolette's brother, Nick, coming in the front door alone. He normally had his girlfriend, Angie, hanging off of him. She's a senior like him—blond, gorgeous, and petite with a big chest. But she always looks sullen, her face upturned and pouting at his. Gorgeous, but needy.

I've always had a crush on Nick, ever since we were little. His hair is jet black and thick and he's the tallest guy in school, but not freaky tall, just perfect and handsome. He letters in Track and Swimming.

His eyes are sea-green and he has ruby-red lips. I never admitted to Nicolette that I liked him, but she could tell. Every girl who wasn't his sister liked Nick, and she used to tease me about it and say, "God, Leah, stare much?" when she would catch me drooling over him.

I never let on, but he could probably tell, too. One summer afternoon after seventh grade, while I was swimming at their house I went inside to use the bathroom. Nick and his friend Tommy were playing Nintendo in the living room and I had to cross in front of their game to get to the bathroom. I was gawky in my one piece, shivering from the A/C. When they thought I was out of earshot I heard Tommy say to Nick (to my surprise), "She's gonna be sexy when she's older."

I looked back over my shoulder and could see Nick's face turn red, and something like jealousy flashed across his face. I stepped into the bathroom and peeled off my suit, but I could still hear them through the door.

"Don't look at her that way, man," Nick said.

"Oh! You like her!!! Nick's got a woody for Leah!"

"Shut up, loser."

Nick saw me and crossed the club. He came straight over to me and looked me up and down with his eyebrows raised. "You look nice, kiddo!" he shouted over the thumping bass, and tousled my hair. Then he grabbed me in a big bear hug and said into my ear, "I'm really sorry about Lucy," and held me for a while. He was wearing a black leather bomber jacket and smelled like heaven. He spotted Nicolette on the dance floor. "What are you guys even doing here?"

I smiled up at him and shrugged.

The music was getting even louder and the whole place was vibrating. Nick stuck his index finger up as if to say, *Be back in a second.* At that moment it seemed like everyone's heads swiveled to the front door. I looked up and saw why: filing in single line, all dressed in dark clothes like a line of black clouds descending, were the Wavers. I'd only seen them one time in person, huddled at the edge of the school parking lot, smoking. They were a tight clique and never spoke to anyone at school but themselves. They dressed only in black clothes and most of them had their hair dyed black or dark purple. They wore white makeup, so to me they looked like the street mimes I had once seen on a PBS show with Mom about Paris. Their clothes were cut in jagged angles and they all wore black combat boots and chains around their waist. It was understood that most students were afraid of them, and left them alone. They were rumored to be on drugs, to be thieves, and some people (like Ali) thought they were in a secret cult that worshipped the devil. She even thought they were behind the black rose in Brandi's locker, and couldn't understand why they weren't already expelled for that. I hadn't given them much thought until I saw them at Monaco's.

I knew the leader's name was Rain. He was tall, Nick tall, and had long platinum-blond hair with black streaks in it and a handsome but tough face. His girlfriend was Sara, a severe-looking girl with deep purple lipstick and short, blunt bangs. She was petite but looked like she could slit your throat with one of her long black fingernails, and always hovering nearby was her best friend, Jess, tall and thin and frail-looking with clear blue eyes smudged with thick charcoal eyeliner.

I was watching them, staring at Rain in particular, when I saw Nick walk up to him and they gave each other a high five. Nick bummed a cigarette off them and followed them upstairs to the balcony. I didn't want him to see me staring at him so I looked over at Nicolette, who was still grinding on the dance floor. I kept glancing upstairs to see what they were doing, but they were just huddled, probably eight of them, in a corner.

Nicolette came up and bumped me on the hip, making me jump. "Hey! Having fun?" I could smell more alcohol on her breath.

I nodded and tried to look chipper. "Is Nick friends with the Wavers?" I shouted in her ear.

She shrugged. "He's been hanging out with them lately. Drives Angie crazy," she said and pulled me onto the dance floor. It was New Order, "Bizarre Love Triangle," and I made a good show of dancing, but I just wanted to get back to her house so we could talk. I wanted to get to Lucy.

––––––––

We got home sometime after midnight. I followed Nicolette to the kitchen, where she groped around for snacks. She grabbed a bag of chips and we headed up to her room. We sat cross-legged on her wrought-iron daybed, sharing the chips until they were all gone. She shook the crumbs off the comforter and then clicked off the lights and gave me a pillow. She was too groggy to pull out the trundle, so we lay curled up on our sides, facing out the window. The moon was bright, the color of wheat, and I began to tell her everything about Lucy. As I was talking, she wrapped her arm around me. I even told her about the bracelet, and guided her hand to it.

"You believe me, don't you?" I asked.

"Course I do," she said in a lazy voice. She had continued drinking at the club—Damien had spiked their Cokes all night with Jack Daniels—and I could smell the whisky on her. I couldn't tell if she was really even awake, but I kept talking about Lucy, about Big Woods. It felt good just to spill my guts to her.

"Do you think the Wavers are dangerous? Do you think … do you think they're a cult? Like Ali thinks? That they're devil worshippers?" I asked, my voice turning shrill. I felt her twitch and begin to snore and I knew she was asleep.

45

Sylvia

Monday, November 13th, 1989

This morning after breakfast, I step outside to check the temperature. The sun is bright and warm, but the air is so chilly that it stings my bare wrist. I stare out over my yard and look at the tall domes of ruby and burnt copper gold leaves. This weekend I had a rare burst of energy, so I spent the morning raking but afterward I didn't have the strength to bag them all up. So I've left them there; I'll probably never get around to it.

And today, I have something else to do.

The wind picks up and plucks through my wind chimes, causing them to tink, and the tops of the leaf piles to get swept away. I wrap my robe tighter around me and go back inside and shut the door.

I climb the stairs to my spare closet on the second floor and run my fingers along the selection of clothes. I settle on a respectable pistachio green pant suit that I haven't worn in ages, and take it down from the rack. It's still in its wrapper from the cleaners and when I peel back the plastic it smells powdery and musty, but it'll have to do. I go to my room and pull out a black turtleneck from my mahogany dresser—the drawer catches and I have to bump it with my hip, cursing it for the millionth time. I select a pair of matching black shoes with thick socks. I put on a little lipstick, pull my hair back in a bun, and get dressed to leave.

———————

St. Mark's Episcopal School sits high on a hill in a pretty neighborhood speckled with old homes so that it feels like its own quaint village. I arrive just before lunch, and park in the visitor's parking space. The school is all done up for fall and Halloween: in the front yard under a soaring oak tree, mountains of pumpkins are hemmed in by hay bales for a makeshift pumpkin patch. The tall classroom windows are plastered with paper leaves in deep jewel tones of red and green, and parked on either side of the front door are two tawny scarecrows, greeting those who walk past. Giant jack-o-lanterns line the ornate stone path leading up to the school and the whole scene is so picturesque that for a moment, I forget why I've come here, and what it is I've come to do.

I walk slowly along the cobblestone path to the entryway; the stones are so well-worn that their tops are smooth and slick like polished rock. A nearby church bell clangs, signaling that it's half-past the hour and a squirrel scurries past, nearly tripping me, and fetches a fat acorn that rolls near my feet.

I walk past the scarecrows, pause at the heavy glass doors, and take a deep breath before pushing them open.

Inside, the school is cozy and smells of cinnamon. A cornucopia of fall potpourri—pinecones, dried holly branches, rosemary, and cinnamon sticks—is splayed out over the receptionist's desk. She's a tiny, stout woman with a tight, graying perm and gold glasses.

"May I help you?" she asks, smiling.

"I'm here to see Principal Spencer," I say.

"I'm sorry, she's in a meeting."

My heart sinks; I know I won't have the courage to come up here again. I'm just turning to leave when the receptionist asks, "But would you like to wait in her office? She shouldn't be much longer."

I follow her down the hall to Roz's office and it occurs to me that she didn't even ask me my name. She must assume I'm an old friend or relative—and probably harmless because of my white hair—but it disturbs me just how trusting people can be.

Her office is lovely. Homey yet professional and crisp at the same time. One wall is a sheet of glass that looks out over a lush courtyard with drooping, ancient crepe myrtles and monstrous hanging ferns. On the opposite wall, Roz has hung a giant wall calendar that features the paintings of Claude Monet, which seem to echo the tranquil garden outside. For each day, she has filled in an exacting schedule, color-coded in red, blue, and black ink by topic: Admin., Teachers, Students. There are thank-you notes from parents and graduates gone off to college taped around the calendar, with pictures of Roz and each graduating class in order by year from floor to ceiling.

But it's the wall behind her desk that threatens to pierce my composure: it's her family wall, and there are framed pictures of Leah and Lucy. Leah and Lucy dressed in their Easter bonnets when they were little. Leah and Lucy at summer camp. A family portrait with Roz and her husband and the two girls, all dressed up, posed in front of a wooded lake scene. And what breaks my heart most of all is how Roz has carefully framed her girls' best works of art. A giraffe painted creatively to look like a zebra from a 4th grade Leah, a homemade Valentine "for my familee, luv Lucy Belle!", and most gut-wrenching of all, a picture that Lucy drew when she was four—a giant face that has freckles, red spots, and a dot, that she titled, "Freckles, Belly Button, and Hurt." My eyes are roving all over this wall and I'm lost in reverie when the door opens behind me, and before I know it I'm on my feet and shaking hands with Roz.

"Hi, please keep your seat," Roz says and disappears behind her giant pine desk that the midday sun has turned the color of weak tea. She's dressed in a smart black suit but looks smaller than I remember, more diminished.

"Do I know you?" she asks, and I see a flicker of recognition cross her face—maybe she saw me on television—and so I quickly say, "I was your nurse. When Leah was born."

"Oh! That *is* you! Of course!" She smiles and takes off her glasses. The edges of her eyes are lined with crow's feet. "What can I do for you?"

A lump forms in my throat, but I manage to say, "I'm here about Lucy."

The corners of her mouth tighten and she lets out a heavy sigh.

"I … I may have some information for you," I say. She just tilts her head and stares straight ahead at me, her mouth a rigid line. I can feel the edges of her weary impatience, so I rush in and quickly fill the gap of silence.

"After I left the Labor and Delivery Ward," I say, "I worked for many years as a nurse in the Psychiatric Unit. And there was a woman who came to us one night. She had been held captive by the Starrville Police. The sheriff, and some other powerful men in Starrville, were operating an elaborate sex ring, and—"

"I'm sorry," Roz interrupts, rubbing the bridge of her nose, "but what does any of this have to do with my daughter?"

"Well, the woman told me that sometimes there were children present," I say, fumbling around and suddenly feeling like the lunatic she perceives me to be. "And I went to the police here and tried to tell them about it but they wouldn't believe me, but I just know that these same men—"

But before I can finish Roz has put her hand up for me to stop talking. "I'm sorry, Mrs. … what was your name again?" Roz asks, the principal in her coming out and suddenly I feel foolish for coming up here, for approaching her like this, at school, out of the blue.

"Mrs. Parker. Sylvia, Sylvia Parker," I stammer. "I know what I saw happened years ago, but I believe these men are still active and—"

"I'm sorry, Mrs. Parker, but I can't take this. I can't listen one second longer. I'm trying to hold onto what little peace in life I've found and I'm afraid I'm going to have to ask you to leave."

"But if you'll just hear me out, I promise I'm not making this up," I try, one last plea, but she's now on her feet, glasses back on, and she crosses the room to open the door without another word.

I walk out of her office meekly, with my head down, tears forming in the corner of my eyes. I'm so embarrassed I don't even say goodbye to the cheery receptionist as she calls out after me.

Inside the station wagon, my face burns. I'm furious with myself for bungling this. I back out of the parking lot and drive away, feeling sadness and shame blistering over me.

46

Leah

Monday, November 13th, 1989
Lucy missing 6 weeks, 3 days

I went to Big Woods again tonight. I still can't believe it, that I was out there just a few hours ago. My mind is still racing, trying to process everything I saw. I'm writing in my diary with the covers pulled up over me, my flashlight wedged between my neck and shoulder so Mom and Dad won't see my light still on. I don't want to have to deal with them anymore tonight.

————

Yesterday just before lunchtime, Mrs. Rossi gave me a ride home. I asked her to let me out a few houses down so that I could walk the rest of the way—she didn't press me with any questions. When I walked through the door, I didn't mention anything about not spending the night at Ali's, and when Mom asked me how it was I just shrugged and said nonchalantly, "Okay, I guess," and went upstairs.

A few hours later the phone rang. Mom answered it and shouted up to me in a chipper voice, "Honey! It's Nicolette!" She sounded so happily surprised that my social life seemed to be returning to normal. All my lying was starting to make me feel guilty.

"Hey," I said, in a low voice.

"Hey! Ummm, did your Mom hang up?" Nicolette asked. I had heard the phone click, but told Nicolette I would call her right back just to be on the safe side. She answered on the first ring. "So, I overheard Nick talking on the phone to someone about a party tomorrow night in Big Woods. With the Wavers."

My stomach clenched into a knot.

"I know it's a Monday, but apparently they have one every time there's a full moon."

"Nicolette, we have to go," I said in a deadpan voice.

"I know, I know. I threatened to tell Mom and Dad about it if he didn't take us along."

My palms were sweaty and tears flooded my eyes. I was scared, but so happy. "So you were awake? You heard what I was telling you last night?" I said, through a stream of snot and tears.

"I heard enough of it, anyway. I never thought you were gonna shut up," she said, trying to make me laugh like she always does when I'm crying. It worked—I snorted out a honking laugh and wiped my nose with my sleeve.

"Thanks a *lot*," I said.

"You're gonna have to sneak out. The party's late. Can you do that?"

"Yes."

"Good. We'll pick you up at nine. Gotta run," she said and blew me a kiss over the phone.

I pressed the pink button down to end the call and sat there, cradling the phone in my hands.

———

It was surprisingly easy to slip out. Mom and Dad were upstairs in bed watching television by eight thirty, so I went into their room and kissed them goodnight. I tiptoed down the stairs, disarmed the burglar alarm, and walked down the drive. The night was clear and cold and I sat on the curb—which glowed fluorescent white from the full moon—and waited for them to pick me up.

Nick pulled up in his 1977 maroon Camaro (I know the stats because he talked about that car endlessly from the time he was twelve until his parents bought it for him on his sixteenth birthday). He leaned over and pushed open the passenger door. Cigarette smoke spilled out of the car. I climbed in and it was toasty. Nicolette was in the back seat with Damien, who leaned forward and passed me a peach wine cooler. I took a swig. It didn't taste bad, so I took another sip, letting the sweet, scorching taste warm the back of my throat. Nick put the car in neutral and we coasted down the hill before he started it back up and sped away.

He had the new INXS tape blaring and the windows were cracked, making my hair whip in my face. I looked over at him and noticed how handsome he looked—the red cherry from his cigarette made his olive skin glow—but even with the alcohol and the music (what would have otherwise been a fun night) my stomach was in knots and my mind was consumed with getting to Lucy.

As we got closer to Big Woods, the streetlights started to fade and the road became darker. Nick turned down an unmarked road that I'd never seen before and killed the lights. The moon was bright enough to see by, but he made a few more turns and I couldn't understand how he knew where he was going, but then it hit me: he'd been here before. He slowed the car and rolled down the windows, flinging out his cigarette before turning down a gravel road. We passed by a gas well that see-sawed in the moonlight. I could hear music, I could feel a thumping techno beat vibrating in my chest. Nick drove around the gas well and then went down an even smaller road, the front of his car bumping and hitting potholes as his gears grinded until I saw a long, glittering row of parked cars ahead of us.

We piled out of the car and followed Nick down the muddy path toward a clearing in the distance. I could see smoke from a fire and the music was so loud that talking to each other was pointless. As we got closer I could hear the lyrics. It was Nine Inch Nails and Trent Reznor was growling about being sanctified. When we made it to the clearing, the breath got sucked out of me. There was a large circle of huge stones—boulders so big they reminded me of Stonehenge—and in the middle of the circle was a massive bonfire. About thirty older teenagers were dancing around the fire as if in a trance. Some wore masks, some were dressed in dark capes, and there were red candles lit in front of each stone, sputtering red wax over heaps of dried flowers. In the corner was a DJ, a guy I recognized from school. I didn't know his name but he ran with the heavy metal crowd, and he was wearing a ripped up Megadeath t-shirt with big chunky combat boots. Next to his booth was a make-shift stage made from old, rotted wood. In the center of the stage was an odd-looking throne made from the same chalk-white stones that formed the circle, and spray-painted on the head of it in black was a skull-and-cross bones.

Nick wandered off and Nicolette leaned in and whisper-shouted, "This is *so* bizarre. Let's just try to act like we belong." She passed me a can of Keystone Light and I slugged some back, trying to look cool, but I choked and the yeasty foam sprayed down the corners of my mouth. She handed me a lit cigarette and I pretended to smoke it and look vaguely pissed off.

The full moon was orange and through the haze of alcohol and the smoke from the fire, it looked like a giant, melting dreamsicle. The DJ put on a slower, chant-like song that I didn't know and everyone started swaying to it—some of the kids had their hands clasped together like they were praying and some coupled off and started making out with each other. I spotted Nick across the bonfire talking to Rain and Sara and Jess. Rain was wearing a black mask, and the girls were wearing long, flowy, black capes with hoods on. I watched as Jess reached up and grabbed the back of Nick's head and started kissing him. My cheeks burned.

Just then Rain leapt onto the stage and ran his hand under his throat, giving the DJ the signal to kill the music. He was wearing a long black trench coat and leather bracelets with spikes. He grabbed the microphone and shouted, "Are you ready?"

"Yes!" the crowd roared back.

"Are you ready, I said!" he howled into the microphone, splitting my ears.

The crowd erupted, and he threw the microphone down and gave the DJ the thumbs up. Strobe lights started flashing everywhere and I felt disoriented—I was trying to keep an eye on everything but it was hard with the pulsing lights. Some of the teenagers started racing around the bonfire, scattering dust and waving sparklers. The song started playing and it was some kind of synth song I had never heard before, with a demented voice shouting about Jesus.

Rain was onstage lip-synching to it and the crowd was shouting out the rest of the lyrics, which were all about the devil. The song then had all this maniacal laughing on it and Rain ripped off his mask and looked out over the crowd, smiling. His eyes were roving all over the crowd and when he spotted me, he stopped singing and just stared at me, holding my eyes for a moment. A shiver ran up my back and I had to look away.

He crossed the stage and sat on the throne and Jess and Sara and three other girls surrounded him. They took out a huge goblet full of red liquid and poured it down his throat, splashing it everywhere. He stood up and shook it off like a wet dog and was lip-synching again about Hell and sinners.

And then he shouted the next part along with the crowd. Something about sex before marriage, and everybody was screaming so I could hardly understand the words. And then Sara straddled him on the throne and was moving up and down on him, her black cape covering everything.

Nicolette was wide-eyed, leaning back into Damien who cradled her from behind, his arms crossed over her chest in a protective X.

I saw Rain make some sort of hand signal and I watched as Sara, Jess, and another guy followed him over to the tree line where they cranked up two four-wheelers and took off.

"I've gotta go pee," I lied to Nicolette and headed for the woods, following Rain and the others.

Away from the bonfire and the strobe lights, I could see the tail lights of the four wheelers and I ran along the edge of the trees, trying to catch up to them. My backpack slammed against my back and my heart was beating so fast it hurt. I ran as fast as I could before I finally had to stop and double over to catch my breath. I could still hear the engine of the four wheelers whining, so I walked as quickly as I could down the path. The moon was still high but the trees were beginning to thicken again, smothering the light and making the path dark.

I kept walking until the music was just a muffled thump, but then the sound of the four wheelers had fizzled out and all I could hear was the night sounds of the forest: tree frogs croaking, night birds in flight, and the wind brushing through the pine trees. The path curved and I looked back but couldn't see the clearing anymore. Up ahead, a wispy smokestack was curling toward the moon and I decided to follow it, hoping that's where they were headed.

Behind me, I thought I heard a branch snap, but when I turned around, there was nothing there. I pulled the cuff back on my blue jean jacket and twisted Lucy's bracelet on my wrist and said out loud to her as if she were there, "I'm going to find you, Lucy. Hold on, I'm on my way." I picked up the pace again until my foot caught on a gnarled tree root and my palms planted in the red dirt. I scrambled up and wiped off my palms on my jeans, and felt tears spring to my eyes, but I brushed them away and kept marching. Now the moon had nearly set and it was even darker, and my own breath was starting to sound like somebody else's. I started doing our chant, *"Christmas, Easter, Happy Times, Christmas, Easter, Happy Times"* until it calmed me. It worked every time.

The smokestack seemed to be coming from my right, and shortly, I came upon a small gravel road and turned down it, hoping it would lead me there. Along the road there was a creaking gas well with a small light and that made me feel less afraid. I was getting closer to the gas well when I suddenly stopped and heard gravel crunching behind me. Blind, white-hot fear shot through me and I spun around with my fists up, my heart piercing my chest. I shouted, "What the fuck do you want from me!!!!"

The figure stopped, too, but then my whole body sighed as I saw his palms, Nick's palms, up in surrender.

"Nick, what the hell?" I said, breathless.

"I didn't mean to scare you ... and I didn't want to intrude," he said, coming closer. "But I saw you leave the bonfire and thought I should follow you." He took off his kelly-green letter jacket and spread it out on the ground. "Come, sit," he said.

"But I'm trying to follow Rain," I said.

"They're long gone," he said, shaking his head, "trust me. Here, share this with me," he said, offering me a sip out of his flask.

The ground was cold, so cold that it reminded me of the cheap window unit in a dingy motel I had once stayed in on the Mississippi coast with my parents and Lucy. We were sunburned and that made the A/C seem even crueler. I leaned back on his jacket and soon we were both laying there, staring up at the sky, Nick lazily smoking a cigarette.

"How do you even know them?" I asked, too embarrassed to tell him much more. He just looked at me and took another drag off his cigarette and blew smoke rings up in the air. We lay there shifting on top of the leaves. It was good to be next to Nick. He radiated warmth and I pushed the question out from the top of my stomach through my mouth.

"So they're like a cult? They're Satanists?" I asked, the word coming out as a nasty hiss. Nick looked up at the sky and blew out a deep sigh. "Well, tell me, please," I begged.

He turned to look at me and brushed a finger across my lips and called me by the nickname he'd given me when I was little. "Be careful, butterfly," he said, his cat-green eyes bloodshot. "They're weird, I'll give you that, but they aren't devil worshippers. And they didn't kidnap Lucy. But you shouldn't be out here alone."

Of course Nicolette had told him everything; I was embarrassed that I didn't already know that.

His breath was hot on my face, and it smelled like I imagined how marijuana smells. I wanted to believe him, but I didn't know what I believed anymore.

Nick dropped me off at the bottom of the driveway, but I guess Mom and Dad heard his car pull away because as I was walking up the drive, the porch lights clicked on, flooding the front yard. They came scrambling out onto the front steps. They looked all around before grabbing me and yanking me into the house. I wouldn't look at them.

"*Where* have you been?" Mom asked, her voice sounding like the high end of a piano.

"Um, I don't know, just *out*, okay?" I could still feel the alcohol in my system and it made me adopt a bitchy teenager-speak that I'd only seen on television. I'd never talked to my parents this way before; it felt cruel.

I tried to walk past them, but Dad grabbed my arm, twisting me back around. "Leah, answer your mother!"

"I was in Big Woods," I spat out at them, still in full character. "I was with Nick and Nicolette—it was just a party. It's *so* not a big deal. I'm home safe now! Isn't that all you care about?" I said, trembling.

"Goddamit, Leah! What in the hell's gotten into you?" Dad barked at me.

"What's the matter with *you guys*?" I screeched back. "Lucy is out there, somewhere, and y'all are just sitting around not doing a damn thing about it!" I was becoming hysterical and could feel a tidal wave of sobs coming on, so I pushed past my parents and tore upstairs.

"You're grounded, Leah Elizabeth Spencer!" Mom shouted after me.

"Yeah, really? Till when?" I shouted. I couldn't seem to shake the attitude.

"Until I don't *know* when," she shouted back.

"And your mother and I are gonna have to decide if you're really ready for your own car and your hardship license. Keep this up and the answer's gonna be no!" I could hear Dad shaking as he said this, struggling to gain the power back.

———————

Even though I'm under the covers, I can't stop shaking. I can't stop seeing Rain's eyes on me—the way he stared straight at me. I try to push his face out of my mind and try to see Lucy's face instead. Lately, I can't picture Lucy at ten for some reason, I can only see her as the five-year-old Lucy—smaller, tender, more childlike. I can imagine her warm hands on my arm and the way she used to pull me around the house to participate in whatever activity was delighting her. I can feel her hair tickle my cheek like it used to when she'd pounce on top of me in bed at night, trying to scare me before climbing in next to me and making me rub her back until she fell asleep. Heat rises in the back of my throat and I can't stop the sobs. Everything I've felt since she's been gone is gushing out. My whole body shakes with the sobs—grief really *is* like a wave, it's not something that people just say—and I cry and cry and cry until I'm emptied out and I fall asleep and hope that my dreams take me to her.

47

Sylvia

ON FRIDAY NIGHT—WHAT would be Delia's last night with me at the hospital—she sprang up in bed and asked for a piece of paper. I tore off a sheet from my notepad and gave her a pen and watched as she drew, her face crimped with concentration. When she was finished and certain that all the details were there, she passed it to me. It was a map of the cemetery, with road signs, landmarks, etc. I nodded and folded it neatly into a tight square and put it in the pocket of my winter coat where I would keep it for years.

Over the weekend, at home, I thought about what I would do next. I went upstairs to the second story and eyed the spare bedroom. I threw open the sash, letting sunlight wash over the modest, wooden bed dressed with a red and white quilt, and I thought—with new sheets from Penny's and a few other touches—the room could do for Delia.

She could stay with me for a little while until I figured out what to do next. We could get her on her feet and she could either go and stay with my sister, Evelyn, for a bit, or maybe I could help her apply to a community college in Dallas. Anything to get her out of this hellhole.

And in the meantime, I could go quietly to the Longview police with her story, have them open an investigation and hopefully find and save the other women.

As I fixed myself dinner that night—a roasted chicken with potatoes—I thought about what I would say to Dr. Marshall, how I could persuade him to go along with my plan. And smiling inside, I pictured telling Delia my plan, and then seeing the look of relief wash over her face.

I would explain things to her on Monday, now that she was stable and clear. I would explain that she needed to act sane in front of Dr. Marshall, that she needed to request a re-evaluation, that she needed to confess that she simply had made the whole story up, that she was really on the run from her abusive boyfriend.

———

On Monday night, I walked down the hall, my heart bursting with the news I was going to give to Delia, but when I got to her room, she was gone. The door was ajar and the lights were on—loud and bright—and the janitor was in there stripping her bed and mopping the floor. My heart started racing, I went out into the hallway and Hattie grabbed me by the hand and led me to an empty break room.

"Sylv," she said, not wanting to meet my eyes. "They discharged her over the weekend."

"Who? Who authorized this? Where is she?" My voice was screechy.

"I know, I know," Hattie said. "Apparently, Dr. Marshall discharged her back to the police. They picked her up Saturday night. Said they had located some of her family in Arkansas—family that had been looking for her, an aunt or uncle or something—and that they were going to take her to them. Dr. Marshall signed off on it—"

"Which police?" I stood there shaking, adrenaline spiking through my body, my mouth going dry.

"I don't know," Hattie said. "It's not written down in her chart." She grabbed both of my wrists and guided me to a hard, plastic bench in the corner and made me sit down with her. "Look here, calm down," she said, her eyes fixing me with a steady gaze. "Let's not think the worst. Maybe she really does have some family that we don't know about, maybe it's—"

But I stood up and tore away from her and pounded down the hall to the nurse's station, where I grabbed the phone and paged Dr. Marshall with an emergency code.

48

Leah

Friday, November 17th, 1989
Lucy missing 7 weeks

The day after the full moon party, Nicolette and I met at her locker just before second period. We let the second bell ring and made sure the halls had emptied out so we could talk in private.

"I heard my mom called your parents. I'm so sorry," I said.

"Yeah, I'm grounded until Friday. But no biggie. You?"

"I'm grounded for almost a month, till my birthday," I said.

"Jesus, Leah! That really sucks." We both had bags under our eyes from staying up late the night before and Nicolette's skin almost looked sickly green in the dingy light. "So, that Rain guy totally creeped me out," she said, her eyes darting from side to side. "I mean, even Damien was spooked. We stayed on the phone with each other until we fell asleep last night."

We were trying to keep our voices down, but our whispers bounced back at us from the hard, cold floor, crisp and loud. "I mean, what were they even *doing* out there? And where do you think they went when they left on the four-wheelers?"

Just then we heard a locker door slam and we both jumped. The noise was close by, maybe one row over, followed by the click, click, clicking sound of someone approaching us. I smelled cigarette smoke and looked up to see Rain walking toward us. He shook back his blond hair and looked us both over for a second, but then his eyes drilled on mine. He fixed me with that same stare from the night before—like he'd caught me doing something—his mouth curled in a dismissive smirk. I stood there frozen in place, staring back at him until he brushed passed us, flinging his cigarette onto the floor and grinding it out with his black hobnail boot.

After lunch that day, Ashley Crawford, a popular, bubbly junior opened her locker and found a bouquet of shriveled black roses.

It might sound weird, but when I heard that, I wished that I had blond hair and blue eyes so I could wait at my locker to catch Rain putting in the roses.

———————

It's Friday night tonight, but since I'm grounded, I'm at home in the living room sitting cross-legged on the couch in my sweatpants with a metal bowl of popcorn resting on my knees. Ever since Monday night, Dad's been staying at the office again. I'm sure it has everything to do with the stunt I pulled, going out to Big Woods. My stomach churns when I think that he's left us again and what it's doing to Mom, but I'm not going to stop looking for Lucy.

Mom and I have barely spoken, but earlier tonight she plopped down next to me on the couch and put her feet up on the coffee table.

I tilted the popcorn bowl toward her and she scooted closer next me, her hand grazing mine as she fished some out of the bowl. I rested my head on her shoulder and let out a deep breath I hadn't noticed I was holding.

She found the clicker behind a cushion and turned on the television. She was flipping through the stations when Lucy's name flashed across the bottom of the screen. We both sat up and Mom grabbed my hand, squeezing it hard. It was the six o'clock news, and the banner at the bottom of the screen read: *Local Church Honors Missing Girl, Lucy Spencer, with Candlelight Vigil.* Mom hurriedly punched the chunky volume control on the clicker, turning up the sound.

A reporter—a pert woman with a polished smile—was standing outside of East Texas Methodist. It was Ali's candlelight vigil. I'd completely forgotten about it.

"Tonight we bring you a story that many in this community have been following for the past few months. Seven weeks ago today, a local girl, Lucy Spencer, ten, went missing here in Longview while she was walking to catch the bus for school."

Snow flurries pelted her face and coated her dark bob like lice. She batted them away while she spoke. "Well, tonight, the good folks at East Texas Methodist are remembering this sweet little girl with a candlelight vigil." The crowd was large—possibly hundreds of people swaying behind her, wrapped up in winter coats and clutching lit candlesticks.

I heard her before I saw her: Ali's cheerleader voice, high and shrill, coming from behind a poster that read "CHRISTIAN YOUTH AGAINST SATANISM." She'd found the camera and made sure to pass behind the reporter.

"Hi dear," the reporter purred. "What can you tell us about your poster there?"

Ali was grinning ear to ear and she set down the poster so the camera could capture her full-on. She was wearing a navy blue sweatshirt that said: FIND LUCY.

"Well, we are all gathered here tonight to remember little Lucy Spencer, who's actually my close friend's sister." I cringed. I knew she'd find a way to own Lucy. "And anyway, we're afraid that Lucy might've been taken by a cult, like all those other children were."

Pastor Mike had saddled up right next to Ali and was beaming at her as if she was his wife running for election. He took the microphone from her and started talking. "We know that our Lord and Savior Jesus Christ will stamp out this evil!" The masses behind him shouted, "Amen! Amen to that!" He nodded quickly and raised his hand to quiet the crowd. "He will banish this darkness! He is the light and the way and we stand up here tonight to bear witness to His greatness!"

The reporter snatched the microphone back, trying to regain control of the coverage. "What are you trying to accomplish here tonight, Pastor?" she asked.

"Well, many things!" he spit-shouted at her. "We want to help find Lucy, of course, bring her home safe. And we're also excited about something our own Ali here is doing. She and her Mom are starting a petition to ban MTV from Longview."

The reporter looked baffled and was about to say something, but he steamrolled over her. "We *know* that some of the music on that station is the work of the devil. We already know the effect it's already had on some of our youth here and we need to stamp it out! We've already got eleven hundred signatures from folks here tonight and we're asking that your viewers stop by the church to add their names to the petition." He continued on, but I had stopped listening. It wasn't even about Lucy anymore. I could feel Mom shuddering—the more hysterical the religious stuff, the more it grated on her nerves.

Mom stood up and clicked off the TV. "I can't watch this garbage anymore," she said and stormed out of the room.

———

I went upstairs and climbed into bed. I couldn't get over the way Pastor Mike was gushing about Ali, that gleam in his eye. He even put his arm around her like she was his girlfriend—it made a pit form in my stomach. And without even thinking about it, I found myself flipping to the back of my diary and under Rain's name as a suspect, I scrawled down Pastor Mike Timmons.

49

Sylvia

DR. MARSHALL ARRIVED TWENTY minutes later, red-faced and furious. "What's going on?"

"A word with you, please?" I asked, and we huddled together in the hall in a weak pool of light. "Who was Delia discharged to?"

"The police from her hometown, Starrville."

I felt like he punched me in the gut. "How *could* you?" I asked, my voice climbing higher.

"You have zero authority here, Nurse Parker," he said. "I'm warning you, let it go," he said, before twisting away from me and plodding down the hall.

———

I punched out from my shift at 7:15 the next morning and walked out into the sunlight, pub blind from the dark basement. It had rained steadily through the night, and a warm spell had blown in with the storm, making the air hot and sticky.

I fished out my keys from the bottom of my purse and my shoulder brushed the branch of a willow tree; drops of rainwater rolled down the leaves, showering me. Birds were trilling in the treetops, singing their morning song, and everything looked cleansed, immaculate, but I couldn't luxuriate in the beauty. My mind was fixed on what I would tell the sheriff.

Driving to the police station, I noticed that all the pear trees were already starting to bloom due to the warm snap, their china-white blossoms opening too early, and I had the bitter thought, *You fools! We will still get another freeze!*

When I arrived at the station, the parking lot was empty, so I pulled into a spot just near the entrance. As I was walking up the flat concrete steps I stepped into a brown puddle of water that splattered dramatically across my white uniform hose.

After the heavy damp from outside, the station lobby felt chilly, so as I sat on a bench waiting for the sheriff, I kept snapping my hose, trying to get them to dry faster.

The sheriff didn't keep me waiting long, and after he shook my hand I trailed behind him down the long, dark, wood-paneled corridor.

He asked me to have a seat and as I was just beginning to explain why I was there, his phone line buzzed and he rolled his eyes in apology, punching the square blinking button and holding up his index finger, indicating that he'd be right with me.

As he talked in a clipped tone to someone who I imagined was a deputy or a fellow officer, I looked around his tidy office. Everything was polished and orderly, and the room had the oaky furniture polish smell of a library. My eyes landed on his wall of diplomas, something I hadn't expected. He had two bachelor's degrees—one in Philosophy

172

and one in History—from the University of Texas in Austin, and also a Criminal Justice degree from Sam Houston State. A thinking man, I thought, and for some reason, this gave me some relief. His voice was also thoughtful and distinguished, not like the rough slang of most of the men in this area. I guessed him to be in his early forties, but this morning, his strawberry-blond hair was freshly washed and combed over to one side so that he looked boyish, almost like a kid playing cop.

He hung up the phone and apologized for keeping me waiting. I found myself spilling it all out to him: how Delia came to us, how she feared for her life, and finally, how she had been released back to the same people who were abusing her. I searched his face for signs of skepticism, but if he had any, I couldn't read them. I felt like he was keenly listening to me, hanging on my every word and the whole time I talked he was jotting notes down in his green steno pad, his ballpoint pen gliding swiftly over the paper, nodding quickly and seemingly taking me serious.

At one point I got choked up and cried as if Delia were my own daughter, and the sheriff—Tommy, as he asked me to call him—hopped up and grabbed a box of tissues off his sideboard, offering one to me.

When I was finished talking, he snapped his notebook shut, clicked his pen, and fixed his sea-green eyes on me. "I'll certainly look into this, Mrs. Parker. In the meantime, here's my card if you need anything else at all," he said, warmly.

I gathered up my purse and thanked him, and stepped out into the sunlight feeling buoyed.

———

That night during my shift, once a hush had fallen over the unit, I huddled in the corner with Hattie and told her about my visit to the sheriff.

Her chestnut-brown eyes went wide. "Sylv, did you really? I'm proud of you, I'm glad you stepped forward. And I do hope we find out she's with family."

The next morning, I clocked out a little bit early, eager to get back to the police station. It was still pleasant out, the morning felt like a warm yawn after the chill of winter. On the way over, I pulled into the donut shop and got a box of assorted pastries and a cup of coffee.

The sheriff led me back to his office immediately. Right away, I could tell his mood was different, chillier. He did accept a donut from me, selecting one filled with strawberry jelly and eating it carefully, but I could tell straight away, it wasn't good news.

"The girl," he said, between bite fulls of donut, "has a bunch of priors, according to Sheriff Meeks."

"But the sheriff is the one—"

But I couldn't finish before he put his hand up.

"They say she's a druggie, has mental problems, has been unstable for some time now."

I didn't believe him, of course. And he didn't come out and say it but I could see it on his face: he thought Delia was a throw-away, a floozy.

"Sheriff Meeks is a fine man, Mrs. Parker," he said, wiping jelly from the corner of his mouth. My own donut expanded in the back of my throat and I had to force myself to swallow it down.

"They've assured me that she's in the best hands possible now, with her family in Fayetteville, Arkansas."

"I'd like some kind of confirmation, some kind of address or something, so I can check in on her," I pleaded.

"I'm sorry, even if I had that information I couldn't disclose it," he said.

"But these men, these men that raped and tortured her," I said, my voice turning shrill. "They just get to carry on? What about their other victims?"

The sheriff looked at me and tilted his head as if he were trying to assess whether or not I was crazy. There was a hint of condescending sympathy in his eyes, but then he turned stone-faced again. "I spoke at length to your boss, Dr. Marshall, yesterday. He assured me that his diagnosis stands—paranoid schizophrenia. I know you had a special relationship with the girl, and so I know this is hard to hear." His mouth emphasized the word *special*. "I'm awfully sorry that she's in such bad mental shape, but you have to believe me, there is no conspiracy here."

I closed the box of donuts and slid them to the side of the desk. I reached into my coat pocket and my fingers found the map. I was just about to show it to him, but something stopped me: the thought that he might be in on it, too. So I tucked it back into my pocket and pulled my purse into my lap and stood to leave, giving him a courteous nod and thanking him for his time as I backed calmly out of his office.

50

Leah

Sunday, November 19th, 1989
Lucy missing 7 weeks, 2 days

Ever since the full moon party I keep having the same dream. I'm headed down a long, blacktopped road—it's almost dusk and I've never been on this road before—and it feels like I'm floating above the road, hovering just beneath the tree line. I want to know what's down the road, it's like I'm being pulled, so I keep going. I pass a small white church, then a rickety farm house with a faded red barn that slants toward a rusty barbed wire fence. I pass an old one-room schoolhouse that's been boarded up, and then the road slopes down to reveal a wide, open valley. My stomach drops as I coast down the hill until the road climbs up again, threading through a canopy of thick trees. It's almost dark when I reach a long, red-dirt drive to the right. I stop and try and go down that road but I wake up each time before I can, and even though I don't see Lucy in my dream, I know it's her. She's trying to show me something.

51

Sylvia

I LEFT THE POLICE station shaking, my hands trembling with my keys, my breath jagged. I drove straight home and tried to clear my head. I walked through the door and chucked the rest of the donuts in the trash—my stomach was in knots and I knew I couldn't finish them. I paced the house, trying to figure out what to do. I thought about calling the police in Fayetteville, to see if they by chance had any information, but I knew she wasn't there. I thought about calling Hattie, but I knew she'd be sleeping and I didn't want to wake her. I tried to lie down on the couch and fall asleep, but my mind wouldn't stop racing, so after a few minutes I got up and tried to busy myself with tidying up.

Finally, the house itself became unbearable to me. I changed into a pair of jeans and an old, faded button-down—my gardening clothes, really—and put on a head scarf and some oversized sunglasses and got back in the station wagon. Once inside, I unfolded the map and pressed it over my steering wheel, then started the engine and backed out of the drive.

I drove to the south side of town and picked up the interstate and headed west toward Dallas. Once I crossed the river at the edge of town, I started counting the miles. Delia had told me it would be about fifteen until the exit. The interstate was quiet in the middle of the day, except for a few eighteen-wheelers zipping past. I got to the exit before long, the green sign that read STARRVILLE / OMEN ROAD. The road in the map hooked right just off the feeder road and I had to slam on my brakes to make the turn, the blacktop road appearing before I had anticipated it.

I could picture Delia making it to the highway half naked and flagging down that trucker who drove her near the hospital before she jumped out of his truck at a red light.

The night she had escaped, she told me that they had untied her from the stone first. She had performed sex acts with them as compliantly as she could, and after the sheriff was finished with her, she looked up at his sweaty face with sheepish eyes and asked if she could go into the woods to relieve herself. The second she got behind the first wide tree, she peered around to make sure no one was looking, then she ran and ran and ran and ran with no feeling at all in her bare feet, just a white hot desire to escape. She told me she kept picturing herself making it to the main road, and that's what gave her the courage to keep running even though her legs were getting scratched up and her feet were bleeding. She kept running until her feet found the smooth tar of the black road.

The road dipped down and to my left there was a thick line of pine trees, their fat waists cinched back by barbed wire. The road plunged down even farther, exposing a wide belly of pasture before being swallowed back up by more trees.

About three miles in, I started scanning for the unmarked red dirt road. I slowed the car and turned right onto the road, which was just a rust-colored lane, really, with thick weeds growing between muddy tire tracks. The bottom of my station wagon chewed on the weeds but I kept idling forward, slowly. I wasn't even sure I was on the right road—it looked like I was driving across somebody's pasture—but then, after climbing a steep incline, I saw the stand of trees that gave way to the dense pack of woods that Delia had drawn on the map. When I got closer to the row of trees, I eased the car into the pasture and parked.

I killed the engine and opened the door, which creaked loudly, but I stepped out and looked around. It seemed like there was nobody else out there.

In the open field, the wind had picked up and the willowy tops of pine trees contracted like clouds. Wild wisteria vines hung from the trees, their lilac clumps swinging in the breeze like clusters of grapes. It was midday and the sun was radiant on my face, but as I walked deeper into the woods the sunlight became watered down, chilling the air and making everything look muted. I walked a little farther until I found the clearing for the little cemetery. Delia was right: you would never know this place existed if someone didn't tell you.

It was tiny—just a handful of graves, maybe thirty at the most—tucked inside a black iron gate with a sign that read, FORSYTHE ME-MORIAL. From the looks of it, it seemed to be an old family graveyard or a cemetery of a forgotten township, and in the green pasture adjacent to it, I saw the large circle of stones, just as Delia had described.

Sunlight filtered through the trees, lighting up the faces of the stones and I thought I could see the rust splatter of dried blood on one of them. I kept listening for sounds to make sure I was still alone, but the wind kept gusting and shushing through the woods so that it made everything feel disorienting. I could smell the charred embers from the fire ring that was in the center of the stone circle, exactly like Delia had drawn on the map, and I stood out there in the howling wind and said just loud enough for the wind to hear: "So this is where these horrible things happened to you."

Just then, something scurried along in the woods behind me. I whipped around to look but saw that it was just a squirrel shimmying up the trunk of a tree. I turned back around and then heard a louder snap of a branch and what sounded like heavier footfalls. I looked over my shoulder and out of the corner of my eye, I thought I saw a dark figure pass behind a tree and stop.

My heart chiseled in my chest and I found myself walking over to a gravesite and kneeling down and praying before it, as if I were visiting a lost loved one. I made a big show of crossing myself and prostrating in front of the grave, and even went as far to sweep pine straw off the headstone. My knees became saturated with the clean damp of wet grass, but I stayed planted there, not wanting to move.

After a while, I stood up and turned in the direction of my car and walked slowly toward it, not looking back but having the strongest feeling I was being watched.

52

Leah

Monday, November 20th, 1989
Lucy missing 7 weeks, 3 days

I'm upstairs in Lucy's room, lying in her bed. Our old pecan tree has been picked clean of its leaves, and the branches scrape against the thick-paned window next to her bed. I've just gotten off the phone with the sheriff. It's cold and black outside and freezing wind seeps through the windowsill, turning my nose red.

By the time I got to school this morning, Ali's story had already bounced around the halls like a boomerang. It was all anyone would talk about. Saturday night, she had gone to a party out at the lake with Brett. When he took her home at the end of the night, they turned down her street and at first, they both thought it had snowed in her front yard—everything was blinding white. But smiling, Ali said she realized her house had been rolled, and only the popular senior boys rolled houses of girls they thought were cute. Hundreds of rolls of toilet paper were draped from the willow trees in her front yard. Even the mailbox and the front hedges were all wrapped in white. But after Brett kissed her goodnight and she climbed out of his car and skipped up the sidewalk, she saw the message, spray-painted in white jagged letters across her bright green lawn:

YOU'RE NEXT, BITCH.

She thought it was because of her petition to ban MTV and was telling everyone at school she thought Rain and the Wavers were behind it. Buoyed by all the attention, she strode around the cafeteria during lunch today, valiantly wielding her clipboard, determined to get up to two thousand signatures.

But just after lunch, when she went to get her books for fourth period out of her locker, thirteen shriveled black roses flew out at her like a flock of ravens. There was a note, too:

Blond hair
Eyes of blue
Picked these roses
Just for you

Don't sleep alone
We're watching your home
And know which one's your window, too.

I heard her high-pitched scream from all the way down the hall—not her usual cheerleader squeal but a shriek of true terror—and saw her hands fly to her cheeks before she took off bounding down the stairs to the principal's office. Soon she was flanked by both Brett and her parents, who had rushed to the school. They demanded that the police be called.

In fifth period, annual staff, I watched from the window as Rain was led out by two officers, his hands clasped behind his back in handcuffs, his streaked blond hair swinging behind him. The officers were wearing hats and even though I couldn't see his face, I could tell by his walk that one of them was Sheriff Greene.

When the last bell sounded and I walked outside, Mom was waiting in the parent pick up line. She was dressed in a long, black wool coat and was leaning up against our Honda. When I got closer, I saw that her eyes were swollen so much that they were just dark slits.

"Come here, honey," she said, pulling me into her. She leaned down and put her forehead to mine.

"What is it, Mom?" I said, panic creeping into my voice.

"Let's get out of here so we can talk," she said, opening the passenger side door for me.

A lit cigarette smoldered in the ashtray, sending wispy curls of smoke up the dash. Mom's unfinished coffee from this morning sloshed between us in a splattered Styrofoam cup as she drove us a few blocks to a nearby park, killing the engine and turning to face me.

"The police found Lucy's coin purse this morning," she said, her eyes roving all over my face.

"Where?" I shot back, frantically.

Mom sucked in a quick breath before continuing, "They found it near a gas well out in Big Woods," she said, her voice breaking before giving way to sobs. The whole car blurred and spun and I felt like I was going to throw up.

After a few moments, Mom let out a long sigh and stared straight ahead as she told me the rest.

An oil field worker had gotten a repair call for a gas well out in Big Woods this morning. When he climbed out of his truck and walked toward the well, something reflected off a nearby tree and caught his eye. He walked closer to the tree and at eye-level there was a giant plastic bag nailed to the bark. Inside the bag was a white cat, dead, with its throat slit and tail cut off. The man immediately radioed his boss who called the police.

When the police arrived, they roped off the area and conducted a search for other signs of animal sacrifice. A few steps into the woods— not more than twenty feet from the dead cat—an officer stubbed his boot on Lucy's lavender-colored Hello Kitty coin purse, half buried in the loamy sand. She always carried it in her back pocket and it was always filled with quarters for the arcade and her yellow, crumpled cafeteria punch card. The card had her name stamped on it and the last day punched was Thursday, the day before she went missing.

"What does this mean?" I asked, through a stream of hot tears.

"I don't know," Mom said, shaking her head. "They haven't found anything else, but I'm telling you all of this because you *have* to promise me," she said, her eyes searching mine for understanding, "that you will *never, ever* go out to Big Woods again."

A chill passed through my body. "I promise," I said, automatically, and for the first time, I almost meant it.

———————

Big Woods. I knew it. I knew I had been right; I knew the dreams were real. But there were probably over a thousand gas wells in Big Woods. Had I been close to the right one that night?

———————

185

When we got home, the house was dark. I flipped on the entryway light and bolted up the stairs to call Sheriff Greene. "He's not in, he's off duty-now," the clerk told me, in a nasally, annoyed tone.

I remembered that the sheriff had given me his card, though, and I fished it off the top of my dresser. He had written his number on the back, in precise, crisp handwriting, so I tried that next.

"Officer Greene," he answered flatly.

"Hi. Um … this is Leah Spencer," I said, my voice going shaky.

"Hey, kiddo. How are you? You okay?" he asked, his voice suddenly bright and warm. His voice was strong and reassuring, like something you'd want to lean against. I blurted out everything I knew—about Rain and about the full moon party and what I'd seen out in Big Woods.

He let me finish before saying in a soft tone, "Yeah, Rain's been on our radar for some time. He's weird, I'll give you that, but he's not our guy."

"But what about the full moon party? The bonfire and the masks … and—?" I stuttered, my throat tightening, threatening tears.

"We've known about these parties and have actually patrolled them." He paused. "Leah, it's nothing but a bunch of social outcasts partying."

"The black roses? My friend and I saw him in the locker bank recently—"

"We searched his locker today. We can't prove that he's the one who's been threatening these girls with the black roses—he probably is—but we did find some cigarettes and a marijuana joint in his locker, so he'll be spending the next week in juvy just for that. But even still, I can promise you he had nothing to do with Lucy. His alibi checks out—he was in detention when Lucy—" He caught himself and treaded lightly. "He was at school that morning. Like I said, he's strange, but he's not capable of—" And he became careful again. "He's not a suspect."

"Which gas well was it where Lucy's purse was found? Where was it exactly? I'd like to know if it was near that party."

"Now you know I can't tell you that, kiddo," he said, a verbal pat on the head. "Look, I'm worried about you. I'm worried about your safety and I hope you know just how dangerous Big Woods really is."

"Okay, but—"

"Leah, I'm asking you to trust me. Can you do that? We've been combing the area all day and will continue to do so. I'll keep you and your mom posted if we find anything," he said.

I hang up the phone and feel hollow, scraped out. I go to bed without eating any dinner and the last thing I see in my mind before I fall asleep is Rain's face, sneering at me.

53

Sylvia

I COULDN'T WAIT TO get to work and to tell Hattie everything. I hadn't slept all day, but I made a fresh thermos of coffee before leaving the house and drove to the burger stand on my way to work to pick up a cheeseburger for dinner. I sat in the parking lot and quickly devoured my dinner and watched as the sun smeared the sky with pink-orange smudges just before it set. When I stepped out of the car, I could already hear the crickets chirping, signaling nighttime.

I punched in and was juggling my thermos and purse and sewing bag, clomping down the hall to find Hattie, when I spotted Dr. Marshall lording over the nurse's station with his back to me. I slowed my pace and when I approached him, the rest of the nurses scattered like birds. He swung around and said, loudly enough for everyone to hear, "You need to leave."

Anger rolled through me and I narrowed my eyes at him. "You can't fire me."

He poked a hard finger in my collarbone. "If we must discuss this, then we better do it in my office." I strained over his shoulder to try and find Hattie but she was hunched behind the station, filling out a chart; she wouldn't meet my eyes.

In his office he slammed the door behind us and stood right in front of me, his stale, hot breath panting in my face. "I can't *believe* you went behind my back and went to the police with this," he said, trembling with rage.

"You can't fire a person for doing what I did. For trying to do the right thing," I spat back at him.

"Listen," he hissed in my face, "I can't prove it, but I *know* you went against my orders and stopped giving that girl her meds."

My stomach clenched but I kept his gaze, narrowing my eyes and giving my best withering look.

"Listen, I'm just firing you, but you keep this up and I'll find a way to prove it and you'll lose your license. You'll never practice nursing again." His bald head was splotchy-red with anger and I felt like the office was shrinking so I shot him one last hard look before turning to the door and leaving that basement forever.

54

Leah

Thanksgiving Day
Thursday, November 23rd, 1989
Lucy missing 7 weeks, 6 days

Dad hasn't been home in over ten days, and I'm pretty sure he's not coming back. Last night, I was in my room reading a book when the phone rang. I scrambled out of bed and headed down the hall to Mom and Dad's room. The door was open, so I stepped inside. Mom was sitting on the edge of the bed with her back to me. She answered on the second ring.

"Hello?" she said, briskly. I could tell right away that it was Dad. Mom reached for her pack of cigarettes on the night stand and shook one out and lit it. "What the hell have you been doing, Carl?" she said, taking a forceful drag off her cigarette as she let Dad finish whatever it was he had to say. "But Thanksgiving's tomorrow, for Christ's sake!"

Her back slumped down in defeat. "Fine. You spend another night there. Spend the rest of the month there. If you can't pull it together for Leah, for us," she said, her voice wavering with tears, "then I don't want you coming home."

She slammed the phone down. My face flushed and tears pricked my eyes. I wanted to cross the room, to go over to her, to hug her, but I knew this was all my fault, so instead, I crept back down the hall to my dark room and cried until I fell asleep.

Since it's just Mom and me at home, we decided to eat our Thanksgiving meal at Luby's Cafeteria. We usually prepare a traditional Thanksgiving dinner, but not this year.

To me, Luby's is comforting. Lucy and I use to eat there every Sunday after church with Grandma and Grandpa. We'd open the heavy glass doors and be enveloped in the heavenly, starchy aroma of cafeteria food. Lucy always wanted to be first in line and she'd stand on her tiptoes and grab a steaming beige tray—straight from the dishwasher—and slap it down on the metal line and glide through, stopping at each station to ogle at the choices. I know it sounds ridiculous, but I'd always feel bad when the servers would ask if I wanted their offerings—a sad little salad, or some wobbly fluorescent Jell-O?—and I'd have to turn them down with a quick shake of my head and an over-polite, "No thank you! None for me today!" with the same dismissiveness as a celebrity turning down an autograph request.

Lucy and I always got the same thing anyway: fried fish with sides of mac and cheese and fried okra, apple pie for dessert and iced tea to drink. When we were seated, Grandma used to say in a rather prim voice, "Well at least, here, you're getting your vegetables," as if Mom never fed us any. Lucy and I used to snicker about it later, behind Grandma's back—the thought that mac and cheese and fried okra were somehow vegetables.

After lunch, glazed over from the food, we'd climb into the backseat of their beer-colored Cadillac. It was always baked from the hot sun and it made us feel drowsy. Lucy would immediately kick off her white patent leather Sunday shoes and peel off her nude panty hose. She'd stretch out and rest with her head in my lap and fall asleep sucking her thumb as we bounced, in the warm safety of their cushy backseat, toward home.

Today the scene at Luby's was dismal. It was only half full with mostly elderly men—lonely widowers dining alone on Thanksgiving, their clothes rumpled but their hair neatly combed over to one side.

Mom and I chose a table by a large window. In the harsh winter light, I noticed that Mom's face was spackled with new wrinkles, and a few new silver strands escape her loose bun, her faded blond hair in need of a touch-up.

Between forkfuls of dressing she asked, "Can we talk about your birthday?"

I tore a large chunk off a yeast roll and was rolling the springy dough between my fingers—a habit that used to drive Lucy crazy—before wadding it into smaller balls and shoving them in my mouth.

"Sure."

"Well, it's just two weeks away. It's on a Friday night. Do you want to do something special? Maybe have a sleepover with some friends?" Her strained effort depressed me.

"Not without Lucy," I said. "No, Mom. It's just not right."

"Leah," she said, shifting cranberry sauce around on her plate. "I hate to say this, but she's gone." She put her fork down and looked up at me. "And there's a possibility she's not coming back."

A cry threatened to strangle my throat but I stifled it. "You're wrong," I said, softly, into my plate. I wasn't mad at her anymore, I just wished so badly she knew what I knew, that she could believe what I believed.

A brassy-haired waitress was barreling down on us with the hulking drink cart. Her front wheel was askew and it creaked as she pushed it across the thin brown carpet.

"More tea?" she asked us in a stiff tone. Her hair was combed back in a severe bun, held up by a hairnet. She looked about as pleased as I was to be there.

"I'll have some more coffee, please," Mom said, "with cream and sugar. Leah?"

"Yes, more tea. Thank you, ma'am," I said and fished a quarter out of my purse for the waitress like Grandma used to do. I set it on the corner of her cart and she winked at me and said, "Thanks, hon," before wheeling the cart away.

"I went to see your father last week," Mom said, stirring her coffee with quick, nervous movements. "And we both agree that we're going to go ahead and buy you the car for your birthday. Especially with your father gone so much"—she let out a long, tired sigh and stared blankly at her plate—"you're gonna need it."

"That's great, Mom, thank you. Really," I said. Giddiness floods my body—I felt light and free and adult, the possibilities already lining up in my head.

"Your father said he would come to the dealership with us, to handle the paperwork. Then, I don't know, I was thinking the three of us could go to dinner, you know, make a night of it?" Mom asked, folding her hands in her lap. I silently vowed to keep things smooth for a little while, so that maybe Dad will come back home then.

"Of course, Mom. That sounds very nice." I pushed back my chair and went around the table and gave her a long, hard hug.

55

Sylvia

I WOKE EARLY THE next morning to the sounds of birdsong and threw open my window.

Two purple martins were playfully splashing around in the birdbath, the water sloshing to the ground, washing away the fine mist of yellow pollen that coated the patio. My honeysuckle was beginning to bloom and the wind picked up and carried its candy scent straight to my window.

Slipping on my house slippers and robe, a sense of rightness and relief washed over me—somehow the full night's sleep had worked everything out in my subconscious and everything was clear: I was meant to be relieved of that job. I could've never kept working under Dr. Marshall after that—and anyway, my real mission now was to find Delia. I wasn't even worried about the money—there was enough now. I had been putting most of my paycheck into savings.

I was just coming down the stairs when the phone rang, yanking me out of my reverie. I answered the lipstick-red wall phone on the landing. It was Hattie; she had just gotten home from her shift.

"Sylvia," she started, her voice full of concern, "I can't *believe* that man fired you. We can do something about it, we can take some kind of action."

"I don't care about that, I really don't," I said. I didn't tell her about the meds and how Laverne had ratted me out.

"But Sylv—"

"Hattie, I'll be fine. But listen, I was going to tell you all of this last night before he fired me, but I drove out to Omen Road yesterday and found the cemetery."

"You *did?*" she asked, her voice full of surprise, splitting the word *did* into two syllables.

"And I saw everything that Delia had told us about—the fire ring, the stone circle, all of it, Hat, it was just like she said. I know they still have her. And I thought, if we both went out there and took some pictures, and came forward, together, that maybe somebody would listen to us."

But Hattie got all quiet on the other end, so quiet that I could hear the dramatic organ music from *Days of our Lives*, her favorite soap playing in the background.

"Hattie? We can still save her."

"I don't know about all this anymore," she said in a deflated voice. "I have a *family*, Sylv."

I couldn't argue with that, so I thanked her for checking on me and promised to come out to her place for lunch soon.

I placed the phone back on its cradle and sat on the steps for a while, watching the sunlight stream through the candy colors of the small, round stained-glass window.

The next night was a Friday, the night they had their rituals, and Hattie or no Hattie, I was going back out there.

56

Leah

**Thursday, December 7th, 1989
Lucy missing 9 weeks, 6 days**

The morning after Thanksgiving, I woke up with a scratchy throat—when I tried to swallow it felt like my tonsils had been stung by a hundred bees. I was cold and shaking with chills but my face felt sunburned.

"It's probably strep," Mom said as she pulled the glass thermometer out of my mouth and read it. 104 degrees. "I'll call Dr. Dixon, see if he can come by."

Everything was closed for the holidays but by midmorning Dr. Dixon was sitting on the edge of my bed, sticking a wide popsicle stick in my mouth and nodding. "Definitely strep throat. I'll start her on a course of antibiotics," he said to Mom.

They stepped out into the hallway to talk, just out of earshot. I was so delirious I thought I heard Lucy's name being muttered, but I didn't have the strength to get out of bed to have a closer listen.

The days and nights blurred together and I drifted in and out of murky sleep. I felt closed in, walled off, the cough syrup making me loopy on top of the high fever. I haven't been to school since before Thanksgiving. Mom took a leave of absence to stay with me and she floated in and out of my room with hot salty soups, Saltine crackers, weak tea, and wet washcloths. I kept asking her about Lucy, but she'd just shake her head—nothing new, no updates from the sheriff, nothing.

My dreams were all fuzzy until last night. I had that same recurring dream, but this time it was different. It wasn't wintertime; it was hot and sticky out. I glided down the blacktop road and the sun shifted behind the trees, melting on the horizon, and this time I was able to turn down the red dirt lane. Suddenly it got very dark and the road bumped over a stretch of wild, jagged pastureland and then vanished into a tangle of trees. I could see a fire in the distance and could hear a low humming sound. My body was glazed in sweat and just before I opened my eyes I heard Lucy's voice, as clear as if she were sitting in the bed next to me, saying, "They only bring us out here at night."

57

Sylvia

FRIDAY AFTERNOON, I STARTED preparing to go. I wanted to get out there as close to dusk as possible, but early enough so I could find a place to hide my car and walk by foot up to the cemetery.

I found a flashlight and my old camera in the back of the junk drawer and made a trip downtown to the drugstore for a fresh roll of film. I stopped at the service station on the way home and had the man check the pressure on my tires after he filled up the car.

I fixed myself a light supper—a toasted sandwich and a cup of tomato soup—and while I ate, I flipped through the glossy pages of a new seed catalog to try and distract my mind from what the next few hours would hold.

———

I left the house at four thirty sharp and was turning down the red dirt road by five with half an hour of daylight to spare. It had rained a little the night before and my wheels slid a little on the slippery red clay while I was going up the incline. My eyes scanned the pasture and beyond. It looked like I was all alone.

I parked behind a giant, shaggy oak tree, its branches splayed out like pudgy arms: the perfect cover for my old station wagon. I strapped the camera around my neck and slipped an old fishing knife of John's down the ankle of my boot.

With the sun setting, the sky was lit up in blues and peaches so that the silhouettes of the oaks looked like dark, shifting figures moving against the skyline. I walked along the edge of the woods, careful to stay far from the road, and tried to blend in with the trees. The previous night's rain helped to soften my footsteps. My plan was to find a spot to hide and wait there until nightfall in the hopes I would be able to snap some photographs and then slip away unnoticed.

Walking near the cemetery, I found an old stone structure—like a mausoleum—the perfect hiding place, and I was just about to reach it when I saw a man dressed in a white robe and hood striding out of the woods.

I froze in place but it was too late, he started running for me. I bent down and grabbed the knife out of my boot and slipped it out of its case, then turned to the station wagon and started running as fast as I could. I looked back over my shoulder and to my relief, the man took off in a different direction. I kept running until I got safely in my car, but then saw that he was running for a white truck parked behind a stack of hay bales that I hadn't noticed before.

I started the engine and turned the car around and was speeding down the red dirt road as fast as I could, the undercarriage banging on the dips, when he came roaring up behind me with his brights on, getting as close to my bumper as he could. He layed on the horn and started hollering out his window and flashing his lights at me, but I didn't slow down until it was time to turn onto the blacktop. Instead of turning left, to the interstate, I turned right and floored it.

He was right on my bumper and I thought he was about to hit me, but then he swerved around and passed me. I wouldn't look his way, but I eased off the gas and let him pass. To my surprise, his truck sped off in the distance, as if he were trying to get away from me.

I pulled over on the side of the road for a few moments to catch my breath. The adrenaline rush had leeched my body of any power. My arms and legs felt slack, but I couldn't seem to slow my heart rate down.

I made a U-turn on the blacktop and headed back to the highway. The moon had risen and was bright, but bluish-black clouds drifted across it, clotting its surface. My body was drenched in sweat so I cracked the window to let in some fresh air.

The road dipped down and just as I was about to reach the basin I heard a car blast out of the woods to my left, its headlights slicing through the trees. I thought it would stop when they saw me approaching, but instead they raced out of the drive and pulled straight across the road, stopping and blocking my path. It was a dark brown El Camino with two figures in the cab. I braked hard, stopped, and threw it in reverse and was trying to back out when I saw the white truck pull up behind me, parking perpendicular like the other car, completely boxing me in. I rolled up my window and kept the engine running. Blood pounded in my temples.

Two men got out of the El Camino and also, out of the white truck, surrounding my car. They were all dressed in the same eerie outfits—the white hoods and robes.

"Get out!" one of the men shouted at me. "Out! Or we will kill you!" He was waving a snub-nosed pistol in my direction.

I opened my door and stepped out with my hands in the air. My camera still hung stupidly from my neck, swinging clumsily over my breasts. The man who shouted at me saw it and ripped it off my neck, the cord burning the skin, and smashed it into the ground and then kicked it with his cowboy boots until it was just a pile of shards.

"Our friend here has told us that he saw you at the cemetery. Tonight and, also, the other day."

"I'm just an old lady, and I'm confused, I was looking for my great aunt's grave," I managed to say.

"Well this is *our* town," said the man from the truck who chased me through the field, giving me a hard shove, making me stumble. "You have no business here." Another man was behind me and put a black-gloved hand over my mouth. I thought he was going to suffocate me, but then he put a burlap sack over my head and pushed me to the ground.

Through the burlap sack, I could still hear the men but their voices were muffled. They seemed to be having some kind of discussion, probably about what to do with me. I was bracing myself for a kick to the gut, or worse, a gunshot, when I heard one of the men say, laughing, "Trust me, she won't be coming out here again."

When I heard his voice, and especially his laugh, my blood went cold. I lay there on my side, still as I could, until I heard them walk away and heard the succession of four doors clapping shut and both vehicles pulling away.

Leah

Friday, December 8th, 1989
Lucy missing 10 weeks

Today is our birthday. I can't believe we're not together. I can't re-member a time when I celebrated a birthday without her. I know I have. I've seen the pictures from my earliest birthdays before Lucy was born—me at one year old with cake smeared all over my face and highchair; my second birthday, me toddling around our backyard in a red pea coat—but all of my memories are of carting her around and us wishing each other a happy birthday all day long. *Happy birthday, Lucy, Happy birthday, Leah,* our own private volley.

My fever finally broke in the middle of the night, soaking my sheets through. Mom has stripped the bed and I'm running myself a bath, filling our coral tub with the hottest water I can stand. I haven't bathed since I've been sick. I step out of my pajamas and slip into the scalding water. I lather up my hair in the tub, then drain the water, letting the suds foam at my feet and run a pounding shower and wash my hair a second time. After I'm scrubbed clean I get dressed in a long wool cardigan and jeans.

Mom has fixed us French toast for breakfast and I devour the buttery, spongy squares—the first real meal I've eaten in days. When she goes upstairs to shower, I step outside.

It's bright and clear and when the sun hits my eyes, it feels like they've been bruised; it's been so long since I've seen daylight. The wind is cold, sharp, and I pull my sweater tight around me as I walk to the edge of our woods kicking football-sized pinecones as I go.

"Happy birthday, Lucy," I say, as boldly and as loudly as I can, but as soon as the words leave my mouth, the wind picks them up and slaps them to the ground.

————

At the car dealership, Mom and I sit at a round, gray table while an old man with a thick cough and polished shoes shuffles through paperwork for Mom to sign. Dad's a no-show.

"Oh! I forgot the most important part. The keys!" he says, pushing back from the table, his polished shoes clicking across the even-more polished floor.

Outside, Mom hands me the keys. "Happy birthday, darling," she says, and tears prick both of our eyes. We were supposed to have an early dinner at Steak and Ale, but without Dad, we've decided to head home and order pizza.

I climb into my new Ford Tempo and for a brief moment, I feel giddy. The car is immaculate with creamy leather interior and that new-car smell, and it's the first car we've had with power windows.

I lower the windows and turn on the radio, fiddling with the dial until I find the top-40 station. "Shout" by Tears for Fears is playing. I turn up the bass and blast it, and dance in my seat. I sing along and am in a happy bliss until the next song comes on. It's that "Rock Me Amadeus" song and a memory of Lucy rips through.

We are younger—she is eight and I'm twelve. The song has just been released and the radio plays it nonstop. One Saturday afternoon Lucy was alone in the den watching MTV and I walked in and the song was playing and Lucy was singing into a pretend microphone, standing on the coffee table, but she got the words all wrong and was singing, "Rock me on my desk."

"What, do you mean like on your school desk?" I teased her and it became a running joke between us.

I'm a hot puddle of tears by the time I pull into the driveway, but I wipe my eyes with the sleeve of my cardigan and try and make myself sound chipper when Mom asks me with childlike excitement, "So, how does it drive?"

————

We sit together in front of the TV eating our pizza, my legs draped across Mom's lap. She has made us a tray of brownies and we each eat two before we climb the stairs to go to sleep. We kiss each other goodnight at the top of the stairs and I turn to go to my room but decide to sleep in Lucy's room instead. I fold myself into her bed and whisper, one last time today, "Happy Birthday, Lucy."

————

In my dream, I wake up in the middle of the night in Lucy's bed. Her nightlight is on and she is sitting cross-legged in front of it, playing with her Lite-Brite. She sees me and smiles and turns it around. In a rainbow of colors, it says *Happy Birthday Leah!* I leap out of bed and hug her and take it from her and make one that says *Happy Birthday Lucy!* I spin it around to show her and she squeals, but then I take it back and write *Where are you?* She takes it from me and furrows her brow, and fiddles with it forever before finally spinning it around.

In the Bad Church.

Then all of the words fade away and it forms itself into other words.

Hurry Leah!

When I look up from the Lite-Brite, Lucy is gone.

———

I wake up covered in sweat. I go over to her closet and her Lite-Brite is on the top shelf, packed away in its box.

I think about the blacktop road from my dreams and the church that I fly by, but the only church I can think of near Big Woods is Shiloh and it looks nothing like the church from my dreams.

I climb out of Lucy's bed and step lightly into my room. I open my diary and record the dream, and then take my pink phone into the closet—I can tell that Mom's already awake—and I call Nicolette.

"Heeeey," Nicolette yawns into the phone. "I'm just waking up. How are you?"

I'm sitting on the floor, leaning against my laundry bin, and say as quietly as possible, "I had another dream. About Lucy." And I try and describe the dream as best I can. "We've got to go back out there." I'm twisting the cord around my index finger, turning it purple.

"I dunno, Leah."

"But you believe me, right?" I say, my throat tightening up with emotion.

"Of course, of course I do. It's just—" she stammers. "I just don't know what *we* can do about it," she says. She sounds scared. "I don't want to go out there again, I don't want *you* to go out there again. I don't want you to get hurt," she says, her voice rising, and I know there's nothing I can say that will make her change her mind.

I think about taking the new car, but I'm only legally allowed to drive it to school and back and to extracurricular activities. But Mom has a staff meeting after school every Monday, so I make a silent plan that I'll go out there then, and I whisper, quietly in my closet to Lucy, "I'm coming. Hold on until Monday."

59

Sylvia

I DROVE AROUND IN circles all night, trying to make sure I wasn't being followed. My heart was racing and I jumped at every pair of head-lights I saw. I even parked outside my church for a while, to see if I had really lost them, and waited until just before sunrise to head home.

I walked through my back door and went upstairs to my altar and knelt and prayed to my long-gone mother, to John up in heaven, and also to St. Michael, the patron saint of protection.

I crept back downstairs to the kitchen and made a quick cup of tea before heading back to the church. They opened the doors at dawn and I stepped inside the musk-scented sanctuary, choosing a pew near the front, and I prayed some more. The night man, Ray, was just fin-ishing up his cleaning and he gave me a friendly nod as he slapped the wet mop against the wooden floors. He was a stout man and the sound of his keys jangling as he worked gave me some added comfort, knowing I was not alone.

When my prayers were finished, I sat back in the pew and tried to calm my mind by staring at the chalky-white monastic walls of our little sanctuary. Ruby-red light was streaming through a window cut in the shape of the cross along the eastern wall, and through another window, I could see the tender, pink tips of a tulip tree beginning to bloom.

I tried to focus on taking slow, deep breaths and after a few moments, I became so relaxed that I thought I might drift off to sleep. So I rose to leave, nodding goodbye to Ray, and made my way to the entrance of the church, pausing at the stone bowl to take some holy water to try and further shake the evil off.

Outside in the sun-dappled parking lot, my station wagon sat next to Ray's gray work truck, but there was not another car in sight. I was still safe, it appeared, but even though I had lost the men last night, one among them knew where I lived.

My only hope was that hidden behind his hood and robe, he thought he was immune from me identifying him. And he would've been, had it not been for his heinous cackle, as wretched and distinct as it was when he was a boy.

───────

And now, I must also pray for something else: forgiveness. I pray that I'll be forgiven for just now sharing this, but it's something I buried many years ago and couldn't bear to tell anyone. I never even told Hattie. The dreadful secret I've been carrying around all these years is this: one of the men behind those robes—the one that Delia knew as the preacher—he is my son.

60

Leah

Monday, December 11th, 1989
Lucy missing 10 weeks, 3 days

In sixth period today, I wait until everyone else is busy with projects, and then cross the room to talk to Mrs. Nicholson, our yearbook staff teacher.

"I've got my license now," I say, matter-of-factly. "Can I get a pass to go and sell ads this afternoon?"

"Of course," Mrs. Nicholson says warmly, tearing off a crisp pink slip and fixing her silver-rimmed glasses on the edge of her nose as she fills it out. "Want to just go on home afterwards?"

This is what I hope she was going to suggest. "Sure."

Big Woods is closer to the high school than my house, so I'm pretty sure I can beat Mom home. It's strangely warm today and I peel off my jacket before getting into the car. I start the engine and notice my hands are shaking. This is one of those times when I wished I smoked like everybody else.

When I reach the road that leads to Shiloh, I turn down it and see a long line of cars slowly streaming by. It's not until I pass the hearse that I realize it's a funeral procession. I pull over and wait for it to pass before heading on to Shiloh.

When I finally get there, I can see that the gate to the graveyard is unlatched and opens to the scene of a just-finished funeral and burial. A black tent is still up with bright green AstroTurf underneath and a team of men is lowering a casket down into the red earth. With people around, the cemetery doesn't look haunted; it looks normal. I park across the road, in front of the school, a hulking red-brick building with the roof blown off and the windows busted out like two eye sockets from a skeleton. Moss clings to the brick and the wind whistles through the empty building. I look across to the church and there's an old man, tall and thin, locking the doors. I walk across the road. The man is dressed in a suit. His fingers are long and they dance over the keys like spiders.

"Help you with somethin'?" he says. From inside the church, I can still smell the smells of funeral food: fried chicken, casseroles, cobbler.

Tears flood my eyes. "I was just, I was just looking for someone."

The man looks at me with a grave look, a look of understanding, and lowers his head. "Sometimes when we lose things, important things, we can't understand why. And we search and search and try and understand it, but some things we can't ever understand, it's just a mystery; it's God's plan," he says, his voice raspy like old paper. He's wearing thick glasses and has a cataract the shade of Mom's milk glass pitcher.

I stand there staring at the steps, twisting Lucy's bracelet around my wrist.

"But I do hope you find what you're looking for," he says, and places a firm, caring hand on my shoulder.

I sink back into the car and feel foolish. Whatever this church is, it isn't bad. I haven't been able to find Lucy so far, so maybe she really is gone, like everyone else believes. Maybe the dreams really are my imagination. I start the car and roll past the cemetery and maybe it's because of all the graves, but I can't get this image out of my mind: Lucy's name, etched on a black tombstone with her birthday followed by a dash and a set of dates I can't make out and I pound on the steering wheel and say, "No no no no no."

I step on the gas and accelerate, but then I see flashing lights in my rearview mirror. My stomach clenches in a knot; it's the police. I ease over onto the shoulder and watch as a chubby policeman heaves himself out of his car and walks toward me.

I lower my window. The officer's badge catches the afternoon sun and in tiny letters, above the badge number, it reads SHERIFF MEEKS, STARRVILLE PD. It hits me then that I've seen this man before, the day we followed Carla Ray around at Caney Creek.

"Leah, isn't it?" the sheriff says. I nod. "I was trailing the funeral procession when I noticed you driving past," he says, "so I figured I'd circle back to see if I could help you with something."

My heart is pounding and even though he hasn't asked for my hardship license, I find myself fishing it out of my back pocket and thrusting it toward him. He waves it off. "That's not necessary, hon, I'm not gonna ticket you."

I'm flooded with relief, but my mouth goes dry picturing Mom beating me home. "I was just, I was—" I start to explain but he interrupts me.

"Listen, I'm sorry about your sister. And I think I know why you're out here, Leah. And I can appreciate that." Sweat pools on his upper lip; he wipes it away with a handkerchief. "But we are patrolling out here all the time, and if we find something, believe me, you'll be the first to know. It's dangerous out here, Leah," he says, fixing his watery eyes on mine.

I gulp and nod in agreement.

"Tell you what," he says, shifting his belt around his chunky waist. "Here's my card. I want you to know that you can come to me, anytime. Anytime at all." He hands me his card and when I take it, he claps his other hand on top of mine. "You take care of yourself," he says, and releases my hand and heads back to his cruiser.

I let out a long sigh and wait until he drives off before I pull back onto the road and head home.

I beat Mom home, but just barely, and when she hustles through the front door, leaden with bags of books and paperwork, I take them from her and set them down. We are standing in the foyer and the last of the daylight catches dust motes flying all around us.

"I love you," I say, and my voice echoes around our big, empty house. I grab her and hold on to her like she's the last thing in this world I have.

61

Sylvia

AS YOU KNOW, I wasn't able to have children of my own, but Hank—short for Henry, named after John's father—came to me as a gift.

He was the result of a teen pregnancy and his mother—one of my patients in the Labor and Delivery Ward (I had started subbing on the floor again on the occasional weekend)—didn't want to give him up, but the poor girl had her whole life ahead of her. Her parents had arranged for an adoption, but it fell through when he was born. The adopting couple had wanted a little girl.

The mother—a frightened, skinny girl named Angela—had long, thick mahogany-brown hair and liquid brown eyes with long lashes like a gazelle's. She confided in me late one night that she got pregnant on Valentine's Day, the very first time she had allowed her boyfriend to go all the way with her, her face marked with fear and shame as she told me.

Hank was a starkly beautiful baby: porcelain-white skin with already a shock of thick, black hair and high, round cheeks like apples that made his little eyes scrunch up even more than a newborn's already do.

During his first few days, Hank was fussy with colic, but after just a few minutes in my arms, he turned from a red-faced, hot ball of tears to a dreamy and calm newborn.

"Well, don't you just have the magic touch," the grandmother said to me one night with pleading eyes. But she didn't need to plead; I was bonded to that baby from the first time I held him, and after the adoption fell apart, I went home after my shift and thought it over and told the family the very next morning that I'd like to adopt him. John had been dead for three years.

Hank was a happy baby, just the dearest thing, and I'd tiptoe into his nursery during naptime just to stare at him. I couldn't believe he was mine. He may have not been my son by blood, but like I told him from the time he could understand, "I may have not carried you in my belly for nine months, but I rocked and held you in my arms for even longer than that."

I took an extended maternity leave and stayed home with him for the first three months, nestling him into me, breathing in his newborn scent, his skin smelling sweetly like peach cobbler.

———

He had a happy childhood, with lots of playmates in our neighborhood, and when he was old enough, I took him fishing and we'd spend weekends camping or playing in nearby parks. But when Hank turned seven, I saw a change in him. At first, I thought it was just because he was an only child with no father—and I blamed myself for spoiling him—but even that couldn't explain his behavior.

He became a bully, and one time I saw him taunting a neighbor's dog who cowered in the corner while Hank poked a long stick at him. I scolded him and snatched him back inside the house. I hate cruelty of any kind, especially to animals and children, but even my scolding seemed to have no effect on him. He just stared back at me with blank eyes and a smirk.

When he was eight, he scared a neighbor girl. They were playing together in the boggy creek that ran between our homes. At some point, Hank had turned on her and made her play this game where he held her under water for longer than was safe. Her parents marched over to the house later with the teary mud-streaked girl in tow to talk to me about it. I was so embarrassed.

I didn't know what to do. I went to church and met with my minister and prayed over it, but in the end, none of his suggestions worked. Even Hattie didn't know what to do for me. I'd take him out to her place with me and she'd just study Hank and shake her head slowly.

His adolescence was a nightmare, with constant trips to the principal's office. When he hit puberty, he pulled back from me almost overnight and fell in with some of the rougher kids at his school. And at home he would stay locked in his room doing God knows what, only coming out for dinner. He was rabid with sex, it seemed, and I'd find hordes of dirty magazines in his room. If I pitched them out, he'd just bring more home, and so I gave up intruding after a while.

I remember taking him to a neighborhood birthday party once when he was thirteen, and I watched him as he watched the younger girls at the party, staring at them with his mouth open, hungry. It wasn't natural the way he looked at them and chased them around, and I wanted to run over to them and cover them up, put pants over their little skirts, but it wasn't their fault he was the way he was. Watching him that afternoon, he sickened me.

Then, in high school, Hank became best friends with a tall and gangly boy named Tim. Tim was fanatically religious and invited Hank to all the events at his church. It was a weird church—the Church of Christ, where they speak in tongues—but Hank loved it and soon he started reading the New Testament, especially the Book of Revelations, and started to talk to me about the end times, his latest obsession.

At least he was talking to me, I thought, but soon he got into yet another fight at school. He assaulted a younger boy. The police were called. The boy's nose was broken; blood was splattered all over his white t-shirt and he spent the rest of the afternoon in the hospital. Apparently Hank had gone into a demented rage where he had bashed this kid's head in at the locker banks. I was just about to yank him out and ship him off to boarding school (another mother had given me the tip) when I came home from work one day with armloads of grocery sacks and found a note waiting for me on the kitchen countertop.

In the letter, Hank told me that he had run away to Dallas to join a missionary and that he never wanted to hear from me again. I was devastated and heartbroken, but he went on in the letter about how he had disowned me, how God was his true father, and how women are the true reason for original sin.

I tried to find him, of course, and I was eventually able to track down the name and telephone number of the church he had joined. But when he got on the line he informed me that I was dead to him, that he had changed his name, to never call him again. I tried to plead with him one last time to come home, but he cut the line before I could finish.

I was distraught, but if I'm honest, by that time, I was also relieved.

It made me heartsick, though, and each November around his birthday I'd feel an emptiness that I couldn't shake. But even that, too, began to fade with time. I would try to picture him in Dallas, or in Houston, or even farther away, doing God's work, and try to imagine that he had finally found some kind of peace.

———

The year before I met Delia, I was holding up a gnarled, burnt-orange pumpkin at a farmers' market on the outskirts of Starrville, eyeing it for a centerpiece, when I heard Hank's voice. I froze and turned to look and saw him, just a few stalls over. He had grown taller (he was twenty-four by then), but he pretty much looked the same, just older, and he was dressed in a stark white button-down with black pants and a black hat. He was encircled by a group of young girls and women, all wearing funny-looking clothes—long prairie skirts, blouses that were buttoned all the way up to the neck, and granny boots—and I could hear him instructing them on what to buy, carrying forth in a loud voice about all the different types of produce and how that was evidence of God's great bounty. I wanted to walk over to him, to reach out and hug him. My son. My child. But I swallowed a hard lump in my throat and turned away. I pulled my straw hat down over my eyes and kept my promise to vanish from his life.

———

But I did go and sit in the station wagon and wait for him to leave. I followed him as he drove down a few twisting roads before parking in front of the Starrville Church of Christ. I watched as he slipped inside the church. A stream of people had gathered outside on the sidewalk and I climbed out and asked one of the children, "Who is that?" And

219

the young boy said, "Oh, that's Papa! I mean, the Reverend Owen Goforth."

So he *had* changed his name. I waited in the car until he left and then trailed him home. He lived on a hilly piece of land in a shabby farmhouse. His car was loaded down with lots of children, and an older girl who I assumed to be his young bride—all of them dressed in those funny clothes—and I shivered when they crossed the cattle guard. I did not want to imagine what went on behind those gates, so I left that day and never returned and tried to force him from my mind.

62

Leah

Tuesday, December 12th, 1989
Lucy missing 10 weeks, 4 days

When I woke up this morning and went downstairs, I found this note
from Mom:

Tonight's the school's annual fundraiser so I won't be home until 7.
Dinner's in the crockpot.

Love you!

So today after school, I don't drive straight home. I cruise the back-
roads behind the school that loop behind the strip mall. The sunlight
catches Lucy's clear tray of cassettes, sitting in the passenger seat, and
I put in her favorite, When In Rome's "The Promise." I haven't let
myself listen to it since she's been gone, but now I feel like I have to.

The familiar drumming starts and I'm singing along until I get to the lyrics about being there for someone who's in doubt and danger. My throat seizes up and my whole body rolls with sobs, but suddenly I'm filled with an urgency I can't explain. I start driving to every single place Lucy and I have ever been together. It's like I'm looking for her, pleading to be led with some sign. I drive past her elementary school, emptied for the day, and then down a few blocks to our favorite park. Kids are swinging and riding on the seesaw and I scan their faces, looking for Lucy. I see a girl who could be Lucy's age, same hair, same height, but I know it's not her. She cartwheels across a field, her face streaked with mud, and then cartwheels back across.

I keep driving. I reach the roller rink, a white brick warehouse painted with swirls of red with a giant sculpture of a roller skate plastered to the side of the building. The parking lot is empty—it's a school night—so I keep driving past and before I know it, I'm almost to the interstate, and to the city limits. I turn down the feeder road and there to my right, at the back of a wide gravel parking lot, is Billy's Sound World. It's the record shop Dad used to take us to when Mom needed to catch up on work on Saturday mornings.

Billy, the owner, is cute in a dangerous, creepy older guy kind of way. He's probably in his twenties and he's not from here, he's from the coast. He's always tanned with blond streaks running through his wild hair and he wears a shark-tooth necklace and drives a black van. Dad likes to come here because, unlike the chain store at the mall, Billy stocks the obscure stuff—The Grateful Dead's bootleg albums, alternative music—and Dad used to ask him about different Beatles trivia. My face would go red and I would be kind of embarrassed for Dad. I could never tell if Billy was patronizing him or if he was as sincere as he acted, but Dad would stand in the corner in his professor pose and regale Billy with stories from his college days in Austin, telling him about shows that he and Mom went to at The Armadillo World Headquarters. Janis Joplin, Willie Nelson, etc. Dad would leave with a stack of records under his arm and Lucy and I would each pick out a new cassette single.

I remember the last time we came in here, it was in the summer, in August, and we had just finished swimming at the community pool. We were both wearing sundresses—mine was yellow, Lucy's was red—with our swimsuits underneath, still damp from the water. Our skin was sizzling from the sun and smelled like coconut sunblock, our hair wild and crunchy with chlorine. I remember that Dad was asking Billy about the White Album by the Beatles, about whether or not he had it on vinyl, and Lucy and I were talking about whether or not we should each buy a single or put our money together and buy Prince's "Purple Rain." Lucy really wanted that tape and she was dancing around me singing "When Doves Cry." I could see Billy watching me, and it felt good to be noticed, but then I noticed him looking at Lucy, too, the way that guys do, and heard him say to Dad, "You've got your hands full with those two."

I pull into the parking lot, and gray gravel dust coats my new car. The parking lot is deserted except for Billy's van. I adjust my jean jacket and apply a fresh coat of lip gloss before heading in.

I push the dirty glass door open and step inside, and a jangle of metal bells hanging together from a rope clank together. Billy is at the back of the store, sliding records back into their sleeves. The place smells musty and in the weak light, I have to squint to get rid of the sun spots.

"Hey!" Billy says and shakes his head back in a nod. "Help you find something?"

"No, just browsing," I say, trying to sound as casual as possible.

Billy turns his back to me and continues filing records. I can't tell if he remembers me, so I stand there in the singles aisle and study the paper spines. After a few moments, with his back still turned, he says, "I'm sorry about your sister."

"Yeah, thanks," I manage to say, but there are no tears. I cried them all out in the car and now I just feel strangely relaxed, zoned out. "Got any new singles?"

"You bet," he says and looks me in the eye, happy that I've changed the subject. "Here, follow me," he says, and I trail him to the front of the store where he pulls out a huge cardboard box and places it on the glass countertop. "I just got these in today," he says, ripping open the box with an X-Acto knife. "Help yourself," he says, pulling a fresh cigarette out of his pocket and lighting it.

I run my fingers over the paper covers, aware that my nails aren't painted, and try to appear like I know exactly what I'm looking for. I settle on Erasure's "A Little Respect"—something light and poppy that doesn't remind me of Lucy—and follow Billy to the cash register to check out.

And that's when I see it, taped to the side of the cash register, a fluorescent teal poster with the edges curling up.

DEEP ELLUM RECORD CONVENTION
AT THE RECORD WAREHOUSE
SATURDAY & SUNDAY DECEMBER 16th & 17th

It's in three days, and my mind is going back to the weekend I spent in Dallas with Nicolette's family last year, shortly before we starting drifting apart. We had meandered through Deep Ellum and went into the Record Warehouse and I remember walking past a storefront a few doors down, painted in a dark purple that said PSYCHIC: HAVE YOUR FORTUNE READ, SEE INTO YOUR FUTURE, COMMUNICATE WITH THE DEPARTED, and it hits me all at once: this is a sign from Lucy, the reason I've driven out here. I need to see a real psychic, not Carla Ray, I need a true psychic to tell me whether or not Lucy is still alive, and if so, how I can find her.

"You going?" I ask Billy, pointing to the flyer.

"Oh yeah," he says, taking a slow drag off his cigarette. "I go to that every year, it's great."

"Mind if I come?" I ask. I bite my lower lip and look up at him, twisting my hair around my finger, trying to look like other girls do when they're flirting.

He looks at me up and down. "How old are you?"

"Old enough," I say, giggling, my cheeks burning red. He cocks an eyebrow at me. "I drove out here didn't I?" I ask, looking straight at him, a dare.

He shrugs and says, "Cool. I could use help loading and unloading the record crates, keeping an eye on my booth. I'm leaving at ten a.m. Saturday morning. Meet me in the parking lot if you really wanna come."

I nod, trying to look nonchalant, and hand over the money for the single. When he hands me my change, our hands brush. I shove the cassette in the back pocket of my jeans and walk out, aware that his eyes are on me.

63

Sylvia

WHEN DELIA FIRST MENTIONED that there was a preacher involved, I was suspicious that it might be Hank, but I shoved that thought away, not wanting to believe it.

The first week after the men threatened me, I lived in fear that he would come for me. I already slept the light sleep of a night-shift worker, but during that first week, it was even more amplified. Every noise would send me shooting up out of thin sleep. But he never came, so after a week I finally built up enough courage to leave the house.

One early morning, I drove over to Starrville and prowled the neighborhood streets. I lowered my windows and tried to divine which house had been Delia's, to see if there was any sign of her, but it was futile, and I finally faced the truth that I'd been dodging since

Delia was taken from the hospital: the minute they got her back, they had killed her.

I buried all of this until the first children went missing a few years later, and then were found murdered. I didn't want to believe it at first; I wanted to believe, like everyone else, that it was devil worshippers in Big Woods, so I went out there, but I knew with dread that it had all been a ruse. Delia had mentioned an oil man, and it all pieced together in my mind: the oil man with a lease in Big Woods would have the perfect spot to stage something. And this town, with all its fanaticism, would easily believe it had been the work of the devil. I kept investigating it, becoming obsessed with it, following the children's stories, hoping for something to point away from Hank and his men. But it never did.

———

One winter's morning, while I was at home, I stepped outside the back door to gather a few logs to build a fire. Snow was just beginning to dust the ground. I brewed myself a pot of coffee and turned on the television and saw Sheriff Greene, in front of the court house, holding a press conference. Another child's body had just been pulled from Big Woods.

There was something sincere in his face—his mustache had started to gray—and he was pleading for the community to come together, for anybody with any information to please step forward.

In the background, clamoring masses held signs that read DOWN WITH THE DEVIL WORSHIPPERS and BANISH SATAN FROM OUR TOWN.

I drained my coffee and changed out of my dingy clothes to head to the police station.

Maybe now, I thought, that there are children involved, Sheriff Greene will listen to me. I couldn't live with myself any longer if I didn't tell someone and also, I didn't know who else to tell.

I pulled on my heavy winter coat and drove straight there. The steering wheel was a cold stone under my gloved hands, and I couldn't stop my teeth from chattering.

When I arrived, the sheriff had already slipped back inside. A television reporter was parked on the steps, interviewing people. The crowd was crazed by this point, and I tried to barge my way through to the front door, but the reporter—she must've pegged me for a family member of one of the victims—stopped me and waved the microphone in my face. "What do you think of the fact that the devil worshippers are behind this?" she asked.

As I stood there on the steps looking out over the heaving masses waving their signs, a boldness overtook me and I blurted out, my voice high and full of emotion, "All I know is that it *isn't* the devil worshippers." The words rushed out of me before I even knew what I was saying. "They know who they are, and they should be ashamed."

The reporter cocked her head and looked at me as if I were insane. Her lip-glossed mouth fell open but she instinctively pulled the microphone away from me and swiveled around to find another person to interview.

I was just about to turn and try and fight my way back to the station doors when I saw a man step apart from the crowd. His eyes were trained on me; it was Hank. He just stood there staring at me, his eyes pressed in a smirk, as if he knew exactly what I was about to do. And I saw the recognition register darkly across his face. He knew I knew he was involved.

I'm ashamed to admit it, but I left. I drove straight home from the police station. I was a coward. I don't remember the drive home, I just remember going inside and feeling emptied out. I locked the door behind me and rattled two baby aspirin out of a bottle and swallowed them. I filled a tumbler with water and went upstairs to my room and got in bed.

The snow was coming down harder, and I remember hoping that the roads would ice over so that he wouldn't be able to reach my house. I must've drifted off to sleep at some point, because just after midnight, I woke up, and all the lights in my room were still on. I was half sitting up in bed, still wearing my coat with the start of a crick pulling at my neck, and I crossed the room and peered around the curtains.

I saw the red taillights of a car smear past and was filled with dread that the roads appeared to be all clear. I sighed and changed into my pajamas and slipped back in bed, pulling a book off the shelf to read and try and quiet my mind.

Just before drifting back off into sleep, I heard a soft knock downstairs, at the back door. My feet hit the floor and I crept softly over to my window and peeked out the curtain but couldn't see a car. The knocking continued. I didn't go downstairs; I knew it was Hank. It was exactly like something he would do to torture me. My heart rattled in my chest and I just stayed up in my room, frozen with fear. The knocking finally stopped, but I stayed awake until daybreak and called Hattie in the morning just to hear a familiar voice.

"Saw you on the news, Sylv," she said, and I winced, hoping that no one had seen me. "Are you crazy? They gonna *kill* you," her voice hissed out the word *kill*.

"I know," I said, and I meant it.

By afternoon, the snow was beginning to melt, and my nerves were shot from listening to the ping ping ping of melting ice turning to water and hitting the metal gutters just outside the kitchen, so I decided to brave a trip to the supermarket.

When I got home I heaved the grocery sacks on the counter and turned to lock the back door behind me. I hung my keys on the key hook and began unloading the groceries. I was bent down, stashing all the produce in the bottom drawer of the fridge when I heard a loud crash upstairs. My heart seized. I tiptoed over to the wall phone to dial 911 and was just lifting it off its cradle when I saw the neighbor's enormous cat scurrying down the stairs. I blew out a long sigh of relief.

"Oh, it's you! How did you get in here?" I asked the cat, my voice all warbly. He must've slipped in behind me, but I went around the house, checking all the rooms, just in case.

When I reached the second floor, in the spare bedroom, I saw where the cat had knocked over my antique pitcher, the pink porcelain in a heap on the floor like fine powder dust. I was just turning to leave to go fetch the broom when a cold breeze shot through the window, first billowing the delicate curtains out, then sucking them ghoulishly back through. I always kept the windows latched, but the lock on that one is painted over and won't turn.

Like the soft knocking, it was Hank, I just knew it. This was his old room and he used to sneak out of this same window in high school. He was warning me, letting me know he was watching me, and that if I made a move, he'd kill me.

He'd kill me, and then the children would never be saved.

—————

I stuck to going to routine places after that. I could never be certain about when he was watching me and when he wasn't. And everybody in town seemed to treat me differently anyways.

One morning I was pulling a bag of spaghetti off a low shelf at the supermarket when I heard a group of women snickering behind me. When I looked over at them, they scattered, but I was certain they had been talking about me. Even the check-out lady with orange hair who used to ask about my day seemed to fix me with an icy stare as she slid the groceries across the scanner and tossed them, haphazardly, into sacks.

It was what I had said to that television reporter, I would soon learn. Even my minister started to treat me differently, as if I were a devil worshipper myself, or a witch. I know I might sound paranoid, but it seemed like the few people I came into contact with seemed to shrink away from me.

Everyone, that is, except for Hattie. So I slowly withdrew from my already quiet social life, only talking occasionally to my sister on the telephone. I even stopped going out to Hattie's place, but she would call me regularly and drop by as often as she could. I shrunk into a tiny existence and lived in my own little world. And once the murders and kidnappings stopped, I thought I would be able to forget everything—I thought the rest of my days would unfold in this quiet, hushed way.

Until Lucy.

64

Leah

Saturday, December 16th, 1989
Lucy missing 11 weeks, 1 day

Last night I shook all the money out of Lucy's teal ceramic piggy bank (thirty-four dollars in crumpled ones; she always squirreled away more than me) and now I am driving out to Billy's.

I'm driving past vacant lots, the ground still sparkling white from the frost this morning, and I suck in sharp, stinging breaths of air. I lied to Mom. I told her Nicolette had invited me to watch Damien play soccer this morning, and begged her to let me drive myself to the game, and later, to spend the day at Nicolette's. "Sure," she said, "but straight there and back to Nicolette's. And let me know if you're not going to be home for supper."

Just before I get to Billy's Sound World, I pull over on the shoulder and apply pink lipstick and black eyeliner. I turn into the parking lot and see Billy leaning into his van, loading up. He sees me, flashes a big smile, and waves. I strap my purse across my chest and walk toward him.

"I didn't think you'd actually show," he says, winking at me.

"Well, here I am!" I say awkwardly.

He's toned and muscular and wearing faded jeans and a black Aerosmith t-shirt under a jean jacket. He locks the record store and we climb into the van. The van is dark and cold. There are no back-seats, it's just filled with crates of records and smells like an old ashtray. The seats are cracked leather and I fasten my seat belt. When he turns on the engine, icy cold air pumps through little black circles and I turn the vents away from me.

"Takes a while for it to warm up," he says. He's playing The Cult, and when we merge onto the interstate, he turns it up so loud that conversation is impossible. I'm grateful. I watch as he lights a cigarette and drains more coffee. His hands shake. He drums on the steering wheel and sings along to the music and I stare out the window and watch the pine trees line up and fall away like matchsticks.

After about an hour, when we reach Canton, Billy pops the top off a beer and passes it to me. It's eleven thirty. I smile and take it, but just pretend to take sips from it. He ejects the tape and fiddles with the dial until he finds a classic rock station and I watch as he fishes out a joint from his visor. He lights it, takes a huge puff, and smelly clouds of marijuana fog over the car. He passes it to me, giving me a devilish grin. I shake my head no.

"I thought you'd want to party," he says, disappointed.

"This beer is great!" I say and take a long swig to prove my worth. It tastes like warm metal and already makes my head swim. The trees thin to a flat nothing and we ride over the vacant, gray planes and I start to sway in time to the music in my seat, trying to look cool.

When we see the sign for Terrell, Billy turns on his signal, exits, and heads for the Dairy Palace. We are sitting in a long line at the drive-thru when he says, "I'm gonna order us a couple of cheeseburgers. You better eat up, not a lot of good places to eat around the convention, and certainly nothing good around the motel."

"Ummm, what motel?" I ask, trying to sound calm but my heart starts to race. My armpits sweat and sting as dread washes over me.

"I got us a room at the Days Inn."

"I thought we were just going up for the day?" I ask, trying to sound calm as a hot panic spreads over my body like a rash.

"Hell no. I don't want to have to load in all this stuff and break it all down and turn around and drive back tomorrow!" He looks over at me; I stare straight ahead. "Chill, I got you your own bed."

"Can I take your order?" an angry lady barks at us over the gravelly speaker.

Billy orders for us and I shift around in the filthy seat, turning to the window. I'm starting to think this was a bad idea. I finger the lock on the door and consider hopping out and running, but we lurch forward in line and he grabs the food and soon we're flying down the highway again.

I think about Mom and my stomach clenches. I feel so foolish for doing this. But then I think of Lucy, of seeing the psychic, and I vow to see it through, hoping I can call Mom later and tell her I'm spending the night with Nicolette.

I wolf down my cheeseburger and fries and am still finishing my milkshake when Billy hands me another beer. I take a few sips and then roll down the window, hoping the blast of fresh, cold air will keep me alert. Out of nowhere, the looming skyline of Dallas rises out of the flat earth and my stomach drops just seeing it. Suddenly we are in a sea of red brake lights and Billy goes ape shit, and starts honking. "Must be a wreck, we're gonna be late," he says, annoyed.

Finally, the traffic jam breaks up and he zips the van through Dallas. He's driving so fast my heart is thundering against my chest and I grab the dash. We come up to a tunnel that looks like it's coated in soot and I make myself memorize the names on the bridge, the three exits—ELM, MAIN, COMMERCE—in case I need to tell someone where to find me and we zoom through the Main Street underpass like we're getting sucked up a chimney.

He finally exits and we go through a few red lights before we pull into the small parking lot for the Days Inn. I wait in the van while he checks in, then I hop out and follow him inside the dingy room. Dark brown floral bedspreads cover the beds and a fluorescent light, still on from the night before, buzzes noisily at us. I head for the bathroom, my bladder burning with urgency, and am embarrassed by the sound of my pee hitting the toilet bowl. I should've run the water, but I cough instead, trying to mask the sound. I wash my hands and fish out my tube of Carmex, warm and slick from my jeans pocket, and smear some on my lips before turning to leave. When I open the door, though, Billy is standing in the doorway, blocking my exit.

Hairs rise on the back of my neck and my mouth goes dry. I stand there looking at the floor, not sure of what to do, but Billy must see the alarm all over my face because he puts his hands up in retreat and scoots aside. "I just need to go myself," he says, a smile spreading across his face.

Without a word, I squirm around him and head outside to wait near the van.

The Deep Ellum Record Warehouse is a giant red-brick loft that looks like an old factory with dusty windows. As we drive past, I crane my neck, trying to see if the psychic is still there, but Billy turns down a tight alleyway next to the Warehouse and we drive to the back. Swarms of hippies unloading their vans mix with shifty-looking characters with spiky hair and tattoos, and the noise of it all—car stereos thumping, honking horns, men shouting hellos at each other—is jarring.

We each grab a black crate of records and I trail Billy into the back entrance. When I set my crate down I start to head for the front door.

"Hey, where you goin'?" Billy shouts out after me.

"I'll be back in five! Just going to look around for a sec," I say and flash him a smile.

Inside, the place is massive with hundreds of tables set up and throngs of people moving shoulder to shoulder so that I have to elbow my way to get to the front door. I step out onto the street and see the psychic shop, still there. It's three o'clock and the sign says that they're open until five. I race back to the Warehouse and Billy slaps a banker's envelope in my hand, full of cash. "I'll finish unloading and you can be in charge of selling."

An endless stream of customers line up—mostly guys in their early twenties—and I stand there, collecting cash, making change, until my hands turn gummy with money. Billy chats everyone up but then starts to wander off to talk to other vendors. I check my watch, it's 4:38. I scan the room for Billy but can't find him so I take the envelope with the cash and thread through the room, looking for him. I find him in a corner, smoking with a silver-haired man who has a raspy, congested laugh and I hand him the envelope.

"I've gotta go pee!" I say, trying to sound desperate.

"Okay! But be back in ten minutes!" he says and as I'm walking off, he shouts, "You're my lucky charm!"

I pound down the sidewalk and try to open the door but it's locked. I see the sign READING IN PROGRESS. At 4:54 a young couple stumbles out, the woman's face is soaked with tears and she clutches her very pregnant belly. I look down at the ground and walk around the couple and step into the shop. A dainty chime tinkles as I push open the glass door.

The room is dark and candlelit. It's almost dusk now, but a fringed lamp in the corner casts a warm glow across the room. Waves of incense smoke drift lazily through the air. Oriental rugs line the bare wooden floors and pink crystals hang from the ceiling, spinning light. A woman comes out from behind a wooden beaded curtain, the strands clapping together behind her. She is a broad woman, with a wide face and long white hair. "I was just about to close, but would you like a reading?"

"Yes," I say, breathless. Bottles of oils line the window and she motions for me to sit in a red velour chair that's pulled up to a table.

"I'm Shira. Care for any tea first?" she asks. Her voice is slightly accented and deep and rich like honey.

"Yes ma'am, thank you," I say. Shira motions for me to take a seat and I sink down in the chair and watch as she disappears again behind the beaded curtain. The room is filled with tropical plants and from a dusty speaker in the corner, the sound of a soft harp plucks the air.

Shira parts the curtain again carrying a yellow metal tray with ornate, mismatched china cups, and a jewel-red teapot. She sets it down on a side table, pours the tea, and passes me a cup, the cup clattering on a saucer as her large, veiny hands shake. She is dressed in a white linen robe and has a small cap of emeralds on her head. She plops down into a throne-like seat on the other side of the table and looks me over through squinty eyes. The table is covered with green velvet fabric and a dimmed, bare bulb hangs above it.

"My readings are fifty dollars," she says, matter-of-factly. I want to cry. All I have is the thirty-four dollars I stole from Lucy.

"But I don't have that much, and I really need—" And before I can stop it, a gush of tears comes streaming out of my eyes and I'm clutching my stomach. I swore to myself that I wouldn't tell her anything—I wanted to see if she was real—so I don't explain.

"Yes, of course. I can see something's troubling you. Well, just give me all you have then," she offers.

I slide my hand into my purse and count out two dollars, putting them aside just in case I need it later, and I hand her the crumpled stack of ones—thirty-two of them. She licks her fingers and counts each one and smiles and nods before tucking the money in her bra.

"So, dear…let us get started," she says.

I keep waiting for her to pull out her crystal ball and when she doesn't, I ask her about it. "No, that is for charlatans. Here, give me your hands," she says and rolls out her heavy arms on the table. I place my hands in hers. Her skin is papery and thin, like the skin of an onion, but her hands are strangely warm, electric. As she folds her hands over mine, she closes her eyes and bows her head. I feel a warmth spreading up my arms and Shira begins swaying slowly from side to side.

"You have a sister," she says, it's not a question.

"Yes," I say, and relief washes over me: she is the real deal.

"She is lost, she was taken from you some time ago. Am I correct?"

"Yes."

She starts swaying faster and her eyes move quickly behind her eyelids. "Tell me more."

I break my vow, give her a few details. "She was kidnapped three months ago on the way to the bus stop."

"And what about your father?" she asks, sweat beads her forehead. "There's something about your father. He's gone, too?"

"Yes, yes he is. He doesn't come home anymore," I say, my head spinning that she can somehow know all of this.

"Yes," she nods. "He feels ... responsible, maybe, for what happened. But it wasn't his fault."

"Can you please tell me more about my sister?"

Her eyes keep moving underneath her eyelids, her hands squeeze mine. She sucks in a few *ohs*. "I see a white gown, she wore a white gown at night. There are other children, they are all holding hands."

"Where *is* she?" I ask, my voice rising. "Can you see that? Is she, is she ... " But I can't finish the question.

Shira shakes her head slowly, her mouth slumps down into a frown.

"I had all these dreams about her, dreams that she was still alive. I *know* she was." And now it's me who's squeezing her hands. "But the dreams stopped a week ago."

"Ah, yes, the dead often appear to us in dreams." It feels like a knife just went through my head, I have a blinding pain between my eyes. I go to pull my hands away, but she snatches them back.

"So, so... she's dead?" I ask hysterically.

Her eyes are moving so fast behind her eyelids now it looks like they are out of control and she starts humming a low, disturbing, buzzing sound. The heat rises up my arms and I'm so hot now that I'm dripping with sweat.

"Leah," she says, in a low voice, though I'm certain I never told her my name. My mouth goes dry. "I cannot say for sure. Your sister is coming through, but it's fuzzy. I see the past, present, and the future, and sometimes I can't tell which is which. Every time I see her, she slips away." She clicks her tongue across her lips which are now dry, parched. I feel like she's withholding something from me, shielding me.

"Just tell me!" I yelp. The light above us suddenly seems harsher and brighter.

Shira's face looks ashen. "It seems, it seems she is very still. When people die, their soul sometimes goes through a transition, where they can contact us before they move onto the next plane."

I jerk my hands away and pound the table with my fists, rattling the teacups. "Is my sister alive?" I shout at her. "Come on!"

She offers her hands to me again and I take them. She starts swaying again, slowly, her mouth moving, making inaudible grunts. "The connection is lost; I cannot feel her energy anymore. This is bigger than me." She opens her eyes and looks straight at me. "I'm so sorry," she says, and pulls out the wad of bills, now soaked, and hands them back to me. "I'm so sorry I couldn't help you. This, this … just rarely happens." She is drenched in sweat, her white hair now matted down to her head as if she's just gotten out of the shower.

I stare straight back, scanning her face. I'm pretty sure she thinks that Lucy is dead but she doesn't have the heart to tell me.

I shove the cash back in my purse and turn to leave without another word. I slam my hip against the door to open it against the cold wind and stumble out onto the crowded, noisy sidewalk. It's freezing out and little pellets of rain sting my face, blurring with the hot tears as I march down the street in the opposite direction of the record convention.

"Goddamit!" I yell to the side of a crumbling brick building as the thought roars in my head: Lucy is dead, and I was late, I was too late. I bite down hard on my lip and the tangy taste of blood fills my mouth, mixing with the hot tears.

I see a payphone at the end of the block and run to it. I step inside the graffiti-covered booth and pull the phone off the hook. It's grimy and waxy and smells like BO. For a quick second I think about calling Nick to come pick me up, but there's only one person I want to talk to.

"Operator," a robotic voice says.

"I need to make a collect call," I say, shaking, and cough out my home phone number. Mom answers on the first ring, saying, "Yes, yes of course I'll accept the charges." When I hear her concerned voice, I fall apart even more.

"Mom!" I shriek, and a searing sob tears the back of my throat, a ripping pain.

"Leah, what's happened? Where are you?"

"I'm in Dallas, I'll tell you everything, just come get me!" I'm convulsing with sobs, holding the nasty phone to my ear.

"Of course! Where exactly are you? Can you see a street sign?"

"I'm at the corner of Main and Exposition. There's a tattoo parlor close by."

"Leah, listen to me. Do you see a restaurant nearby? Somewhere safe you can wait?"

I scan the street and spot a Waffle House a few blocks up.

"Just find a quiet table and wait there. Do you have any money?" I nod and tell her about the thirty-four dollars. "Good, honey. Give the waitress a twenty and explain to her that you need to sit there for a few hours. Keep ordering stuff. I'll pick up the tab when I get there. I'm leaving now."

The Waffle House is packed and noisy; everybody is escaping the chill of the streets. I look around the room for the friendliest-looking waitress and ask to be seated in her section. There's a short wait, but soon the hostess shows me to my table, a small window seat in the corner and slaps the plastic menu down on the table. The table is still moist from the last wipe down and I peel the menu off and pretend to scan it.

"What would you like to drink, sweetie pie?" a smoky voice asks from behind my menu. I set it down and look up. The waitress is heavy set and has perfect, short curls hugging her head. Her name tag reads MABEL. Her skin is the color of caramel and she has electric, hazel eyes that turn worried as she scans my face. I don't even have to pull a twenty out; she pats me on the shoulder and says, "Stay as long as you like." I gulp back more tears and manage to order a hot chocolate.

The front door keeps opening as more people spill in. At one point I see the manager motioning toward my table, asking Mabel why I'm still there, and I hear her say, "That girl's hungry! Must have a hollow leg, she's orderin' the whole menu. Best customer I've had all day," and I see him nod in compliance.

Mabel brings me a slow but steady stream of hot food: hash browns smothered in gooey cheese followed by a spongy stack of waffles, a side of bacon, and then she starts pouring coffee. Miraculously, I eat it all. I hadn't realized how hungry I was.

I sit and listen to the sizzle of the hash browns cooking, to the rhythmic scraping of the metal spatulas along the grate, to the ding and slam of the cash register. Mabel keeps returning, going through the whole litany of food, "Now. What kinda toast we havin'?" she purrs, taking her time. "We got whole wheat, sourdough, or just plain white." I order the sourdough and she brings out a plate of it and a colorful tray of butter and jellies.

I'm on my second warm up when I look up and see Mom through the window, marching to the front door. She's made it in two hours on the nose. Her hair is piled on top of her head in a messy bun and she's dressed in a dark navy trench coat over jogging pants, as if she just dashed out of the house. She opens the door and a concerned line creases her forehead as she scans the room for me.

"Mom!" I say, and it comes out as a cry. She rushes over to me and grabs me into a hug and I start convulsing with sobs, and we stand there in the hot, cramped Waffle House surrounded by strangers, Mom smoothing my hair down, her eyes roving all over me. I turn to look for Mabel and can see that she is watching us, but she respectfully turns away. We walk over to her and Mom pays the tab and on top of that I hand Mabel my entire wad of cash.

———————

In the car, I'm quiet as Mom navigates us out of Dallas, traffic pinballing all around us. The ashtray is choked with a glut of stubbed-out cigarettes. Mom must've chained-smoked the whole drive up. I pull down the mirror in the visor and look at myself. I've cried so much my makeup is all smeared—rivers of charcoal are etched in my face. I wipe them away.

When we pass the Town East Mall, the last sign of Dallas, I tell Mom everything: about Billy, about Shira, and what she said about Lucy. She stares straight ahead at the gray interstate for a moment, taking it in, before turning to look at me.

"Honey ... I think," she sucks in a quick breath, strangling a cry. "I think it's time we both let go."

My hands are folded together in my lap and my shoulder is leaning into the door, my head resting on the cold window. Our tires chew up the gray highway; the dividing lines in my vision blur into one. I am broken, empty, and all of a sudden letting go doesn't sound like such a bad idea.

65

Leah

Sunday, December 17th, 1989
Lucy missing 11 weeks, 2 days

When I wake up, my room is already lemon-yellow with the sun. I can smell the smoky smell of bacon frying, and my stomach gurgles and rumbles. After I brush my teeth and pull my frazzled hair back into a ponytail, I drift groggily down the stairs to the dining room, still half in a dream state.

"Morning, sweetie," Mom says and kisses the top of my head. I sink into a chair and Mom pushes a cup of chocolate milk at me before stepping back into the kitchen to finish cooking breakfast.

My eyes are still adjusting to the morning light, which is much brighter in the dining room. The sun is shining and it reflects off the silvery pools of rainwater below in our courtyard, and I've just turned back to my milk when I see a figure moving out of the corner of my eye. I whip back around and look out the window and see the top of white, wild hair, walking toward the front of the house. My heart starts pounding.

"Mom!" I call out in a high pitch, but before she answers there is a knocking at the front door. I creep around the stairway and hear the front door creak as Mom answers it. I'm about to rush to Mom's side, but I hear her say, "Oh, it's you again."

And something in Mom's voice makes me pause at the wall, just within ear shot to hear their conversation. Maybe Mom knows I'm snooping because I hear her voice as it moves to the top step of the porch and gets picked up by the wind. I can only hear snatches of words, so I inch closer. I hear the woman say, in a pleading voice, "But I know what happened to her." And then I hear Mom raise her voice and move to close the door, but not before I hear the woman say, loud enough for me to hear, "712 Melton. That's my address if you change your—" and then the door slams shut.

66

Sylvia

Sunday, December 17th, 1989

I'm driving over to the Spencers' house. I can't believe I'm doing this, but earlier this week, one night while I was dicing onions for a stew, I had the small, portable television on in the kitchen. It was muted because I was listening to the radio, but I always like to watch *Wheel of Fortune* so I had it on while I was chopping away, a candle burning next to the cutting board to try and cut the fumes from the onions. Just after the show ended and a commercial ran, I looked up to see Sheriff Greene on the six o' clock news. I set the knife down and was washing my hands so I could turn up the volume when a banner ran across the bottom of the screen that said: MISSING CHILD'S PURSE FOUND IN BIG WOODS.

I gasped and Sheriff Greene was talking but my head was spinning so much I couldn't make out all of his words. They flashed a picture of

Lucy—it looked like a school portrait—and then followed that with footage of Big Woods and then the hotline number to call, just before the segment ended. I managed to piece together that they had discovered Lucy's purse in Big Woods, evidently just before the Thanksgiving holidays, but were only just now making it public, as a plea for help. They were painting it as the same scenario as all the other cases, but I know the truth.

As I dried my hands with a towel, my mind was already made up: I would try and talk to Roz again. I couldn't let her think that Lucy was out in Big Woods when I knew differently.

———

It's early, and the town is quiet, but I'm driving over there now hoping to catch Roz at home, hoping that it will be more disarming this way, and I'm also hoping that the husband might come to the door. Maybe he will listen to me.

I found their address easily enough in the phone book, and it's a neighborhood I know well so I'm turning down their lane now, driving under a canopy of trees whose leaves have been shorn off by winter. My body is coursing with adrenaline, but I know this is the right thing to do. At least that's what I keep telling myself. If I can just get the whole story out this time, then I will have done all I know to do.

I approach their drive but think better of turning in and park on the street instead. Their house is a two-story white Colonial set back on a high hill. It must've been a showplace in its day, but this morning it looks like it's fallen into neglect. The yard is littered with curled, dead leaves and tall, spindly weeds choke the walkway leading up to the front door. The husband must've let the yard go, and I think to myself that their house looks marked by tragedy.

The shutters are all open on the front of the house, so as I'm making my way up the drive, I decide to try the side door, instead. Maybe I won't be shooed away as fast if they can't tell who's out there. But as I'm walking along the side of the house, I feel like a prowler so I turn, with my head down, and walk up to the front door.

I stand as close to the door as possible and rap the brass knocker a few times, still keeping my head down, hoping to look as demure and nonthreatening as possible. I hear footsteps padding toward the front door but I don't dare look through the window to see who it is.

The door opens slowly and it's Roz, looking annoyed and standing there with a maroon bathrobe on, an eye mask parked on top of her tangled hair. I hope I haven't woken her. I look up at her, hoping to be invited inside, perhaps, but she steps outside toward me instead, leaving the door just cracked behind her.

"It's you again," she sighs. I beg her to please listen to the rest of my story. She seems to contemplate hearing me out, but then looks over her shoulder as if she's concerned about who else might be listening.

"I told you to leave us alone," she says. She doesn't sound angry, just weary and resigned. Before she shuts the door and slips back inside, I manage to shout out my address.

67

Sylvia

Christmas Eve
Sunday, December 24th, 1989

Had I known the girl would go out there on her own, I would've never told her all that I did. I thought she could get her parents to listen, urge them to go to the police.

I see now that it was foolish, telling her all that, but once I started I couldn't stop. To have just one person who believed me after all this time, who listened ... I couldn't help myself.

But now she's missing, too, and I feel terrible.

They found her car, a sky-blue Ford Tempo, on the side of Omen Road, parked in a shallow ditch. She's been missing since Friday afternoon.

It's 6:45 in the morning. The police have just left my house. I was sitting in the half-dark kitchen at my wooden table in a thin nightgown,

250

heating oil in a frying pan when I heard them knocking. I grabbed my forest-green sweater and pulled it around my shoulders before making my way to the front door. I looked through the peephole and saw Sheriff Greene standing there with two other officers, their radios crackling and bleating on my front porch.

I opened the door and cold air shocked my bare ankles, the wind violent and cutting, so I invited the officers in and they took a seat in the living room on my ratty brown sofa, the side lamps giving off weak, warm light.

My hand flew to my mouth when the sheriff told me that Leah had vanished, and I was still trying to wrap my mind around it all when he mentioned that they were there to talk to me because Roz told them that I'd stopped by their house last Sunday. He didn't come right out and say it, but it seemed like I was under suspicion, and I knew that having Leah's diary would make me seem even more suspicious, so I kept it to myself.

————

But let me start with last Thursday, the day that Leah came over. She stopped by the house late in the afternoon, a few hours after lunchtime. I was surprised to hear a knock at the door. It startled me—it wasn't Owen's soft knock, but I still crept quietly to the front door and checked the peephole before answering.

I recognized Leah from all the constant news coverage of her family. She was pretty and slight with shiny light brown hair and her pert nose was covered with a delicate spray of caramel freckles. I invited her inside, but she declined, saying, "No thanks, I'm fine out here," and took a seat on the wooden porch swing. We'd had a warm snap and it was lovely out so I didn't try to persuade her otherwise. I sat across from her in my tattered wicker chair and told her everything:

about Delia, about the cemetery, about Omen Road, about how the police wouldn't listen to me. I even told her I was her delivery nurse—which surprised her—but I didn't tell her about Hank. It seemed like it would be too much. She was quiet, as if she was taking all this in, only asking me a few questions, namely about the location of the cemetery.

I stepped inside to make us some tea and returned with a tray of candies. She was very polite, and after she selected one, she said she'd better get going, she needed to get on home but had wanted to hear what I had to say. When she left, she turned back and gave me a gentle hug and said, "Goodbye, Sylvia, and thank you." When she pulled back from me, there were tears in her eyes.

———

I feel silly now that I didn't think that was strange, the way she said goodbye, and that it didn't occur to me to call her mother, or to even question that she was out of school in the middle of the day.

And then the next day while I was upstairs stripping the sheets off the bed for the laundry—my usual Friday routine—the doorbell rang. I rushed downstairs but by the time I opened the door, there was no one there. I looked down and saw that a gift had been left for me, wrapped in shiny red wrapping paper out on my stoop. As I stepped out to pick it up, I glanced down the street and saw Leah's blue Tempo pulling away.

How sweet, I thought, the girl brought me a Christmas present, and for a moment I let myself enjoy the fantasy that she and I might become friends of a sort. I went back inside and sat down at the kitchen table and unwrapped it.

At first I was puzzled. Why would she bring me her diary? But once I read it—which I did in one sitting, breathlessly—I understood. She knew I was the one person who would believe her.

And I did. I read about the dreams and when I got to the part where Lucy appeared to her in a dream and told her that she was in the bad church, I knew without a lick of doubt that Hank—or Owen, rather—had her in the church cellar.

But my throat closed up when I thought about telling all that to the sheriff just now.

"Have you had any contact with Leah Spencer?" Sheriff Greene asked, his voice weary.

"Yes, yes I have," I said, my mouth going dry. "She stopped by this past Thursday."

All the officers looked up at me then, in surprise, and they each straightened up, cats coiled above their prey.

"This would be the twenty-first? And what was the nature of her visit? Why did she stop by?" the sheriff asked, jotting down notes in his notepad.

I started to speak but couldn't find the words. I looked down at my hands, they were shaking. I didn't want to talk about this in front of the other officers, so I looked squarely at the sheriff and asked, "May I speak to you in private?"

The other officers looked befuddled, but Sheriff Greene didn't miss a beat, picking up my meaning. "Excuse us," he said to his deputies, as he followed me down the hallway toward the kitchen, closing the door behind us.

I leaned against the countertop for support, afraid I might swoon. "I believe I know what happened to Leah," I said in a low voice.

The sheriff nodded for me to go on.

I drew in a deep breath and continued. "I told her everything. I told her about that girl from years ago, Delia, about the police in Starrville, about the sex ring," I said, my voice shaky. "I told her, obviously, and unfortunately, exactly where the cemetery is."

This time, he didn't look at me like I was crazy; he just studied me for a moment, chewing thoughtfully on his mustache.

"So I believe those same men have her," I offered, my voice now bolder. "Those same men who took Delia."

The sheriff met my eyes and held my gaze. I was shaking, and he placed a gentle hand on my shoulder. I couldn't tell if the gesture was condescending or conciliatory, if he was being sincere or merely trying to comfort a senile old woman.

"Thank you for cooperating with us, Sylvia," he said, his voice stable and calm. "If you think of anything else, give me a call."

He turned to leave and I was just about to tell him about Owen and the church cellar, but I couldn't. I couldn't force the words from my mouth; I'm not certain he would've believed me anyway. And there's no time for that anymore: Leah is out there, and she's out there because of me, because of what I've told her. So I'm going out there, too.

And there's also something else that held me back from telling him, something that's harder to name, something even murkier, but that something is this: I want my face to be the one Owen sees before he's captured and exposed.

He's a monster, I know, but he's a monster I couldn't stop, and monster or not, I'm still his mother and I might just be his soul's one last shot at salvation, if only I can talk to him. Maybe I can reason with him—tell him I'll do my best to protect him, convince him to hand the girls over to me. If they are even still alive. I don't know, I'm not thinking clearly and there is still a small, irrational part of me that hopes he's not involved, that he stopped all of this after Delia, that he doesn't have the girls at all. So I must go out there.

But because I know that's unlikely, and because I know he'll kill me if he does have them, I cross the room and go over to the rolltop desk. I sit down and tear off a sheet of fresh stationery and compose a letter to Sheriff Greene.

Dear Sheriff Greene,

I didn't tell you everything. I have my reasons and I hope you'll understand.

I believe a man by the name of Owen Goforth—the Reverend Owen Goforth—has the girls and is keeping them locked in his church cellar. The name of his church is the Starrville Church of Christ. Look there.

He is not a good man. How do I know?

He is my son.

My hands are shaking and I realize I've been holding in my breath as I've been writing. I sign the bottom of the letter and seal it, and climb the stairs.

I step into my bedroom and pull Leah's diary off the top of my dresser. I mark the pages that I think the sheriff needs to see, and then place it together with the letter.

I get dressed in heavy winter clothes and then go over to my bedside table. There is a framed picture of John, taken on our honeymoon—his eyes are a glittering blue, his smile flirty with new love—and I lift the picture and press it to my lips, then hug it to my chest before setting it back down. Tears are spilling down my cheeks and I sit on the edge of my bed, sobbing.

255

I wipe my eyes and take a few deep breaths and stare out the window. The roof of my neighbor's house is lined with sparkling Christmas lights, still on from the night before. I watch the branches of their bare trees rattle in the wind, and think of Leah and Lucy out there in the cold.

After a few moments, I pick up the receiver on my powder-blue bedside phone and punch in Hattie's number. I'm not going to tell her what I'm up to; I just want to hear her voice. It rings and rings though, and when she doesn't answer, I leave a message and say goodbye. I want so badly to say goodbye to someone.

68

Sylvia

I'M IN MY STATION wagon, driving through town, headed for the post office. It's so cold out that even with my heater blasting, the car is an ice box, my cheeks red from the chill. Before I left the house, I wrapped the diary with the letter in brown packing paper, covered it with stamps, and addressed it to Sheriff Greene, care of the Longview Police Department.

I pull into the post office parking lot and ease up to the blue drop box, the legs of which are wrapped in red and silver tinsel. I roll my window down. Wind punches me in the face and I drop the package down the shoot; it lands with a dull thud. I take a deep breath. I hope I'm doing the right thing.

The drive to Starrville passes in a quick blur—my mind swirling with thoughts of Leah and Lucy, about what I'm about to step into—and before I know it, I'm turning down the bumpy country lane that leads to the church.

I slow the car. My breath is quick and shallow, my palms sweaty with fear. I arrive at the church and see just a few cars parked out front. In the front lawn there is a handpainted wooden sign that reads, CHRISTMAS PROGRAM: SUNRISE SERVICE 7 A.M. & REGULAR SERVICE 11 A.M.

It's 8:35 a.m. I pull to the curb and park under a hulking oak tree. The front doors to the church are open, but it looks empty. The congregation has already filtered out into the gray light. I scan the remaining crowd for Owen but don't see him. There are just a few kids monkeying around on the chipped and weathered swing set, their parents chatting on the sidewalk as they play.

My heart is thudding in my chest but I open the car door and head down the cracked, weed-choked sidewalk. My eyes fixate on the cellar door, which is next to the church, separated by a path, but I walk past it. I want to have a peek inside the church first.

I step into the musty sanctuary and walk casually up the center aisle. The hymnals are all neatly tucked in place along the backs of the wooden church pews, and there are just a few church bulletins scattered about, papering the floor.

When I reach the pulpit, I turn in front of it and head down a dimly lit hallway that leads to the church offices. I'm jumpy and feel like at every turn I'm going to run into Owen.

It seems that I'm alone, though.

I stop outside a broom closet, and for some reason my hand is drawn to the knob. Shaking, I twist it and fling open the door. A dirty mop is resting in a bucket of gray water and the shelves are lined with cleaning supplies. I'm starting to feel silly. But when I close the door, a short, prim woman with a matronly, squat face is on the other side and my breath catches.

"Help you with somethin', ma'am?" she asks, eyeing me suspiciously.

"Yes, as a matter of fact," I say, the lie pouring out of me with no effort. "I'm looking for my mother."

Her thin, dark eyebrows knit together in confusion, but I stammer out the words before she has too much time to think. "As you can imagine, she is quite old. She lives in the nursing home, just there in town, and I was supposed to come and visit her this morning for Christmas. And well," I say, wringing my hands dramatically, "I was late. And with all the chaos of the holiday, and all the visitors in the lobby, she slipped out before anybody noticed."

"Oh dear," she said, sucking in a quick breath. "By all means have a look around. But I haven't seen her, and in fact, I'm the only one here. Well, me and the Reverend. But he just slipped out back, actually, headed for home."

Goose bumps line my arms and I feel like I'm going to be sick. I crane my head around hers to look out the warbled glass of the back door, but I don't see Owen.

"I'm going to look outside now, thank you," I say and step around her and walk toward the back door. I push it open and climb down a small flight of stairs covered in dingy outdoor carpet. I scan the grounds for Owen but I don't see him anywhere. He must already be gone.

"Mother? Mother?" I call out to the edge of the woods, just in case the woman is listening to me.

I walk over to the cellar and kneel down next to the door. There's a rusted lock on it, but it's not latched. I can feel the woman's eyes on me, and when I turn back to the church, I see her move past a window. Now she's coming out the back door and is heading toward me.

I get on my feet and smooth back my hair. "I know this must look ridiculous," I say, smiling, "but I'd like to have a look in the cellar. Mother can get awful turned around sometimes."

The woman's eyes trail to the cellar door. She pauses for a second too long, and my blood turns cold. She looks at me and narrows her eyes. Sweat beads on my upper lip. "I know this is silly," I say, my voice small and raspy, "but it really would make me feel better if I could just check the cellar."

The woman stands there parked, her spotted, wrinkled hand on her hip, but what can she say? She looks down at the cellar and nods with permission, walks over to it, and removes the lock. I feel like she is going to continue hovering over me, but when she opens the white buckled doors, the smell of rotting flesh hits us both in the face and she grabs her stomach and says, "Must be a dead rat. I'll leave you to it." She turns and walks away.

69

Leah

I THOUGHT THE OLD lady was kooky at first. She answered her door in a faded blue bathrobe and looked so startled and confused that for a moment, I thought I might have had the wrong house. I glanced down at the slip of paper I'd scribbled her address on to make sure I was in the right place and I was just about to open my mouth to ask when she stepped out and said in a bright voice, "Forgive me, Leah, I'm just so surprised to see you. But I'm so glad you've come."

She opened the door and invited me inside, but I asked if we could sit on the porch instead. I didn't know what to expect and I felt more comfortable outside.

"I heard what you said the other day, when you came to our house," I said. "That you know what happened. And I thought ..." My voice wavered. "Well, I hoped, anyway, that you might be talking about my sister."

The old woman just nodded and pulled her fingers through her white, frizzy hair and rocked back and forth in her chair, her eyes fixed on a faraway location. She then let out a calm sigh before going into a long, wild story. She had been a nurse, she told me, and had once met a terrified young girl who said she'd been held captive by a group of powerful men. She went into this girl's history, her name, her background, and I was just about to interrupt her and stand to leave when she started telling me about the cemetery.

"They conduct their dark rituals out there, on Friday evenings," she said, her eyes wide. "It's out on Omen Road." She then described, in vivid detail, the stretch of Omen Road that leads to the cemetery— you pass a church, then a red barn—and I knew all at once that she was describing the road Lucy kept showing me in my dreams.

My pulse was racing and I sat up and asked her to go on. At one point she stepped inside to make us tea, and when she came back out she had a crumpled map to the cemetery that she let me study as she pushed a tray of butterscotch candies across the table at me. It was strangely warm outside, the day drowsy with heat, and while I listened to her speak, I felt like I'd slipped into another time.

"I tried to tell the sheriff," she said, her face darkening.

But no one had believed her. I knew how she felt.

She also told me that she had gone out to the cemetery herself and had seen the signs of the rituals that the girl had described to her. "They all thought she was crazy," she said. "But I, I knew she wasn't. And then," she continued, "I lost her."

She told me, with real terror in her eyes, that she had gone out to the cemetery once at night, looking for the girl, and that she had been threatened by men in hoods and robes—and that the men knew where she lived. And the whole time we talked she kept glancing around as if she were looking out for them.

262

I felt such gratefulness and warmth toward her that when I stood up to leave, tears misted my eyes and I hugged her neck tightly and thanked her.

Once I knew where Lucy was, I couldn't wait around to convince someone to believe me; I had to go find her. I went straight home from Sylvia's and began packing the car. I pitched my puffy black coat in the backseat, in case it turned cold, and set out my mint-green high-top Reeboks. I wanted to pack light, but I tossed a blanket in the trunk and had visions of wrapping Lucy in it and driving her home.

———————

As Mom was leaving for work the next morning, I tried to act casual, but my heart fluttered and I almost faltered and told her my plans and begged her to go with me. But instead, I pulled her into me as hot tears flooded my eyes and gave her a good, hard hug, one last time.

I stood in the chilly entryway and watched as she drove away before stepping outside and locking the house. A cold front had blasted through and the sky was a dull gray, the sun hidden behind a patchwork of low, shifting clouds.

Sylvia had told me that the men gathered at the cemetery on Friday nights after sunset. I wanted to be in place long before then, so my plan was to get there earlier. I slipped away from school during last period, unnoticed—so many kids were already gone, the Friday before Christmas, that I knew my teacher wouldn't question it—and drove across town to Sylvia's before heading out. I pulled to the curb and quietly closed the car door behind me. I set my diary—which I'd wrapped neatly as a gift—on the top step of her front porch and rang the doorbell before leaving.

I wanted her to have it. I wanted someone to know what I'd been through, someone who would believe me. And I wanted some record left behind in case I went missing, too.

On the interstate, I had the heater up so high that I grew stuffy in my jacket so I cracked the windows and let in freezing gusts of air. The road was empty and a shudder rippled through me when I passed the city limits sign, the sides of the highway thickening with pine trees.

I unwrapped a Twix bar, half melted from the heat in the car, and ate it in three bites before crunching my way through a bag of Cheetos. I was licking the orange dust off my fingertips when I saw the exit for Starrville/Omen Road, and before I knew it I was driving down the exact same road, lifted from my dreams, driving toward Lucy.

The steering wheel became slick in my hands, my palms glazed with sweat, and soon I found the red dirt road leading to the cemetery. I slowed the car but drove a half mile past it and parked in a ditch. I wanted it to look like my car had broken down, not like I was out there snooping.

I climbed out and hiked along Omen Road, the tree tops shifting above me, their wispy branches shaking in the wind, the cold stinging my lungs. I prayed that a car wouldn't pass, and when one did, I kept my head down, pulling my jacket up around me.

I checked my watch—I still had about thirty minutes of daylight left. By the time I reached the red dirt road, though, night was falling fast so I started walking even faster. The road climbed up a sharp hill and when I reached the top, the wind battered me from all sides.

In the distance, I could see the wrought-iron gates to the cemetery and as I approached I didn't feel fear like I thought I might. I felt a yearning so vast to see Lucy again I thought my chest might rip in two.

I stepped into the cemetery. It was shrouded in tall pines and only fingers of light filtered across the crumbling graves. The giant circle of stones and the fire pit were there, just as Sylvia had described, and I zipped up my jacket and shivered. On the back edge of the cemetery I found a huge chunk of iron ore and positioned myself behind it, so that I could peer around the edge of it, unnoticed. The clouds had scattered and the night was clear. It was so dark out there that the stars hung from the sky like lit chandeliers.

Two hours passed and my body ached from crouching behind the rock, so I got up and moved around, my breath making smoke circles in the cold air. I was pacing back and forth, trying to warm up, when I heard the engine of a truck approaching and saw a beam of headlights slice through the trees. I ran and crouched back behind the rock.

It was a black Blazer, and two men in white hoods and robes hopped out and opened the back door and dragged a woman out by her wrists. It was hard to make the figures out, but when they dragged her in front of the truck, I could see in the headlights that the woman was wearing handcuffs. She was naked from the waist up and her hair was long and wild. Bloody scratches covered her chest and arms and she was screaming and kicking at the men.

I watched as the taller man took out a pistol and whipped it across her mouth before throwing her to the ground.

The two men circled around to the back of the truck and started unloading firewood. While one man built the fire, the taller man tied the woman to one of the stones facing the fire. Blood drained from her mouth and her head just hung there limp, like a ragdoll's.

It was so cold I couldn't stop shaking. I worried the men were going to hear my teeth chattering.

The bonfire crackled to life and I slipped back behind the rock, afraid they'd see me. I heard the creak of a car door and then heavy metal music that sounded like Metallica, blaring through the open windows of the truck.

I peered around the rock once more and gasped as I saw the taller man raping the woman. The ropes crisscrossed her breasts and it looked like they were cutting into her chest, making her bleed from there, too. I had to look away, so I turned my back flat against the rock and stared into the dark, tangled forest, my stomach hardening into a knot as the scent of the fire drifted to me.

Then I saw another pair of headlights bounce over the trees beyond the clearing. I peeked around the stone and saw a white van bump over the pitted road. A man in a white robe jumped out of the van and before he pulled the hood over his head, I could see that he had thick, black hair that was smoothed over to one side like someone from the fifties. He slid the side door of the van open and led two children out by a rope. My heart seized in my chest. He had fastened the rope around their waists and at first I thought the girl might be Lucy, but as he led them closer to the campfire, I could tell it wasn't her. This girl had stringy red hair and she looked younger than Lucy, maybe six. The other child was a blond-headed boy, maybe five years old, who couldn't stop shaking. This seemed to make the man angry so he gave them a shove toward the fire and I watched as the light from the flames licked their frightened little faces.

As the man walked back to the van, I was holding my breath, hoping that he would lead Lucy out next, but he just slammed the door and spit into the ground. It hit me then that Lucy was probably already dead, that he'd already killed her, and I was suddenly filled with such a white-hot lightning rage that before I knew what I was doing I stood and was running to the campfire, screaming, "What have you done with my sister?" my voice sounding primitive and strange to my ears.

The taller man spun around from the unmoving woman tied to the stone and marched over to me, his robe falling to cover his undone pants. He pulled out his pistol. "You got no business bein' here," he said.

I couldn't be sure, but I felt like I'd hear his voice before, and dread crept over me when I placed it: he sounded exactly like the sheriff from Starrville, Sheriff Meeks. He stopped right in front of me and started waving the gun in front of my face.

"STOP!" the man from the van shouted at him. "It's okay." He walked over and stood between us until the taller man retreated. He then turned to me and pulled off his hood. He had chalk-white skin and dark freckles. His lips were full and looked red as if stained by cherries.

"You must be Leah," he said. My stomach flipped. "We've been waiting for you; we knew you would come," he said, his mouth spreading in a wide smile that showed a row of crooked buck teeth.

I stared at him with seething hate. "Where is Lucy?" I asked through clenched teeth again, prepared to fight him to my death.

He looked me up and down, his eyes lingering on my small chest. I felt like I was going to be ill. "Come with me," he said. "I will take you to her."

I thought he was full of shit, but I followed him to the van anyway.

70

Sylvia

MY MOUTH IS PARCHED, I feel dizzy, but I grab the railing and head down the stairs. I walk down slowly, into the dank cellar, the putrid smell growing stronger, and I cover my mouth and nose with the sleeve of my coat. When I reach the bottom step, I see a white cord dangling down. I yank it and a bare bulb casts a dull light over the cellar. I squint—there are darkened places near the back that I cannot see—but at first glance, the cellar looks empty except for a few old tins of paint and a rusted out gasoline can.

I creep along the pitted dirt floor to the back wall. It's empty, too. Something like giddiness floods over my body and tears spring to my eyes. Maybe it's not Owen. Maybe I'm wrong, I think. Maybe this is just his church, as simple as that, and he has nothing at all to do with any of this. My head is spinning, and I'm just about to lift my hands up and give thanks when I hear muffled voices outside. Then the creak and groan of heavy footfalls on the stairs, followed by the flat sound of the cellar door slamming.

Hairs rise on the back of my neck. I don't have to turn around; I know it's him, and I know what this means for me. And I know my last thought will be of Leah and Lucy, so I say a quick prayer for them and soon I hear his voice, low and wretched behind me.

"Mother?"

71

Leah

HE PULLED THE CHILDREN along by the rope and I trailed behind them, looking back over my shoulder at the other two men who were both consumed again with the woman.

"I'm the Reverend Goforth," he said in his strange voice, a mix of baritone edged with a feminine shrillness. "But you can call me Owen, or, if we get along, Papa."

He slid the dented side door open to the van and pushed the children inside. The seats had all been torn out, and there was just a thin wooden bench lining the driver's side of the van. The children scrambled to the bench, but I hesitated. A fierce pang for Mom and Dad tore through my chest. For Dad's sturdy arms, roping me into a tight hug. For Mom's warm hands, silky with lotion, rubbing my back before bedtime. Their faces blurred in my mind and a hot cry strangled the back of my throat and I thought, How can I do this to them?

They've lost Lucy, and now they're going to lose me, too. What am I doing?

But I looked at the faces of the filthy children and thought of Lucy, who was one of them and who might still be alive out there somewhere. I grabbed the sides of the van and stepped in.

Owen slammed the door shut behind me and climbed in the front. A sheet of chicken wire divided the front of the van from the back, but I felt his eyes watching me through the octagonal silver holes.

As we thumped along the cemetery road, the boy (I would later learn that his name was Nate) huddled next to me. He smelled like piss and campfire smoke. When we hit a deep rut, we all clamored together for balance, and Nate clasped his tiny, sticky hand around mine.

I just assumed that we were headed to the church, so I was surprised when Owen slid the door open and we stepped out into the middle of a pasture. The moon was just a sliver so it was hard to see, but then a dim porch light clicked on, washing over a small, ramshackle house. A young girl in a long denim skirt and a button-up shirt walked over and whispered something in Owen's ear.

"Follow Heather, children," he commanded to us and soon we were walking across the dewy field, tall grass licking at our shins. After a few minutes, once we reached the top of a hill, Heather bent down and pulled a key out from her sock, and twisted it into the ground and wrenched open a wooden door. Warm light shone from underground, and Heather stared at me blankly and motioned for us all to descend the wooden steps leading down. The girl scrambled down first, and Nate tugged at my pants until I followed him down. The steps down were rickety and long, about twenty feet. It seemed to be some kind of underground cave, deep and dark, lit only by a kerosene lamp.

When I got to the bottom step, I heard the door shut and lock above us. The first thing I noticed about the cave was the smell: decaying earth, rotting food, and gasoline. My eyes scanned the cave for Lucy, but all I could see as my eyes adjusted was a brown-haired girl curled up on a cot. She shifted when she heard us.

"Do you guys know where—" but I couldn't finish. As soon as the words left my mouth, I heard her voice, the most glorious sound I'd ever heard.

"LEEEEEYYYAAAHHHH!" Lucy cried and scurried out from the very darkest corner of the cave and came running at me. Her blond hair was longer than I'd ever seen it, shaggy and a few shades darker. Her eyes were sunken in and her legs were sticks. She leapt into my arms and wrapped herself around me. She was so light, lighter than I ever remembered her being. I broke down and started sobbing and just said, "Lucy, Lucy, Lucy," over and over again to somehow make the unreal moment more real. I buried my face into her greasy hair, which smelled like dried apple juice and old sweat.

Eighty-four days. Twelve weeks exactly. That's how long it had been since I'd seen her. Tears gushed out of both of our eyes until we were just one hot pool of gooey, snotty mess. When we finally untangled ourselves, Lucy looked up at me and said, "I knew you'd find me!"

She led me by the hand around the cave. It was no bigger than our kitchen, but it was dug out so far underground that the roof of it soared above our heads, making it feel roomier than it was. Other than the kerosene lantern that rested on the staircase, there were only tiny white cots in every corner of the cave and a tall plastic bucket that served as the bathroom.

Heather, I would soon learn, made sure to wipe the place clean every night, placing forks and knives and bowls and the little food they were rationed into a cardboard box and marching it upstairs before she locked the place down.

Lucy introduced me to the other children. "This is little Nate," she said, "he doesn't know how to talk, so we don't know where he's from." Nate looked up at us from behind his curly blond bangs and gave me a sheepish smile.

"And this is Julie," Lucy said. "She's from Louisiana. She's been here the longest." Julie looked at me with huge brown eyes and just nodded her head. She was shy, I could tell, but I asked her for her last name—Benoit. I was trying to collect as much information about everyone as possible.

The little brown-haired girl was back on her cot, her thumb in her mouth, eyes turned to the wall of the cave. "Isabel, meet my sister, Leah!" Lucy said, cheerfully, as if she were introducing me to her latest best friend from elementary school. The girl just stared at me and rolled back over on her side. "She's not trying to be mean, she just doesn't speak any English," Lucy said, shrugging her shoulders. I would later find out Isabel's last name—Chacon—and even though I only knew "restaurant" Spanish, I would deduce that she was from Hot Springs, Arkansas.

———

Later that night, after all the other children had fallen asleep and I was curled up on Lucy's cot with my arms clasped around her, her sharp shoulders blades digging into my chest, she whispered in my ear all she had been through.

Owen took her when she was just around the corner from the bus stop. He threw her in the backseat and she kept looking out the back window, her eyes frantically searching for Dad, until he finally hit her so hard she crouched down.

He drove her to his church and told her to act as though she belonged with him; if she didn't, he said he would kill her. He led her around to the side of the church to the cellar and forced her to climb down the steps before he locked her in. She decided not to scream, and instead stayed huddled against the steps with thin blades of light slicing through the rotting wood.

"I thought that first day the police or Dad or someone would find me," she said, "but when they didn't, I got really scared he was gonna kill me."

She obeyed each of his commands and did exactly what he told her to do. "Soon you will see," he told her every night while he set her in his lap, running his fingers through her tangled hair, "you will understand that we are meant to be together."

At first she was the only kid in the church cellar, but after a few weeks, he started to bring the other children down there. They all tried together, once, to bust open the door and break free, but none of them had the strength to pop off the rusty lock.

She had no idea how long they had lived in the cellar—every day was just a darkened blur of breakfast, lunch, and dinner—but one night they were all startled awake by Heather shaking them, telling them to get up and follow her. She led them to the dirty white van and slammed the door behind them. Owen drove them to his land and through the chicken wire, he told them that the "end times were near, and they needed to move."

———————

I knew that we were probably going to die in this dark pit, especially if Sheriff Meeks was involved, but I was okay with it, because at least we'd be together, at least Lucy knew that I had come for her.

Lucy, thank God, was spared from having to witness what went on in the cemetery. Owen took her with him, let her ride in the front seat beside him, but parked far away from the cemetery and ordered her not to look. She didn't. He forced the other children out of the van and they'd come back shaking, cold, disturbed.

Julie told her what they had to watch, even if neither of them fully understood it.

According to Owen, Lucy was the chosen one, and he was keeping her pure so that she could be his bride one day. "Heather's his bride," Lucy told me, "and he has four other ones that live in the house. I never met them, but he told me they would be my sisters one day."

Lucy seemed to understand that she needed to play the part. She told me that she trusted I was coming, that she had seen my messages to her in her dreams, too. Sometimes at night, she'd stay away and fix her mind on something so hard, like the road from my dreams, until she believed the message had reached me.

That first night, I couldn't quit sobbing, listening to all she had been through, and it was Lucy, this time, who consoled me, bringing my hands up under her chin and saying over and over to me in a soft sing-song voice, *"Christmas, Easter, Happy Times."*

———————

Owen would come to the cave most nights, Lucy told me at bedtime a few nights later, and in the glow of the kerosene lantern, he would read passages from the Bible and talk about how there were signs that the end of the world was near, and that soon, very soon, they would need to move again, to a piece of land he knew about in Oklahoma. On those nights, Lucy worried that I wouldn't find her in time, so she'd made a plan to try and break free and run when they pulled them out of the cave for the move.

"And now that you're with me," she said one night, her voice raspy with thirst, "I know we can!"

I shook my head. "No, Lucy, we need to escape now."

"But there's no way! She takes everything at night so there's no way to break through the door or anything!" she said, her voice turning into a squeal.

We laid back on the cot and stared at the dank ceiling. Lucy's cot was in the very back of the cave and the ceiling sloped down so that if I stood up on the cot, my fingertips could reach the roof. I stared up at the compact, red clay, shiny and slick, and automatically started twisting Lucy's butterfly bracelet around on my wrist.

Lucy saw me doing this and her mouth dropped in disbelief. I fingered the sharp tips of the butterfly wings and it hit me, too: this is how we would leave here.

"See, you were right," I said to Lucy, smiling, hot tears streaming from my eyes. "I would need this."

And that night (it was Sunday, I forced myself to keep track of the days), we started to dig into the rich, thick clay while the other children slept. I'd stand on the cot and hoist Lucy on my shoulders and she'd tear through the meaty clay, dropping clumps in my hair, coating the bed. I didn't want to think about how far we'd have to dig to escape, but that first night she dug so much she threaded her entire arm inside the hole.

We saved a thick plug to cover the hole each night and made sure we shook out the sheets and stuck the largest clumps back into the wall.

72

Leah

TWO NIGHTS LATER, ON Tuesday, the day after Christmas, after one of Owen's sermons, he shut his thick, worn Bible and said, "Tonight, Leah, I would like for you to come with me." Dread spread across my chest and I looked over at Lucy, who gave me a quick, secret nod as if to say *Do whatever he wants*. I stood and followed Owen up the stairs, leaving a fuming Heather behind with the kids.

The thought of being separated from Lucy again tore through me, but I climbed the steps. Outside, it was night. A few feet away from the door to the cave, Owen had built a huge fire. I was afraid that somehow he found out we had tried to escape, but he sat down on a red wool blanket and patted the space next to him.

"Come here, sit down. I just want to talk to you, to get to know you better, Leah," he said. He had this unnerving way of never breaking eye contact. I felt queasy but sunk down anyway and stared into the fire.

He asked me all kinds of questions about myself, about my sexuality, if I had ever been kissed or touched before. I lied and said that I hadn't, not yet anyways, and he smiled and shook his head as if he'd just won a big prize. He stood up and started stirring the fire, poking a long stick into the logs, sending a spray of orange embers flying.

He told me that Lucy had said I would come for her, had warned them about me, and here I was. He shook his head as if in wonder. "I have been waiting for a sign that it's time to leave, time to move on from this place, and you, Leah, you are that sign."

He had a dark green jug and took a long swig off it, wiping his mouth afterwards. He shook it toward me, asked me to have some with him. "It's wine," he said. I didn't trust him but I took a small sip to appease him, the wine actually feeling good as it warmed my damp body.

"Your sister is very special," he said, his eyes shining with glee. He told me that when he found her, he wasn't even looking for more children. He was driving through Longview and just happened to be cutting through our neighborhood to run an errand. But when he saw her—all alone, walking down the street, her head shaking with golden curls as she listened to her Walkman—he said it was like seeing an angel, and he knew that she was the chosen one. His plan was to groom her to be his virgin bride, to keep her innocent until her thirteenth birthday, when he would perform an elaborate ceremony. It would be a long wait, he said, but he knew she would be worth it.

The wine soured in my stomach but I stared at him as if I understood, and then he led me back down to the cave.

73

Leah

THE FOLLOWING NIGHT, WEDNESDAY, as Heather was slapping all of our empty cereal bowls together, stacking them into her box (dried Cheerios were all we got for dinner, with slices of processed cheese), she announced to the wall that we'd be leaving Friday, just before daybreak. "I want everyone to be ready. No fussing or whining, this is already hard enough on Papa." And she looked at me accusingly, as if I were the sole reason four children (now five) were living in an underground pit and being forced to move on.

Lucy and I panicked. We knew there was no way we could dig ourselves out in time, and we were exhausted from staying up the past three nights. "We have to try," I told her. So that night, I lifted her up on my shoulders and as my knees knocked together from exhaustion, I thought of Mom and Dad and tried to imagine us all together.

———

The next night, after Heather latched the door and the rest of the children were asleep, Lucy wriggled on my shoulders and started digging again. After a few moments, I looked up and showers of powdery earth dusted my eyes and then started roaring down onto our heads. The dirt was mixed with grass and once it stopped falling, we both gasped and looked through the hole to a tiny circle of night sky.

Adrenaline flooded my body and Lucy climbed down and gave me a tight, sweaty hug. I grabbed her face and kissed her and we sat there for a second, grinning crazily at each other. She then crept quietly around the cave to make sure everyone else was still asleep before climbing back on my shoulders, her small feet muddy and cold. I stood on the cot and she stuck her arm through the hole and clamored her way through it. I was staring up when she stuck her dirty face back through and said, "C'mon, Leah!" But even on my tiptoes, my hands only made it part of the way through. I felt like a moron. I couldn't believe we hadn't thought about this earlier.

Panicked, I grabbed our thin sheet and tied my shoe to the bottom of it and threaded it through the hole to Lucy.

In the distance, we started to hear a dog barking.

"C'mon!" she cried, and tried to pull me through with the sheet, but she wasn't strong enough.

Her voice was so loud that she woke Nate and he stumbled out of bed, dreamy-eyed and looked over at me. I wanted to lift him through the hole and take him with us—I wanted to take all of the children, actually—but I knew they'd slow us down and so I vowed to get to safety first and come back for them.

I walked over and crouched down and smoothed back his bangs, "Go back to sleep, sweetie," I whispered, kissing the top of his head and stroking his back until his eyes drooped and he gave way to sleep.

Walking back to our bunk, I passed by the piss bucket and prayed it would be tall enough for me. I set the urine-crusted bucket upside down on our bed and climbed on top. I could reach farther, but I still wasn't going all the way through without someone pushing me upwards like I had Lucy.

"Lu, you're going to have to get me through!" The dog was barking louder now. "Tie the sheet around your waist and crawl," I shout-whispered at her.

She dropped the end down with my shoe on it and I grabbed the sheet and she slowly pulled me through the hole until I could hoist myself out. I laid on the cold, wet ground for a moment, panting, my lungs burning.

I untied the sheet from Lucy's waist so it wouldn't slow her down, then tied it around my own and grabbed her hand and we started running. Behind us, the dog was getting closer and we heard a door from the house slap open, and a light came on, but we were down the hill and I doubted we had been spotted.

We ran across the pasture and even though it would've been faster, we didn't drop each other's hands; we weren't letting go. So we ran lopsided together across the field—which was vaster than I had imagined—and down the wet slope of pasture, and didn't stop running until we came upon a tall barbed-wire fence. So tall that we couldn't get over it.

We stood there, both of us bent over, winded, trying to catch our breath.

"Can we throw the sheet over and try to climb it that way?" Lucy said, her eyes filling with panic. The dog was at our heels, barking and barking.

I was just about to unravel the sheet and fling it over then fence when I heard Owen, his voice jagged with anger, shouting, "GIRLS!"

I opened my mouth to respond but my voice evaporated, my heart pounding in my ears. He was almost upon us and I could see the bulk at his hip—a shiny pistol grabbing the moonlight. I held Lucy's hand. We were both shaking. I was trying to decide if we should make a run for it when Lucy cried out, "Papa!" and broke away from me and sprinted toward Owen. I watched as she leapt into his arms and leaned her face into his. At first I was confused, but then I heard her brilliant lie.

"Heather didn't give us enough to eat for dinner, Papa!" she said, cocking her head to the side, twirling her hair with a finger. "And the cellar door was unlocked so Leah and I went up to the house to find you but the dog started chasing us and I was so scared!" She buried her head into his shoulder and I could hear her crying.

Owen rubbed her back and ran his hands through her hair, consoling her. He kissed her on the cheek; my stomach was filled with revulsion and he looked at me then and must have saw the open disgust on my face because his eyes narrowed into thin slits and I knew that he didn't believe us.

My feet were leaden but I walked over to them and Owen placed a rough hand on my shoulder, guiding us up the hill with Lucy bouncing on his hip.

We reached the cave, but he marched us past it toward the house. When we got to the porch, I saw Heather from behind the screen door, her mouth crimped into a tight line. She stepped aside as we walked into the house, stomping off down a darkened hallway.

Owen shut the door behind us. An ugly corner lamp cast feeble light around the living room. The house was small with unfinished wood floors, and my eyes roved over it, taking it in. Above the tatty sofa hung a framed cross-stitch picture of the Serenity Prayer. The coffee table was drab with only Owen's thick Bible splayed open across it. I could see into the next room, which was the kitchen, and could smell a whiff of Pine-Sol mixed with the flat smell of stale frying grease. The white stove gleamed, though. The house appeared spotless: the shabby yet kempt look of a country preacher's home.

Still carrying Lucy, Owen jabbed a sharp finger into my back, pushing me into the hallway that Heather had disappeared down. He led us to a bedroom in the back of the house. He flicked on the light. The bedroom was dreary and odd with three twin beds parked next to each other, all of them covered with dark olive bedspreads. The room smelled musty, closed-up, and he ordered us to sit down on the bed next to the far corner before he left, shutting the door behind him.

I looked around the room for some place to escape, but the only way out was a window that was lined with black iron bars. In the hallway, I had noticed duffel bags lining the floor, the house presumably packed for the move in the morning.

From the next room, I heard what sounded like an argument building. Heather hissing at Owen. Owen shouting back. I could only catch certain words but I heard him say, "No … the girls and I are leaving. Now!" Followed by the sounds of slamming doors.

A bad feeling crept over me. I knew it was odd that it was just the three of us going. I knew he was going to take us back to the cemetery and kill us, or have someone else kill us.

I pulled Lucy into me and kissed the top of her head. I sucked in a deep breath, trying to soak up our last few minutes together, trying hard not to let her see me fall apart. I thought of Mom and Dad, and my vision blurred with tears, and then I saw Owen open the door.

"Come, girls," he ordered, his gaze vacant and trained on the floor. "We leave tonight. You will be riding with me, the rest will follow behind. Heather's fixed a plate of sandwiches; you can eat in the van."

I clasped Lucy's warm hand in mine and led her out of the room. Owen waited for us to pass then trailed closely behind us. When we got outside, the van was already running, spewing streams of white exhaust across the black night sky.

As we got closer to the van, I squeezed Lucy's hand, sending her an urgent signal for us to run. But Owen stepped between us and lifted Lucy up, tearing her away from me. He opened the passenger door and set her on the seat and slammed the door shut. My stomach turned to acid and I wanted to punch him, to rip his hair out, to fight him as best I could, but then I saw his hand move to the pistol, adjusting it in his waistband, his face darkening with rage. He slid open the side door and shoved me. "Get in."

A hot lump formed in the back of my throat, my eyes pricking with tears, and I looked up to the sky and said silently to myself, *Goodbye, Mom. Goodbye, Dad,* before gripping the sides of the van and climbing in.

74

Leah

THE VAN WAS STIFLING—the heater was roaring and the windows were fogged up. I watched as Owen shooed the grungy dog away with a kick and he was just about to slide the door to the van shut when I heard a loud noise above us.

Owen froze and stood there, looking startled, and as the sound got closer, I could tell it was a helicopter, the womph, womph, womph of the blades cutting over the noisy engine of the van. Adrenaline coursed through me and soon the van was bathed in a blinding white light.

I turned and saw Owen sprinting back to the house, the searchlight trailing him. He leapt onto the porch and disappeared inside the darkened house.

I jumped out of the van and opened Lucy's door and grabbed her, hugging her into me. The helicopter started to descend, and Lucy and I crouched down to the ground together, shielding each other from the sharp gusts of wind from the blades.

Before we knew it, two officers in black SWAT team uniforms were at our side leading us into the warm, safe helicopter. They wrapped us in heavy blankets and slapped warmed bottles of water in our hands.

"We've got 'em!" one of the officers radioed back. "Ten-four!"

"There's three more kids down there! In a cave!" I shouted above the loud noise.

"Don't worry," one of the officers said, "we'll get them, too." And I then saw another helicopter dive bomb out of the air and three black Suburbans bust through the front gate, all racing for the house.

As we were lifting off, I saw Owen running out into the pasture, his hands turned up, and he fell to his knees with a look of pure terror in his eyes.

Lucy was frightened of the take off so she jumped her bony butt into my lap and I wrapped my arms around her waist and rested my head on her shoulder. The two officers who rescued us sat on either side of us, and across from us was Sheriff Greene, who shouted at me, "Hey, kiddo!" and gave me the thumbs-up.

I looked down and saw Owen's house, and the land, shrink away and blur out of focus. We coasted above the trees and their broccoli tops became a blur.

It was too loud to talk in the helicopter, but Sheriff Greene kept grinning at me, his head resting on his hand as if in disbelief.

The helicopter circled over the municipal airport and stopped, hovering over the landing strip before finally descending. As we sank down to the ground, as if in an elevator, Lucy leaned forward and strained out the window. I tucked my head around hers, to see what she was looking at, and together we saw our parents, their hair thrashed wild by the chopper, huddled into each other, waiting to take us home.

––––––––

Sheriff Greene would explain it all to me the next morning, over steaming cups of hot cocoa around our breakfast table, after I had gotten some rest. Mom and Dad had Lucy to themselves upstairs, Lucy still curled in a deep sleep, nestled between them in their bed.

How Carla Ray hadn't been that far off, after all. That Owen's church, as it turned out, was very similar to the church in Kilgore we had searched—an eerie parallel.

How it was Sylvia—his voice catching on her name as he said it— who tipped them off about Owen.

How Owen squealed on everyone the minute they booked him: Sheriff Meeks, his deputy, and the oil man. How Owen confessed to the kidnapping of eight children total, and admitted they were all part of the plot to stage the children's murders in Big Woods, on the oil man's lease.

And the sheriff would tell me, also, that it was Sylvia who had given him my diary, marking the passages for him to read. And as he said this, he would get choked up and swallow a cry and look across the table at me and say, "I'm so sorry I didn't believe you."

––––––––

The night before I left to find Lucy, I'd had one last dream, and it was this dream that told me she was still alive, and that she, too, could also see me. It was simple, and short, and in it, I heard her voice, clear as a bell. She said, "Tell Dad to come home; I'm coming home."

75

Leah

Thursday, January 4th, 1990

Lucy and I are sitting cross-legged on the kitchen floor in our pajamas. Our hands are sticky with cookie dough, our hair is dusted with flour, and we sit parked in front of the oven, waiting for our next batch of chocolate chip cookies to be ready. Snowflakes the size of thumbprints pelt the wavy glass windows and stick for a moment before dissolving.

Mom and Dad are in the next room, around the breakfast table. I can hear the rustle of newspaper as they trade different sections to read and the pleasant thud of their coffee mugs striking the wooden table.

We've spent the past week like this: all of us huddled at home together, spending bottomless days in our pajamas. Dad cooks all day, frying bacon in the morning and making teetering stacks of pancakes. He then chops vegetables and marinates assorted cuts of meat for stews while Mom leads Lucy and I in various baking projects: Christmas cookies iced in red and green frosting, trays of gooey chocolate brownies, and sugar cookies topped with candy-colored sprinkles. Yesterday we spent the afternoon making Shrinky Dinks. We made so many that they're heaped on the center of my bed like a stash of jewels.

We spend our evenings together in the living room, playing board games and roasting marshmallows in the fireplace for s'mores.

Lucy sleeps in my room now, and I wake up during the night to find her tangled around me, her bony legs beginning to turn back into a healthy plump. We've spent the past seven days luxuriating in the basic fact of our togetherness. Braiding each other's hair, painting each other's toenails, and taking languid naps together on the couch.

So it's not until just now, as I click on the oven light to check the cookies, watching the dough flatten with heat and the chocolate chips begin to melt and pool, that I think of Sylvia for the first time since our rescue. Her face pops into my head and I'm seized by a longing to fill up a Christmas tin and bring her some cookies.

Lucy cracks open the oven and stands on her tiptoes to peer in, leaving cookie dough smear on the handle.

"Not just yet, Lu. But they're almost done," I say, hopping up and going into the breakfast room. "Can I take Sylvia some cookies later today?" I ask, leaning against the doorway.

No one has left the house all week except when we all took a single trip to the grocery store to stock up.

Mom closes the paper and sets it aside. Dad grabs their drained coffee mugs and moves to the kitchen. I plop down in a seat across from Mom.

"Sweetie," Mom says, glancing toward the kitchen. "There's something I need to tell you." I hear Dad slide the sheet of cookies out of the oven and then he scoops Lucy up and tickles her, chasing her up the stairs, out of earshot.

"Sylvia," Mom starts, her eyes trained on me. "Sweetie, Sylvia died."

I gulp and the room spins. My lips start to quiver as I ask, "How? When?"

Mom stands and walks over to the sideboard. She takes down her wooden letterbox, opens it, and slides a clipping from the paper to me.

It's Sylvia's obituary. Mom stands behind me as I read it, her steady hands planted on my shoulders. It's short, with no cause of death mentioned, only saying that she passed away on Christmas morning. Sylvia Louise Parker. Age 75. Proceeded in death by a husband, John, and survived by a sister, Evelyn, in Florida. There was no funeral, no memorial service for Sylvia, and this pains me, but the obituary mentions that her final resting place is in the cemetery at St. Paul's, where she used to attend church.

I'm openly crying now, my body shaking with sobs and Mom leans down and grips me into a tight hug, letting me cry it out. When I'm finished, she smooths my bangs back and tucks my hair behind my ears.

"The sheriff thought you had been through too much already," she says, "so we decided to wait as long as possible before telling you."

"But what *did* happen?" I ask, my voice hoarse from crying.

Mom hesitates, but then she tells me everything.

Sylvia was murdered by Owen, Mom tells me with a shudder. She had come looking for us herself. She had read my diary, marking the passages about the dream of Lucy being underground, and in the margin next to it, in her careful cursive, Mom showed me where Sylvia had written *Owen. Starrville Church of Christ.*

She must've known about him, somehow, and before she left Longview for Starrville she had written to the police, mailing them the letter with her suspicions about Owen.

They received her letter Thursday afternoon, December 28th. The mail was delayed because of the holidays. Sheriff Greene and two officers went straight to Owen's church to conduct a search. The church was closed up and deserted with a thick lock bolting the front door. They circled around to the cellar, prying off the lock, and that's when they found her.

A hard pit forms in my stomach and I sit there clutching my belly, rocking back and forth. Sylvia didn't tell me about Owen, I realize, because she must've known how dangerous he was. I wonder how she knew him, and the same longing to see her, to hug her neck, overcomes me.

"We have to go visit her grave," I say.

"Of course." Mom nods. "We can go this afternoon, if you like."

———

Lucy is in the den, curled into a ball on the couch, napping with her head in Dad's lap while he reads a book. Her cheeks are rosy, her hair sweaty, and her thumb is plugged into her mouth, an old habit she's resumed since coming home.

Mom and I wave goodbye to Dad and step outside. The snow has begun to melt. Jagged pieces of frost-bitten grass slice their way through the perfect white crust.

We drive across town to a small white church that I've always passed by but never stepped foot in. We park the car and circle around the church, heading for the cemetery, which sits high on a grassy hill.

I'm wearing my darkest Sunday School clothes with my black wool pea coat, dressed as if for a funeral, out of respect for Sylvia.

Mom takes my hand and we cross the churchyard, and as we approach the cemetery, Mom pauses and lets me walk the rest of the way alone.

The iron gate creaks as I open it and I walk along a row of graves toward Sylvia's; it isn't hard to spot, it's the only one that still has a red dirt mound in front of it.

Her tombstone is next to her husband's matching one. Both are simple gray marble slabs bearing their names and time spent on earth. Her death date is freshly chiseled, *December 25th, 1989.*

Even though it's cold, the clouds part and warm sunlight cracks through, making me feel heated and almost dizzy.

I kneel down and place a small bouquet of white irises next to her name, and hot tears pour out and puddle on the marble as I quietly give thanks to the woman who saved us.

Acknowledgments

Big Woods would not exist without the crucial encouragement of the following women in my life, my best friends: first, my mother, Liz Hinkle, who not only gave me this story, but the support (both financially and mentally) with which to write it. Thank you for housing us, feeding us, and pushing me each day to finish the first draft. You've been my biggest cheerleader and inspiration since day one.

To my first responders and readers, Beth Matlock and Amy Thompson. You both read this book as it was being written and I thank my lucky stars for that. Beth, my big sister and guide in life, thank you for all of your critical edits and for seeing and believing in this novel when I wanted to give up. Also, thanks for the timely trip to Big Woods with Leigh! Here's to more starry nights at Terramar Beach. Amy, my b/f/f/e/a/e/a, how can I adequately thank you? Your razor-sharp feedback is what transformed *Big Woods* from a family drama into a thriller. Thank you for insisting—constantly—that I make it spookier and for reading it over and over at the drop of a hat. It's as much yours as it is mine. And thanks for creating the series with me—fingers crossed! You're the best b/f/f ever!

Susie, my little sister and heroine, thank you for being the brilliant and stunning badass that you are—I borrowed all of Lucy's moves from you. I couldn't have written the book, or her character, without you. You're always, always there for me, in the biggest of ways, and I finally get to put it in print and settle the score once and for all: "I love you more."

Big thanks to my amazing friend, Carmen Costello, who insisted twenty years ago that I was a writer and kept after me until I began to believe it myself. And for showing me, by example, how to live the artist's life. (And for that creepy drive down Omen Road!)

I'm a lucky writer in that I not only got to befriend one of my favorite novelists of all time—the incomparable Amanda Eyre Ward—I got to study under her as well. Though I took Amanda's yearlong novel/ memoir class in order to finish my nonfiction project, *Big Woods* was born instead. Thanks, Amanda, for your fierce belief in this novel, your brilliant notes, and for making the ending so much better.

Much love and gratitude to my father, Charles Cobb, whose endless support has kept me buoyed over the years. Thanks, also, Dad, for the suggestion that I write a thriller. I love you! And special thanks to Joni for all the love (and the macaroons!).

Many thanks for my wonderful agents, Ellen Levine and Alexa Stark, for plucking *Big Woods* out of the slush pile and taking a chance on me. Your incisive notes help shape the novel and I appreciated your calm fearlessness during the submission process.

I'm endlessly grateful to my fabulously supportive editor, Terri Bischoff, who is both warm and brilliant. Thank you so much for saying yes. And many thanks to the stellar Midnight Ink team, especially Jake Ryan-Kent, Nicole Nugent, Anna Levine, and also to my rock star publicists Dana Kaye and Samantha Lien.

A special thanks to the rest of my wonderful family, especially Uncle Buddy who was an early reader. Much love and thanks to Paul Matlock, my brother-in-law, and my darling nephews, Xavier and Logan whom I love dearly.

Enormous thanks to my husband's incredible family, especially Larry and Martha Lutringer (Mimi, your prayers are working!) for the wonderful support and love. A massive thanks to Jake Scherrer for having our backs in such a huge way. Always.

Infinite gratitude to Dorthaan Kirk whose friendship and guidance I could not live without. Thank you, Nana, for supporting me all these years and for keeping the faith. You are my forever role model!

BRIGHT MOMENTS! Thanks also to my Houston family, Charlotte and Shan Williams and family also to my New Jersey family, April and Yolie Harper, Iris Mitchell and all the Grands! And I'm greatly indebted to Rahsaan Roland Kirk, my forever muse.

Thanks to my longtime friend, Jessica Powell, for reading *Big Woods* early on and giving me such helpful notes. And for thirty years of friendship! My wonderful friend, Kim Downey, also read the novel early on and encouraged me, and is always there for me. Love you lady and much love to Chris and Elliot Downey. One of my oldest friends, Shannon Crawford, was also an early reader and I can't thank you enough for all the love always. (And for placing that book in my hands on my 16th birthday).

Big thanks to my extended family, Tommy and Sheryl Thompson, who make everything way more fun! Love you guys. Huge thanks to Rex and Delena Richardson for years of love—Mama D, you're the sweetest person I know and your unconditional love means the world.

To the wonderful Keegan Boos (love you Butzi!), and to Slade Barnett, for years of encouragement and being my writing partner in crime. To Trevor and Noah—love you guys so much.

Other amazing friends that have helped me enormously: Carole Geffen (you're the best, C.J., for too many reasons to list here), Jackie Reynolds, Lauren Cammack, Lori Danielson, Betty Neals, David Ward (little soul brother!), Bo and Laura Elder, David Hess, Mark Braun and McCombs, Bob and Shirley Drinkwater, Adam and Colette Dorn, Leigh Schlett, Stanley Smith, Robb Bindler, Kellie Davis, and Karin Shelton. Special thanks to Ron Shelton and Lolita Davidovich for countless support, for nurturing me, and for naming me Maybird. And big love and thanks to Dave and Joyce Dormady for years of warm friendship and support—(thanks, Joyce, for reading *Big Woods* and cheering me on). To Tanda Tashjian, the first person I shared this idea with, thanks for telling me to write it.

I'm deeply grateful to Henry and Patricia Tippie, for their generous support. And I owe a big thanks to George and Fran Ramsey for their selfless and generous support during the writing of this novel.

Massive thanks to Dan Mallory for being so generous with me and for the incredibly kind and life-changing quote. Also, many thanks to the wonderful Anna Hogarty.

Special shout-out to Luis Alberto Urrea who saved my writing life many years ago and to my Cabin 20 mates—gems all of you—Kathryn Kopple, Roxanne Pilat, Eag and Charles Redner—and especially Ed "El Po" Chacon-Lontin, and Cathy "Fast Horse" Safiran. Thank you Cathy, for being such a huge inspiration with your rich writing, and for giving voice to Sylvia. Also, for your early read of *Big Woods* and your unending faith in it. Huge thanks to El Po for always being there, for showing me, by example, how both to write and to row. You helped unlock my voice and your friendship has been a beacon in both dark and light times. I can only hope to write as well as both of you one day.

Special thanks to my dear friend, Tracy Strauss—birthday twin and writing sister—for encouraging me to enter this novel into a contest and for years of friendship. Your writing is an inspiration to me. Many thanks to Stacia Campbell, for countless texts and conversations that made my life and writing life so much richer.

Many thanks to Arielle Eckstut and David Henry Sterry for selecting the pitch to *Big Woods* as the winner for the 2016 NaNoWrimo. For the past seven years, I've leaned on you so many times, Arielle, and am eternally grateful for your guidance and support.

To the wonderful writing community in Austin, especially Suzy Spencer, my dear friend and mentor, and endless supporter, I couldn't do it without you. Also, big thanks to Owen Egerton, Marit Weisenberg, and the Writer's League of Texas. Thanks to Katie Guiterrez for enthusiastically reading *Big Woods* and giving me incredible notes—and hours of your time and friendship!

Thanks to the entire Zhang family, for keeping me and my family feeling great, and a special thanks to my dear friend, Li Zhang for our treasured friendship.

Huge thanks also to Johnny's team, especially Kristen, Kayla, Sam, Annabelle, Dominique, Dani, and Erin.

And finally, the biggest thanks of all goes to my lovely husband, Chuck Scherrer. Your unwavering belief in me is both astounding and most likely undeserved. But I'll take it. Thank you for chopping the wood and carrying the water and making every day a celebration with your incredible, beautiful personality. I love you madly. And to Johnny, our sunshine boy, whose smile lights up the galaxy—I'm so proud of you and your daddy and I love you more than all of the stars in the sky.

© Jessica Doffing Photograpy

About the Author

May Cobb is a freelance writer who won the 2015 Writer's League of Texas Manuscript Contest. Her writing has appeared in *Austin Monthly* and the online edition of *JazzTimes*. *Big Woods* is her debut novel.